THE FIELDS WE CALLED HOME

A NOVEL

CARRIE BURROWS

♡ Enjoy!
Carrie Burrows

ISBN 978-1-7368826-0-3

Ebook ISBN 978-1-7368826-1-0

Cover designed by www.carmenmaciel.com.

To all the families who sacrificed and moved for the sake of America.

CHAPTER 1

a year ago, Katie Johnson would never have imagined she'd be driving a back Texas road with all her belongings in tow on this hot, sultry late May morning. With no AC in her old red four door sedan, she swept a strand of dark blond hair away from her sticky forehead and glanced at the clock on the dash. 10:00 a.m. Katie released a deep sigh and pressed her foot down on the accelerator.

Thud! The ominous noise ricocheted from the back of her sedan.

Thump, thump, thump! The car wobbled in an unbalanced dance as her stomach sank.

Katie's sweaty palms gripped the steering wheel tighter as she maneuvered her car to the shoulder of the two-lane road and crept to a stop. She put the old girl in park and ripped her sunglasses from her face. Fingers to her temples, she took a deep breath. Not today. Not now.

Letting out a sigh, she opened her door. It creaked in protest.

"You and me both, ol' Betsy." She got out and walked around her car. The right, rear tire was flat and looked like it was melting into a puddle on the hot Texas pavement.

Katie's frustration built. From the look of it, the tire would have to be replaced.

Her phone beeped from the pocket of her white skirt. She pulled it out and glanced at the time. If she just swallowed her annoyance and started changing the tire, she might still make it to the ceremony. Maybe late, but that couldn't be helped now.

Perspiration ran down Katie's brow as she popped open the trunk and sifted through her belongings, thankful she'd moved her big items to Gatesville two weeks ago. With a grunt, she heaved her overstuffed zebra-striped suitcase onto the black asphalt, then gripped the handle of the matching overnight bag and tossed it onto the ground as well. Katie's shirt stuck to her back as she lugged out a box of books, a broom, a bag of dirty laundry, and a plastic container stuffed with assorted junk from her old apartment. She pushed aside the remaining loose items enough to uncover the dusty spare tire and jack.

She yanked the black tire jack out of its hidey-hole and dropped it in the shin-high buffalo grass. Something tickled her arm and she screeched. A giant green grasshopper catapulted from her arm back to the grass. Still feeling the legs against her skin, she grimaced at the insect and shivered.

"Dumb grasshopper." She stared at its beady eyes. "I should use you as fishing bait. Now, go back into the field where you belong."

Changing a tire didn't intimidate Katie but being on the side of a country road did. With a glance at her flip-flops, the thought of whatever else might be living in the thick Texas weeds made her skin crawl.

Images of snakes and scorpions ran through her mind and made her dig through her things. Finding a bright pink beach towel, she huffed. "This will have to work."

Before getting on the ground, she glanced at her skirt—that probably wouldn't remain white after this—and made sure all uninvited guests were gone.

Two small cars whizzed past her stirring up good ol' Texas dust. Yep, the skirt wouldn't make it through unscathed. Taking a deep breath, she positioned the towel on the uneven grass. She crouched down onto the towel and began cranking on the jack. Sweat poured down her back as she made little progress lifting the sad, distorted tire off the ground. A diesel engine roared in the distance. Great, just what she needed. An oversize pickup truck would probably blow her off the road as it passed. Preparing herself for the deluge of dust, she squinted and kept cranking. But the chugging engine slowed.

Katie turned and watched as a farm truck came to a stop behind her car. The driver's door opened and shut. "Ma'am?" A man in a cowboy hat, with an easy Texas drawl, walked toward her.

She shielded her eyes from the sun as she inspected her visitor.

"Would you like some help?" The tall, brawny stranger looked to be in his late twenties or early thirties.

She noticed his clean dark pleated jeans and rugged brown boots as he approached her.

After her sixteenth birthday, Katie's dad had refused to give her the keys to her first car until she learned how to change a flat tire. Now fourteen years later, changing a tire was not a problem, but doing so in a skirt on the grass with the possibility of snakes nearby made her cringe. Katie clung to the handle of the jack as the debate raged in her head. Her mind told her to say no to this stranger because she could certainly handle it on her own, *but* the ceremony would start soon. Besides, she didn't have the time nor the energy for this today.

"If you have a few minutes to spare that would be awesome, but I don't want to keep you from wherever you are headed."

She got to her feet as ladylike as possible under the circumstances.

Her visitor nodded. "Not a problem, ma'am. I've got a few minutes. Just let me grab a couple things from my truck."

"Sure. Thank you."

He stepped back to his truck and was hidden by the driver's door. After a few seconds, he slammed it shut and returned— tools in tow. His sturdy shoulders and forearms highlighted his athletic frame. The nice dress shirt must be in the truck, because now just his white t-shirt remained. A full head of thick dark hair was now exposed without his cowboy hat on.

He laid out his tools next to the car and knelt on the ground.

Katie watched him work but then turned away. What if he caught her staring? That wouldn't be good.

A humming noise drew her attention back to the man. Tanned, calloused hands broke loose the five lug nuts with little effort as the chorus of a country song drifted on the wind. No doubt now the man could change a tire. A wash of relief filled her chest. How sad she'd questioned it in the first place.

In about four minutes, he stood and wiped his hands on a grease-stained rag he'd brought with his tools. More evidence this wasn't his first tire-changing rodeo.

"That lil' donut will work for now." Her good Samaritan tossed the rag down with his tools. "But I would suggest getting a new tire soon. Are you from around here? If not, there's a place in town I can recommend."

"I'm not from here. I'm from the Dallas/Fort Worth Metroplex, but I'm moving to town today actually. By the way, I'm Katie." She extended her hand toward him.

"Luke." He looked at his gritty fingers and laughed, "How about we skip shaking hands? I don't think you want to get this grime on you. You might ruin your nice outfit."

She felt warmness rising in her cheeks. Oh, how she hoped he didn't notice her embarrassment.

"You are right. Well, I'm sorry, but I have an appointment in a few minutes." She reached for her phone in her pocket. "Shoot! I'm going to be late. Could I pay you for your time?

Before Katie could turn around to find her wallet, Luke started for his truck with his belongings in his hands. "No need," he called out as he placed his loose tools in the back of his tool-box. "It was my pleasure. And welcome to Gatesville." He wiped his hands on his rag and then put his cowboy hat back on. He then tipped his hat toward her and climbed into the cab of his truck.

Katie turned toward her small car to hide her growing smile.

"Snap out of it, Katie! You are thirty years old. Not some teenager." She scooted into her seat and buckled her belt.

The roaring diesel passed as she lifted her hand in gratitude toward her first new friend in Gatesville, Luke.

She shook her head as heat filled her cheeks again. *To think that last time I was thankful for a tow truck to rescue me off the freeway. It is nice to be back in the country where cowboys still come to your rescue.* With a look into the rearview mirror, she laughed at herself. *I could get used to this!*

Katie turned the key in the ignition and pulled out onto the small country road. Driving toward Oakmont cemetery, she prayed the little tire would hold until after she made it to Fort Hood and the special annual ceremony. She couldn't miss it.

The Sunday before Memorial Day, the gates at Fort Hood opened to civilians. Katie had not been in years, but she knew her grandma would be seated in her rickety metal lawn chair waiting for the ceremony to begin. With another glance at the clock, Katie cringed.

Less than thirty minutes. She'd never make it in time.

CHAPTER 2

*K*atie scanned for signs marking the way to the ceremony. She'd been hoping that something would trigger her memory by now, but recognition didn't come, and unease built in her stomach.

Taking a deep breath, she focused on the scenery around her. Blooming wildflowers and sprawling oak trees lined the side of the road. A few remaining fading patches of bluebonnets waved shades of indigo and white in the fields. Native yellow-and-scarlet firewheels, along with red Indian paintbrushes, added pops of bright color to the majestic scene. Springtime in Central Texas made her heart happy. Other than the thick humidity, Katie would call this place paradise. Why did she let her job—well, her former job—keep her from visiting this gorgeous countryside? She had so many precious childhood memories of taking family photos in fields of shin-high bluebonnets. Why did she let unimportant things deemed as priorities get in the way of coming back more often?

A chestnut Army sign surrounded by lush flowers displayed a simple "Fort Hood – 1 mile." As she glanced at the clock on her dash, she realized the ceremony would start in ten minutes. It was one mile to the base and even longer to reach the cemetery. Her eyes darted to the odometer as thoughts of her grandma worrying about her streamed through her mind. It wouldn't be too bad to go ten over the speed limit for a minute, would it?

She sped the next mile while her eyes darted between the odometer and any possible law enforcement waiting to tag the next driver with a ticket.

Twelve years ago marked the last time she'd attended this annual event. She'd been an eighteen-year-old high-school graduate. How had so much time gone by? Why had she let it? Probably linked with the passing of her dad ten years ago, she'd quit finding time to visit her grandma, especially on special weekends like this one. It had been too hard. She knew she couldn't make up for all the past years, but she could be here now for Grandma. Katie assumed the attendance would be different since the last time she visited. The faithful members of this group who had started this homecoming reunion were now in their 80s and 90s. They wanted to remember their communities which had existed long before Fort Hood, and they continued this tradition faithfully every year until they passed away.

Ahh. Finally, the marker. She felt guilty about speeding even that short distance.

She turned onto the side road off the main highway at an entrance into Fort Hood. Years ago, they'd entered through the main gates where all the guards were stationed; this year Grandma had called to tell her to go in through this side entrance, which made her a little nervous navigating her way around the base.

Grandma never got lost inside Fort Hood. She could point out exactly where buildings, trees, and even outhouses used to stand. Katie followed the mundane white signs with black stamped letters spelling, "Oakmont Cemetery" and looked for her destination.

The normally active and live firing range was eerily silent for

Memorial Day to allow former residents of the area to visit. Sparse patches of charred vegetation and leftover missile remnants were visual reminders of the main use for the post. Katie noticed a few guards standing near their Army trucks, assuming they were available for guests.

The dirt road opened to a wide field covered in tall buffalo grass and blooming wildflowers. Katie stopped and rolled down her window. She gazed in the distance at the rolling hills with patches of oak, cedar, and mesquite trees. The time did not matter. This could not be forgotten. She reached for her phone and swiped it to camera mode. She stopped the car just long enough to snap several pictures of the scenery and started driving again.

Another sign stamped with the same black letters signaled for her to make her last turn. She waved at a guard standing at a truck, thankful to pass someone on this lonely road.

The bumpy road jolted her up and down. She noticed the stationary cows enjoying the shade watching her from a distance. The cows. She had forgotten about the cows roaming the property. So many details of *the move* were foggy to her, but she did understand many ranchers were still allowed grazing rights on the base.

"Whoa!" A large pothole jerked Katie's attention back to the road. She maneuvered the car around two more massive potholes and continued past a creek. She drove up one last hill.

There was her destination. In its same glory as the last time her eyes had been upon it.

A few hundred granite headstones dotted the landscape before her. Graves that preserved the remains of loved ones from generations past. On the far edge and the lowest point of the cemetery, a knoll surrounded the two-acre plot—attempting to shield the land from missiles being fired. The large grassy barrier kept most of the live-fire at bay, but several granite markers bore the effects of being unintentional targets.

The cemetery overlooked a green valley that was surrounded by cedar covered hills. Several vehicles lined the road; Katie followed suit and parked behind a blue truck.

She climbed out of her car and took quick strides to join the others outside the chain link fence surrounding Oakmont Cemetery. The nasty combination of wind and sweat turned Katie's hair into a rat's nest. With her fingers, she combed out the tangles and pulled her thick locks into a low ponytail as she headed toward the chain-link gate. She tried to smooth the deep wrinkles of her skirt, but the three-hour drive had pressed them into the fabric.

Katie scanned the back of the small crowd trying to spot her grandma from behind. Not in the back row. Not the middle section either. She shielded her eyes so she could see better. There in the front row. Her tiny grandma sat in her striped folding lawn chair. Her ruby, red shawl covered her shoulders. Of course. Always cold even in this heat.

Katie crept around the edges of the crowd and knelt next to her grandma. She reached for the older woman's hand and watched a smile spread across her face. A long and full life graced her complexion with lines—lines that Grandma announced on more than one occasion that she was proud of because it meant she'd laughed, smiled, and cried. The ninety-five-year-old woman embraced her hand. How good it was to be near her grandma again. She understood what it felt like to ache the loss of a dear loved one. Today, she would be far from that feeling.

A balding gentleman in his late eighties wearing pressed western-cut blue jeans and a pearl snap shirt cleared his throat and welcomed the group.

"I consider it an honor to speak before you again on this Memorial Day weekend," the older gentleman began as he tried to amplify his raspy voice. A pair of prominent flags flanked the older cowboy. The wind whipped the regal flags back and forth

g a reminder of the unfailing patriotism and loyalty this
f men and women had for their country.

are here to remember those who lived bravely on this
land long before the government took ownership. Our parents,
grandparents, great-grandparents, aunts, uncles, cousins, and
friends worked hard to survive and make a living on this very
land we stand on today. They plowed fields, harvested crops and
raised cattle and other livestock. They worshipped God in
church together, sent their children to school together, and
buried their loved ones together here in this cemetery. When it
came time to serve their country during war and desperation,
they stepped aside for the establishment of Fort Hood. I consider
it a blessing to have been born and raised right here by this cemetery in the community of Oakmont. I am sure many of you do as
well."

Katie glanced over at her grandma and smiled. This woman,
her namesake, lived up to every bit of her name, Grace Katherine
Johnson. She called Oakmont, Texas her place of birth. In her
early twenties, she'd held her head high when she was displaced
from the only home she had known.

Grandma's family as well as hundreds of others were ordered
to leave their homesteads for the development of Camp Hood.
The only ones left behind were those buried in the community
cemeteries. A forever reminder of why Grandma sat there today.

Grandma shared few details with her family over the years
concerning the move from Fort Hood, which had occurred
seventy-four years earlier; however, Katie knew where to find
her grandma the Sunday before every Memorial Day.

"Before the gates to the cemetery open this year," the raspy
voice called out, "let us take time to pray. Let us pray for our
country. Let us pray for our soldiers overseas and those stationed
here at Fort Hood. And let us give thanks to our precious heavenly Father as we remember our family and friends buried here."

The older cowboy removed his hat, placed it over his chest

and lowered his head. He proceeded to pray, and Katie and her grandma joined him by bowing in reverence. After a scratchy and hoarse, "Amen," Katie gave her grandma a long hug. There was that scent. Rose perfume. She could smell it all day.

"I'm so glad to finally be here. Here let me help you get up." Katie offered before the older woman tried standing on her own. She helped her grandma steady herself and then grabbed artificial flowers next to the lawn chair.

Grandma led the way toward the chain link fence and gate that surrounded Oakmont cemetery, assisted only by her cane. Katie noticed a black sign with silver print at the entrance of the cemetery. She scanned the words realizing it retold the story of Oakmont community. It marked the land as a Texas Historical site. One new addition to the old cemetery.

"Well, how was your drive from the Metroplex, honey?" Grace asked as she headed into the cemetery.

Katie laughed. "Let's just say I am glad to be here. One of my back tires decided it was time to be replaced, but other than that, the trip was fine."

Grandma's eyes widened.

Katie patted her hand. "Don't you worry one bit; I was rescued by a tire-changing angel-cowboy." Katie's words trailed off as she spotted the very man she'd spoken of a mere ten feet away. And he was walking toward them. She could feel her face glowing, and it was *not* from the effects of the beaming sun.

CHAPTER 3

"Well, hello there!" Luke's thick Texas accent warmed her insides. "I saw you sitting beside Mrs. Johnson and realized we were headed to the same place. I guess if I'd known I could have given you a ride here."

Katie shrugged her shoulders, not knowing what to say. Luke's square jaw line and shaved face made him that much more attractive. It would've been nice to leave her flushing cheeks in the past along with all her other teenage awkwardness. But no. Here she stood in front of a handsome stranger—who'd already come to her rescue once—at a complete loss for words and blushing like a schoolgirl.

Grandma filled in the awkward silence. "This is my grand-daughter, Katherine. She goes by Katie. I'm assuming you two have already met?"

Katie forced her lips open. "Uh…um…yes. Luke assisted me in changing my flat tire a couple miles outside Fort Hood." She shifted her eyes away from Luke's amused face. "He was kind enough to stop and help me; otherwise, I would have been much later."

Katie lifted her eyes toward Luke. "Thank you again and

please don't worry about it." She smiled. "So how do you know Grandma?" She looked back and forth at the two.

Luke chimed in first. "Your grandma and my grandparents were neighbors. My grandparents have since passed away, but my parents still live a few miles east of your grandma's house."

"So, then, what brings you here today?" Katie raised her eyebrows. *Why was someone of her generation at the cemetery? Was he related to original settlers here as well?*

"My grandpa was born and raised in Oakmont. My parents invited me to join them today because I just recently moved back to the area. Sadly, I missed these reunions while I was in college and then serving in the military."

"Katherine just moved here as well," Grandma piped up. "She's staying with me until she finds a place of her own while she works at the school. You know they need a good teacher like her. She knows all about history. She has even been all over the world. Last summer, she went to...what country did you go to again?"

"England—and Grandma, I'm sure there are plenty of great teachers already working at the school. I'm thankful for the opportunity."

"That's great you got a job here. Welcome to the area." Luke beamed a perfect white smile in her direction. "What will you be doing at the school?"

Moved by the sincerity in his voice, Katie smiled back at the opportunity to talk about her new passion. "I'll be teaching history at the high school."

"Luke." A strained voice called out from a short distance away. "Could you come help us?"

Luke turned and Katie followed his gaze. An older gentleman stood beside a stack of chairs and a pickup with the tailgate down. The need was obvious.

"I'm coming. Don't you try to lift those on your own." Luke turned back to them. "Grace, it was nice to see you." Luke gave

Grandma a gentle side hug. "And Katherine," Luke nodded his head to her and gave her a smile. "Nice to meet you...again." He backed away and then headed toward the older man.

Katie smiled. She hoped to run into Luke again before school started.

Katie glanced down. She noticed an empty shell laying on the ground a few feet from them. She knew light green artillery shells were a common sight in the fields since it was still a live firing range the rest of the year. Several headstones had been damaged or destroyed and replaced with new ones.

"Look, Grandma, at this shell. Be careful to not trip on it." Katie pointed down trying to change the subject from the dark-headed cowboy. A large grassy mound stretched around the cemetery, but shells still made their way into the fenced area.

"Well, honey, I am glad you finally got to meet Luke. I have always known he was such a good man. Every time I see a picture of him in the newspaper, I cut it out and give it to his parents." Grandma stepped carefully over the shell.

The two walked in silence, glancing at the names on each headstone. Katie noticed some of the granite markers were doubled. One old and one new. The older ones had been damaged by something. Probably these shells in the field.

"Here we are." Grandma tapped the end of her brown wooden cane on two aging gray headstones. The older woman stood motionless for a moment. Katie handed her grandma some flowers. She gave her some space and let her eyes drift over the engraved names of the deceased.

Grandma stooped her frail body and pushed the tip of her artificial red and blue wildflowers into the moist dirt in front of the weather-worn granite headstone. The bodies of Katie's great-grandparents rested below the surface. Her great-grandfather had passed away years before the war, but her great-grandma died a few years after Fort Hood's development. The Army had made an exception and allowed the family to bury her great-grandmother by her husband's side. She was only one of five buried there after 1942.

In the blistering morning sun, Katie assisted Grandma in placing more red and blue wildflowers on other graves marking loved ones. Two of the headstones included Grandma's siblings who never made it past infancy. She couldn't even fathom losing a child, much less a sibling. A sadness drifted over Katie as she thought of all the family members her grandma had lost over the years. One by one. Marker by marker. Mother buried next to child. Husband next to wife. Sibling next to sibling. Katie took in each name. Each date – the date of birth and the date of passing. She knew a story could be told between every dash.

After fifteen minutes, the two paused under a lone bushy cedar tree in the middle of the cemetery. Katie's dry throat craved some water, but she stood quiet and let her grandma have her time.

They stood in silence, and she watched her grandma gaze past the cemetery.

~

GRACE'S EYES spanned the empty fields and rolling hills. The scenery surrounding the cemetery had transformed from small communities and farmland into a military training facility.

Her beloved community of Oakmont had dissolved more than seventy years earlier; now the 200,000-acre property belonged to Fort Hood. Thousands of men and women across the United States came to this place to serve their country.

"Do they wonder about life before Fort Hood? Do they understand why there are cemeteries scattered throughout the base, but no homes or buildings? Do they know hundreds of families used to call this place home?"

"Who, Grandma?"

"The soldiers and all those who come to train here. Do they

ever wonder about the land they are driving over and if a building, house or church used to be there? Do they question why the cattle are still roaming? Or even why that pomegranate tree is planted over there?"

Grace saw images of buildings and homes in her mind, but the cemeteries were the only physical remains of her beloved town. Her grandparents had been gone over six decades, yet they had left such a positive impact on her life. She wondered if she would leave the same legacy. She leaned on her cane with one hand while the other grasped for Katie's fingers as the young woman joined her in front of the last headstone. She lifted her granddaughter's hand and kissed the top of it as she blinked away tears.

As Grace stood in the middle of the cemetery with Katie, her mind drifted to her mother, Georgia Alabama. Everyone called her Georgia for short. In the last years of her life, Mama had wisely and repeatedly told her to air out her dirty laundry before her mind did it first. Now here Grace was in her final years of life, and she could not remember much of the past. The present was hard enough to keep up with. Her mind was not as sharp as it once was, but she did not want her loved ones to know it, for fear she would have to leave her beloved home and move into a nursing facility.

Standing in this cemetery, however, things came to life around her. As she intently stared down the hill just on the other side of the fence, she could almost see him on one knee, proposing to her. Her heart felt confusion, shock, and surprise all at once.

"There he is. On one knee. Just waiting for my answer."

"Who, Grandma? I don't see anyone on one knee."

"Edward."

CHAPTER 4

"*E*dward, I *am* honored." Grace loosened her hand from her admirer's grip and brought it up to her chest. "But you surprise me with such a question now. I told you I wanted to teach for a year, and I have only finished the first two months."

"I'm ready to marry you now. I know you asked me to wait, but please say yes, so we can at least be *engaged* to be married. You can have the rest of the year to plan the wedding." His eyes danced as he pleaded his case. It was almost convincing.

Edward elevated the ring toward her. His eyes widened with the optimism of his twenty-two years and held a steady gaze on her as he waited.

Grace, twenty-one and optimistic about the future, knew it might be selfish of her to want to teach for a year, but she'd worked hard to earn her degree and wanted to use it. She feared getting married would prevent her having a job outside the home. While she didn't always see eye to eye with Edward, she *did* love him. Maybe she shouldn't deny him this? Clutching the sides of his face with her hands, she kissed him on the forehead. She released her grip and returned his gaze. "Yes, Edward. Yes, I will marry you!" Grace's insides somersaulted with butterflies. She was getting married!

Edward slid the simple gold band with a small square diamond on her slender finger. *Ahh. It fits perfect.* Then with his long legs and lean arms, he reached around Grace's waist and spun the dark headed beauty around. As Edward set her back on her feet, the laughter and squeals of children rang in the air. Small heads peeked around the live oak tree less than twenty feet away. Grace assumed these children must have followed the couple unnoticed, since Edward had surprised her after the students were dismissed from the schoolhouse down the road.

"I guess you heard the news? Edward and I are getting married!" Grace raised her voice loud enough for the children hidden behind the bushes to hear her. The girls giggled and ran off, leaving them to relish the moment alone. Grace's heart fluttered feeling her excitement.

Grace had been born and raised in Oakmont like her parents. She was the first to attend college and left Oakmont for four years. It was during her final year of college she met Edward. City-bred, neither Edward nor his parents understood what it was like to live in a small farming community.

He had followed his father's love of journalism and become a staff writer for the local paper in Gatesville. She'd never convince him to live in the country. He had grown up with electricity his entire life, whereas her family had electricity put in their house only two years ago.

Yet, there was something about Edward. His work ethic and passion for journalism increased her admiration for him. He did not care about farm production, but rather about his grades and his accomplishments throughout college. She had heard stories from others about his leadership in the classroom. Every time she visited his office, she studied his diploma hanging on a back wall and the numerous awards for his writings even while he was still in college. He graduated with honors from college and then became a sought-after journalist for several local newspapers. He opted to work for the *Gatesville Tribune.*

The couple met when Edward visited Grace's college to write an article about one of her beloved professors who was retiring. Grace didn't hesitate to volunteer and share personal experiences about her aging professor and mentor.

The minute she entered the room, she watched him glance up at her from his work and do a double-take before his head ducked. She captured Edward's attention. She knew it. She took a seat and articulated her admiration for her professor as Edward scribbled words in a journal. She spoke with confidence and directness; however, she found Edward quite awkward and self-conscious, constantly clearing his throat and twisting his words. His legs bounced during the entire interview.

The young journalist's nervous twitches brought an amused smile to her lips. She felt sorry for Edward and continued to converse with him long after the interview was over. The longer they talked, the more she felt drawn toward him.

Edward convinced her to go on a first date with him and then she agreed to a second and a third. After a year of dating, Grace knew he loved and adored her.

Now she gazed into her fiancé's dark chocolate eyes as her hands intertwined with his sturdy grasp. Her love for him had escalated over the year from awkwardness into deep passion. She loved him and yearned to live life with him. Edward squeezed her hand, ending the moment as he led her back to his car parked near the schoolhouse.

The sharp screech of a Model T horn interrupted the newly engaged couple. *Aoogha! Aoogha!* Grace froze as Edward jerked her out of the path of the oncoming car.

Aoogha! Grace heard a hearty laugh coming from inside the older vehicle as it pulled up next to them.

"What do we have here?" James Lloyd teased. Their mutual friend grinned from ear to ear.

Edward just scratched his head and smiled without answering.

"Well, did ya pop the question or not?" James cocked his head to one side. He wanted answers. Nope. Not yet. She kept her mouth shut and moved her left hand behind her back. The auburn-haired young man squinted at her. He had many admirers throughout the years with his thick square jaw line and handsome features, but to her...he was a lifelong friend. And nothing more than that. They had known each other since childhood. His family lived on the edge of the Oakmont community and the two grew up going to school in Oakmont until eighth grade. His fireball energy made her tired and her cautious nature made him restless as young friends. He was always ready to tackle anything coming his direction. Somehow, their friendship had made it through all the squabbles of childhood.

From their hours upon hours shared together she knew his heart well. Too well. She'd never felt him a soulmate. He would be the perfect husband for someone one day—just not her.

A year ago, James started working with Edward at the news-paper. She'd wondered how it would turn out. The two hit it off fast. James was inquisitive and Edward was fastidious; together they created outstanding articles.

"Where in the world did you come from? And how did you know we would be here?" Edward walked toward the stalled car.

"You told me you were going to do something today you have never done before and you would never do again." James smirked. "And also, I saw a box on your desk with a time written on a piece of paper next to it." He shrugged his shoulders.

Edward turned and grinned at her. She smiled back and swallowed her laugh. One day impatience would get the best of that guy.

James raised his thick eyebrows. "Well, are you two going to keep me waiting or what?"

Laughter escaped her lips. "Okay! You win." She could not hold back from James any longer. Her ring glinted in the late afternoon sunlight as she raised her hand toward her friend. "Does this answer your question?"

"Well, I'll be!" exclaimed James as he hit his horn again. *Aoogha!* "I knew it!"

She wasn't sure if James was more excited about the engagement or just the fact he'd solved the mystery. Either way, his enthusiasm was contagious.

"You're welcome to join us for a few minutes before we head to her family's house." Edward motioned his head toward Grace. "My car is parked down the road at the schoolhouse."

"Nah, I'll leave you two alone. I'm on my way to Owl Creek to get a story about a record catfish some guy caught." James waggled his eyebrows. "You know, big news and all." He laughed.

Aoogha! "See you two love birds later!" James threw over his shoulder as he chugged away in his old Model T.

They waved and then turned to walk back to the schoolhouse. *It really happened. We're engaged!* Grace's heart pounded. In less than a year, she'd be married.

Edward squeezed her hand. "Are you excited?"

"More than you could imagine." Girlish laughter bubbled up through her throat. All her dreams were coming true.

After they passed the last bend of cedar trees, she spotted a thick-waisted woman shielding her eyes in the afternoon sun, looking their direction. Mrs. Smith stood with a broom in one hand on the front porch of her general store. She must have heard the news from the schoolgirls—perhaps even her youngest child, Rebecca—and was anxious to hear the details. News seemed to always travel fast here in this small town.

The Smith family had lived in Oakmont since the town was established around 1910. The Railroad announced back then it would build tracks through the area, which brought people to settle in the area. As it turned out, the Railroad changed plans and never made it into the community, but by then several buildings had gone up, including the school where she taught, the two churches, the old wooden tabernacle where they held community gatherings, the blacksmith shop, cotton gin, the old mill and Smith's General Store. Most of the structures and business owners had been there since 1910. Many descendants of the farmers and ranchers on the outskirts of Oakmont though had been living on the land since the county was formed in 1854.

The gray-haired proprietress of the General store appeared in her early fifties. She was the mother of five children—two of whom had passed away early in life. Mrs. Smith stopped shielding the glaring sun and began using both hands to gesture Edward and Grace toward her. There was no ignoring Mrs. Smith.

Grace felt more eyes upon her. She glanced at the blacksmith shop. The owner and his customer both nodded their heads toward them. *How many people did they go tell? The entire town?*

Then she noticed townsfolk stepping out of the store and joining Mrs. Smith on the front porch. Everyone appeared ready to hear the story. She glanced at her stunning ring and then her beaming fiancé. *There's no being quiet now. Might as well make it a celebration.*

She smiled to herself as she gazed toward Smith's, then the blacksmith shop, and the cotton gin; beyond that toward the river she could see the gristmill. She loved the people, the smallness and the closeness of her community of Oakmont. This was where she'd been born, where she was engaged, and where she would be married.

"Grace Katherine!" called out Mrs. Smith. "Honey, do come

over here! I think you have something to show us." As a young girl, Grace had spent her stockpiled pennies every few months on sugary candy stored at Smith's General Store. As she grew older, she spent her money on small gifts for others and fabric for herself. Mrs. Smith knew Grace and her family well, especially her mother, whom she adored.

"Good afternoon, Mrs. Smith." Grace lifted her hand once again.

"My word! This is beautiful! Your fiancé must have worked and saved a long time to give you something so exquisite." Mrs. Smith peered up and down at Edward through her rimless glasses. "Rebecca, Helen, and Henry," Mrs. Smith hollered over her shoulder. "You three git on out here. Y'all come quick and look at this."

Grace cringed at the attention being drawn toward her.

Mrs. Smith's kids wandered over to the porch with the two girls being the first to arrive. "Oh, Miss Willis! It is beautiful!" twelve-year old Rebecca said as her hand flew over her mouth. The wide-eyed child always seemed so eager to follow in the footsteps of the teacher she admired most, Grace Katherine Willis. Rebecca slung her light brown hair out of her eyes so she could better inspect the shiny diamond. "This is exactly the ring I want one day!" The others chuckled at Rebecca as she stared at the ring with her jaw dropped.

"Miss Willis, I do agree with my sister. It sure is a nice ring and quite stunning on you," fourteen-year-old Helen said, eyeing the piece of gold jewelry. Helen was the older, softer-spoken of the two sisters. Grace was glad to have her one more year at Oakmont school before she would start riding the bus to the larger high school in Gatesville.

"Thank you, girls," Grace responded. She could feel her cheeks turning various shades of pink as she withdrew her hand to her side.

"So, when are you two going to get hitched? Tomorrow? Huh?" Rebecca questioned as her mother's piercing brown eyes stared at her. "What?" Rebecca shrugged. "Tomorrow would be a great day! It is a Saturday and there is no school and there is this beautiful piece of white fabric in our store. I was just looking at it today and we could sew it tonight and oh what a beautiful bride you will be!" Rebecca drew a breath of air after her monologue. She grabbed Grace around the waist, giving her a huge squeeze in a motion seeming to seal the deal.

"Who's going to be a beautiful bride?" A husky voice came from the doorway. She knew that voice well. A moment later, Mrs. Smith's oldest son, Henry, appeared. His broad shoulders and thick arms always made the twenty-year old look as if he belonged in the fields around Oakmont rather than in the modest building housing his parents' general store. And his eyes. He captivated every girl around with his light-green eyes and dark blond hair now hidden under his dark cap. After Henry had completed high school two years ago, he'd become his father's apprentice, working in the store and pumping gas. It wasn't a secret; Grace had always known he hoped to one day call the family store and gas pump his own.

"Rebecca." Henry glanced down at the girl with one eyebrow raised. "Are you inquiring too much of Miss Willis and now bothering her?"

"No, I'm not." She glared at her older brother as she pulled away from Grace's waist. "I'm simply wondering if Miss Willis is going to get married tomorrow!" She crossed her arms. She was young, but she had the feisty Smith family gene. How could anyone resist her with her sweet chocolate eyes?

"Tomorrow?" Henry's eyebrows shot up. Grace had always thought of Henry as a companion, but he had viewed her as someone more than a friend. He'd had a crush on her all through high school at Gatesville. She graduated and left for college while he stayed behind to finish. She'd heard his lovesick heart healed a year later when a new girl moved to town and they fell in love. Rebecca often boasted about her brother wanting to marry his sweetheart after she graduated from high school. Glad someone came and swooned him off his feet much like Edward had done her. Still, she wondered if any tinge of jealousy remained.

"No, not tomorrow, but soon." Grace threw her head back and released a soft laugh. She hoped they were long past the years of his teenage infatuation with her. "Thank you, Rebecca, for offering to make my dress, but we will be getting married in the spring after school gets out."

"But if it were up to me," Edward piped in, "I would marry her tomorrow!" He gave Henry a wink. "Hi, I'm Edward. I'm not sure I have met you." He extended this hand to greet the other man.

"Ah, so you're the guy my sisters have been talking about," Henry said and let out a laugh as the girls giggled. "I'm Henry," the young man said as he reached out to shake Edward's hand. "Glad to finally meet you."

"And Henry, while we are doing introductions and all, are you the gentleman who might be able to help me fill up my car with a little gasoline?" Edward pointed to his 1935 Chevrolet sedan parked near the school. "I ran out of time to get gas before I left Gatesville and I'm not sure now if I will be able to make it back."

"Why yes, sir!" Henry smiled. "Just pull 'er on up here and I'll help ya out!"

Relieved to have Henry occupied again, Grace continued conversing with the girls and Mrs. Smith while Edward went to get his car.

Boots shuffled up behind her as she felt the presence of someone nearby. She turned and found Mr. Lloyd, James' grandfather, who owned 200 acres on the edge of town, scratching his white scraggly beard and releasing a low whistle.

"My, Grace Katherine! You done well!" he chimed in as he passed by the group on the porch. "That ring looks mighty purty on you!" The elderly Mr. Lloyd tipped his hat and then hobbled his bowed legs down the steps as he headed home. Always a genuine man with a kind heart.

Two women bustled their way in right behind Mr. Lloyd and paused next to Rebecca. "Grace Katherine, did I hear right? Are you wearing a ring on your finger?" questioned the older of the two women, Mrs. Carter. It was not a dream. There really was a gold band on her finger.

"Yes, Ma'am." Grace flashed the ring in the direction of the two women.

"My that is a beautiful diamond." The other woman, Mrs. Miller, clutched her chest. "And the ring fits your hand perfectly."

Mrs. Carter and Mrs. Miller were sisters whose husbands owned a considerable amount of property side by side, totaling almost 1,200 acres together. They were a constant presence in the store, always looking for new things to gab about since their children were grown and out of school. Grace always found their stories intriguing. Might as well let them have some fun going on about her engagement.

"I heard you all talking about getting married tomorrow," Mrs. Miller commented. "The two of us both got engaged one day and married the next day." The woman pointed to Mrs. Carter and both nodded their heads in agreement.

"Did you hop in a car and drive away after you got married?" Rebecca asked.

"Yes, honey." Mrs. Carter said with a straight face before she began chuckling. "We were married in a car!"

"You were?" Helen gasped as her mouth formed a wide oval.

"No, honey!" Mrs. Carter said. The older women began snickering. Grace knew that laugh. They were teasing the two girls.

"A buggy! We were married in a buggy!"

Rebecca's mouth shut. Her face drew in, smeared with a look of confusion.

"Honey, people only rode horses, when we were married.

Cars didn't exist," Mrs. Carter explained, giving the child a pat on the shoulder.

"We got married on a Wednesday, the sixth of November. Close to the small community of Flat," Mrs. Miller said. "That's down where the preacher lived. We were married in a buggy right in front of his house."

"A double wedding!" Mrs. Smith clasped her hands together. "My goodness! I love this story. I'm not sure I've heard you two tell this."

Mrs. Smith with a twinkle in her eye placed her hand next to her mouth and called down to Henry pumping gas. "Henry! Are you listening to this? You and Bessie and Grace and Edward could all just hop in a car and have a double wedding!"

"And don't forget the double honeymoon!" Henry quipped without missing a beat. He finished putting gas in Edward's car and seemed to shake his head at his mother's notion.

"Oh yes, sir, it was a double honeymoon," Mrs. Carter commented. Grace wasn't sure if the woman was still teasing or not. The young girls leaned forward waiting for her next sentence. "Back home in the cotton patch."

Laughter and giggles overcame the adults and children in the small, huddled group.

"You ladies are too much for me." Grace grabbed her side. Laughter did her soul good. She reached her hand toward Edward who was walking up the steps to join them. "Now, we are going to tell my parents the good news before word gets to them that we will be having a double wedding this time tomorrow. See you ladies later."

She allowed Edward to escort her down the steps of the general store, leaving the older women alone to tell more stories from the past. Somehow, they always managed to connect the past with the present. Oh, the contagious joy they brought her heart.

Edward opened the car door and helped Grace in. He walked

to the driver's side, got in, and started the car. Grace rolled down the window and waved goodbye to her friends.

"Bye, Miss Willis," Rebecca and Helen called out to their teacher.

"Bye!" She continued waving out the window as the car pulled away.

CHAPTER 5

The fall breeze brought leaves trickling on the fading grass as they drove through the town headed to Grace's home. A leaf landed on the car before being swooshed away by the wind onto the dusty road. Each season played a necessary part in the cycle of life. A deep sense of comfort rose in her on this fall afternoon as she watched the season change. As they drove through town, she waved at her friends. The farmers. The landowners. The children. The mill workers. Each contributed a necessary element of a quaint and intimate hamlet.

There in the distance she caught sight of the hobbling Mr. Lloyd. He was probably about eighty and had also played an important role in the development of the community. Edward tapped his horn. The old man lifted his leathered hand before he turned toward the dirt driveway leading to his home.

Every day on her walk to and from the schoolhouse, Grace made it part of her routine to look for Mr. Lloyd sitting on his long front porch. She usually found him whittling on a wood project. Within a hundred yards of his house sat an almost century-old dog run. As a child, she'd spent many afternoons playing hide-and-seek with James, his grandson. They would run around and around James' great-grandfather's old home. James would tell her *secrets* about Indian raids. His grandfather would then ramble on about *the settlers fightin' for Texas.*

Mr. Lloyd also told stories to the two children about his father, one of the first settlers in the area. He'd built his home after his land was given to him for serving in the Republic of Texas. He proudly wore his Texas pride. She often wished she could have seen Texas in the early days.

After Grace and Edward passed Mr. Lloyd, she continued gazing out the window. Rows of wheat and corn came into view. Roughly 200 acres of land, owned by the Springer and White families. Grace and her twelve-year-old brother, John Jr.—also known as J.J.—met the Springer and White children on the road in the mornings as they walked to school. They often played tag or catch with a ball.

Grace felt the tires meet the wooden planks of the Henson Creek bridge. She glanced at the clear bottom of the creek bed from the car. Her breathing slowed as her mind drifted to sultry summer days of her childhood, using the cool refreshing water of the creek as a relief from the heat. Many families sought solace from hot summer days in the surrounding creeks.

She found herself dreaming of her childhood days as Edward's car came in view of her family's quaint whitewashed Victorian home. The house contained all the rooms in one story and boasted a grand wrap-around porch and two chimneys. Grandpa's craftsmanship had held steady since the mid-1890s. They'd lived there for almost thirty years before deeding the home to Grace's parents when she was a young child. Sprawling live oak trees, cedar trees, and pecan trees lined the dirt driveway to the house. The growing life within the trees seemed to symbolize the thickness of the bond of love within that white-painted house.

As they drove closer, Grace spotted her mother bending over and gathering vegetables in the garden close to the house. Always working hard. Always tending to the needs of her family. Georgia Alabama, named after the two states her great-great-grandparents had come from, was a still-shapely woman who had birthed six children. Two of her babies never made it past a day old. Like clockwork, once a month after the sun rose above the nearest hill and all the morning chores were finished, Georgia—as most everyone called her—walked the serene dirt path to Oakmont Cemetery to visit the simple rock headstones where her babies were laid to rest.

Georgia's silky dark-brown hair, which Grace inherited, swooped into a lower bun exposing a few fleeting streaks of gray. Her favorite waist-high blue-and-white floral apron protected her beige dress from plant and food stains. Mama often told her the apron looked like fields covered in beautiful bluebonnets in the spring. Mama's favorite flower. She always said seeing the bluebonnets every year brought an escape from the hard realities of life. They might even line the streets of gold in heaven.

Grace watched her mother lift the lightweight apron and wipe sweat off her forehead, and head toward the back of the house. Somehow fall had let them down again this year. The cool crisp autumn air had yet to arrive. Behind her mother, shirts of various sizes waved back and forth as they hung from line stretched across the side yard. In the country, washing and drying clothes was still manual work done outside the home despite having indoor plumbing and electricity.

Grace swept her eyes across the fields beyond her family's home. Two hundred acres. She knew her father, John Willis Sr., was out somewhere in the field checking on his cotton. He probably would arrive home after the sun set. It was nearing time to harvest cotton. The schools in the area would release the children to help with the large task, but he still had to prepare so he was ready when the day arrived.

Not all of the land was good farming land since hills covered much of the terrain. However, Father made the most of his low land filled with rich soil perfect for farming. The original tract of land her grandparents owned was 500 acres, but they'd deeded a fourth of the land to her uncle and sold another portion at a time when money was tight.

John worked long days and seldom spoke except when necessary. It wasn't shyness. Maybe more thoughtfulness before he spoke. What would he say about her engagement? She knew he didn't always show fondness toward Edward, but he'd at least be happy she was getting married. Right? At twenty-one she had already been surpassed to saying wedding vows by many childhood friends.

Grace spun her ring around her finger. She stopped the diamond on top of her finger as she extended her hand in front of her. The small diamond seated on a thin gold band sparkled in the sunlight. Edward must have spent a couple month's earnings on this ring. At least. The jewel mesmerized her as she stared at her hand.

Edward shifted the car into park. He reached over to his fiancée and interlocked his long fingers between her smooth fingers. She focused her eyes on their united hands before turning her head toward his dark eyes. His lips twisted upward trying to hide a smirk on his lips. She squinted her eyes trying to decipher his smile.

"Edward, you look like you are up to something. What is it? I've already had one surprise," Grace's voice trailed off as Edward quieted her with his finger to her lips.

"Shhh." Edward could not seem to hold back his smile. "Wait here." He hopped out and rushed to open Grace's door.

"Okay, now close your eyes. I will lead you."

Grace closed her eyes as Edward gripped one hand in front and placed his other hand on the small of her back, escorting her up the familiar squeaking steps. Their feet echoed on the hollow porch. *Is that shuffling coming from inside that house?* An image of J.J., her youngest brother, spying on them popped into her head.

The old screen door creaked open. Scooting and moving of more feet tempted her to open her eyes. *Is that a whisper too?* Edward's hands slid to her slender hips, guiding her into the entryway of her home.

The movement stopped. Silence. She felt Edward leaning in close to her ear and whisper. "On the count of three, I want you to open your eyes."

"One, two..." Edward's voice got louder as he stretched out the final number.

"Three!" he exclaimed as she opened her eyes.

"Surprise!" Her entire family stood crowding the entry way. She caught her breath and froze. What was everyone doing here? Her heart filled her chest as she realized they were waiting to congratulate them. She gazed upon her brothers, sister, parents, and her granny. Her Mama could not contain her joy as tears flowed freely down her cheeks. Ruth, her younger sister, wrapped her arms around her. Out of the corner of her eye, she could see her brothers giving Edward firm handshakes. What about her father? There he stood next to the banister in the hallway. *Was that a brief smile?*

CHAPTER 6

*K*atie paced the small waiting room lined with soft, gray-cushioned chairs, with a candy bar clutched in one hand. The memorial service at Fort Hood had come and gone. It was now mid-week. After running errands in Grandma's massive sedan the past few days, she was more than ready to hop back into her little car and have a new tire put on her own car. Maneuvering the beast around gave her more than one headache.

She stood waiting at one of two dealerships her grandma had mentioned. They would replace her tire for her. The shop was not too busy, and the manager told her it would take about thirty minutes. Katie wandered around the tight lobby space looking at pictures of the sales team members holding dedication and achievement awards.

A crooked rectangle frame on the mustard color wall caught her attention. Instead of men dressed in suits displaying golden plaques, this frame held a picture of a man wearing a tan cowboy hat, dark western-cut jeans, and a light sports coat, gripping hands with a young man in an Army uniform. The soldier stood a few inches taller than the gentleman in the cowboy hat.

His built shoulders and arms filled the sleeves of his uniform. His eyes were young, and his clean-shaven face and strong jaw line reminded her of Luke. She bit into her chocolate candy bar and took a step forward. She tilted her head to the side and studied the photograph of the handsome soldier.

"Katie?" a male voice questioned near the entrance of the room.

The smooth deep voice reminded her of someone she recently met. With a mouth full of candy, Katie knew who the voice belonged to before she turned her head.

"Uh, hi, Luke." She stuttered and swallowed a big piece of chocolate. She stepped back away from the frame.

"What are you doing here?" She could feel the warmness rising in her ears. *Please don't show any pink.*

"Well, I would ask you the same question, but I am sure I know the answer." His eyes twinkled. "My dad and uncle are in business together here at Brothers Automotive."

Embarrassment flushed her cheeks. Grandma hadn't warned her of the possibility running into him. "Oh, I didn't know. Do you work here with them?"

"No, I am just up here to meet my dad for lunch today. I didn't mention this to you the other day, but I got a job in the school district too and will start in August."

"You did?" Katie felt her eyes go wide. "What subject will you be teaching?"

"I will teach two classes of high school economics, but my primary role will be as an assistant football coach."

"Oh, wow, you are a man of many talents." She figured he'd caught her staring at his picture on the wall, so she pointed to the frame. "I'm guessing that is a younger Luke in the military uniform."

He took a step closer to the frame and glanced at the picture inside. "Yep, a much younger me that didn't understand how much life would change by serving my country."

"So how long did you serve in the military?"

Luke shrugged. "I went to college and played football for a few years and then served for a few years after that." He seemed to not want to talk about his past. "I think your car might be ready. I saw it on my way in here to grab a cup of coffee. Do you mind if I walk you to the front?" Luke poured himself a cup of coffee from the glass carafe.

"Sure." Katie tried to not to sound too excited about seeing Luke again.

"Hey, Luke!" A sales associate with thick dark brown hair resting on his collar stood at in the doorway holding the town's newspaper. "Look who is on the front page of the paper again!" The wide-mouthed sales associate tossed the paper at Luke.

Luke caught it with ease but did not look as amused as the other man. "Thanks for sharing, but I've seen it." Luke put the paper under his arm and walked toward the door.

"Katie, this is Wes. Wes, this is Katie. She's new to town and will be teaching at the high school in the fall," Luke introduced the two. His eyes flitted toward the door as he turned his shoulders to the entrance. He looked uncomfortable, ready to bolt from the room.

"Nice to meet you, Wes," Katie extended her right hand.

"Nice to meet you, too, ma'am. And welcome to Gatesville." The young associate eyed her as he gave a firm handshake. "Oh, and maybe I will see you downtown at the Spurfest this weekend? There will be homemade ice cream, carnival games, and an evening concert. It is one event you will not want to miss being new to town and all."

"I will have to check my calendar." Katie made her way to the door next to Luke. "I do have so much to learn about Gatesville. I really appreciate you letting me know." Katie gave Wes a courteous smile.

"Well, I know this is kind of forward, but if you give me your number then I can give you a call later this week and see if you are interested in hanging out. You wouldn't want to miss it. Really." Wes appeared genuinely interested in her.

She knew she had nothing on her calendar except to spend time with her grandma. Maybe it would be okay to go with him.

"Well," Katie started and looked at Luke hoping he would help her out. She didn't even know this guy. Luke caught her plea.

"Hey now, Wes. Katie probably just wants to hang out with her grandma this weekend. Katie's car is ready now, so I am leading her to it." Luke headed toward the door.

"If I end up being free then I know where to find you and how to contact you. Thank you again." Katie halfway lifted her hand. She felt bad leaving him hanging, but she normally did not give her number out to men she did not know—even in a small town.

Without speaking, Luke led her down the hallway. It seemed Wes' words about the paper had put him in deep thought and she did not want to disturb him. His shoulders seemed to droop some. Should she perk him up? Maybe a funny joke about being on the front page. Nah. Her corny jokes might only annoy him. She was curious, though. Why did he look so uncomfortable about being on the front page?

Relief filled Katie when she saw her car through the window at the end of the hallway.

"There's my car. I guess I'll get my keys at the desk. Thank you, Luke." Katie broke the awkward silence.

Her voice seemed to interrupt his thoughts. "It was great running into you today, Katie. I wonder where the next place is that we will see each other?" He grinned as he halfway joked with her.

"There aren't too many more places to go here in Gatesville, so maybe it'll be the dirty ole' hole-in-the-wall Burger Shack next." Katie grinned right back at him.

"Hey, I like the Burger Shack. That's my favorite burger place in town!" Luke exclaimed as he acted offended.

"It's the only burger place in town!" Katie laughed.

"If you don't find it too repulsive of a place then how 'bout we meet there on Friday for lunch? It'd be much nicer to meet you somewhere than having to wait and see where the next spot is that I happen to run into you. Or do you have to check your busy calendar first?" Luke winked at her.

Katie stopped laughing and felt her cheeks flushing. She knew she couldn't hold off on an answer.

"Well, I do have a very busy schedule." Katie lifted her chin. "But I do suppose I could make time for you and your favorite burger place," she teased him, trying to hide the embarrassment and excitement she had in her stomach all at the same time.

"Okay, then how 'bout we meet at 11:30 so we can beat the rush? You know it's everyone's favorite," Luke teased her back.

"That sounds great. I will see you at 11:30," Katie's voice trailed off as she locked eyes with Luke. Goodness. His eyes were dangerously gorgeous. She just might fall for him if she weren't careful. This guy just wanted a friendly meeting and she could hardly keep her composure around him.

"Okay, then! You better be ready for a great burger, shake and fries. The finest Gatesville has to offer!" Luke smarted off as he made his way to the offices in the back of the shop.

CHAPTER 7

*R*eflecting on her brief conversation with Luke made the seven-mile drive back to Grandma's house pass in a blur. She tried not to overanalyze the short visit, but it was so nice to have made an acquaintance in Luke.

Katie drove up the gravel drive to the century-old, white-washed, wood-frame house. Grandma had lived here as long as she could remember. The huge front porch was a favorite spot for the family to gather. It was no surprise to find Betty—Grandma's home health care worker—sitting on the porch taking care of her charge. The middle-aged woman came each weekday morning and stayed through the early afternoon. Her bleach-blond hair contrasted with her dark-tanned skin, and her smile could melt the heart of the most stubborn soul. Betty helped Grandma get ready for the day, take her medicines, and eat a nutritious breakfast and lunch.

An agreement made two years ago between Grandma and Katie's mom, Mary—Grace's daughter-in-law—allowed Grandma to live at home. Katie cringed thinking about Grandma losing her freedom, but something needed to take place to help her aging grandma. If only she could have moved to Gatesville sooner. The time and desire weren't right though. At least Grandma still lived at home even if things weren't the same as they used to be when she was younger. Driving her car didn't happen often and baking pies occurred almost never.

Mary had agreed to Grandma living at home as long as she had someone come check on her at least once a day. After weeks of dealing with Grandma's stubbornness, she had convinced her to have a home healthcare worker come check on her.

Katie could tell Grandma thoroughly enjoyed having the company of her home health care worker. Betty always had listening ears for her.

Katie parked her car in the shade under the rusting metal carport and joined the two women on the front porch.

"Hi, Grandma. Hi, Betty." She greeted both ladies with a smile.

"Hi, Katie. Looks like someone is happy to have her car back." Betty pointed toward the carport. "Your grandma told me you were in town getting a new tire."

Katie gave a slight smirk. "Ha, yes! I definitely am glad to have my car back. And Grandma," said Katie as she patted her knee and laughed. "I am so thankful you let me borrow your car, but that trunk is so massive. It is nice to have my little sedan back to whiz around." Parking and backing up in that thing were near impossible.

"You're welcome, Katie, anytime you need it you just go ahead and borrow it. I only drive it to and from church and then to the grocery store once a week. It's probably about time for me to sell the thing, but I like having my freedom." Grace lowered her eyes. She spoke sobering truth.

"Well, ladies," Betty interjected with her thick country twang. She could have sung backup for a country band. "I'd better grab my bag and get on my way. Ms. Grace, now make sure you eat a good breakfast in the morning before I see you tomorrow. Don't be telling me none of this 'I drank my coffee and that was my breakfast,'" chastised Betty. She gave Grandma a stern glance before winking at Katie.

"It was great seeing you, Katie." Betty stood up from her spot, grabbed her bags resting against the wall, and headed toward the steps. "I'm sure glad you are here to give your grandma some company; maybe you can keep her in line." Betty laughed.

"I think it is more like I'm glad to be here so she can give me company," Katie said. She sat on the porch swing next to her grandma and wrapped her arm around the thin woman, giving her a gentle squeeze.

For the past six years, Katie had lived alone. Her last roommate was post-college while she was working on her masters. She vowed never to live with another person unless she got married. Delegating bathroom and kitchen cleaning almost drove her crazy. But being alone stirred in her a deep longing for community. Having time with Grandma brought the best to both worlds. Time with her beloved grandma—even if she didn't cook anymore.

Grandma used to whip up the best meals of mashed potatoes, chicken fried steak, and gravy in her younger years. Now, Katie attempted to cook for her grandma even though she found the microwave as the most helpful appliance. She'd given up even cooking even mac and cheese on the stove top. She prepared simple meals – salads, sandwich wraps, frozen lasagna - but Grace didn't mind. She seemed happy to have Katie there.

"Well, I am glad for both of you to have company now. You ladies have a great day and enjoy this beautiful sunshine." She got in her car and then drove down the dusty gravel road, leaving a cloud of white dust in the air behind her.

Katie looked down and noticed a newspaper in her grandma's lap. On the front page, the smile of a handsome young man caught her attention.

"Is that Luke on the front page of the paper?" Katie gasped as she grabbed it from her grandma's lap and opened it all the way.

Sure enough, it was him. Wes, at the dealership, mentioned someone being on the front page, but he hadn't shared any details.

It was the local paper, but she was still impressed he'd made the front page. "Why is his picture in here?" Katie questioned her grandma as she scanned the small print under the picture.

"He's back in town. Everyone is glad to have their hero back in Gatesville," stated Grace nonchalantly.

"What do you mean *their* hero?" Katie sat up straight. What else didn't she know about Luke?

"Oh, you know, honey. Just glad to have the hometown boy back after he served overseas. He got a couple of medals and now he's home again."

"Huh." Katie relaxed in her seat. There must be more to his story. She was a high school teacher ready for a change away from a stale and stagnant life. Ready to get away from life in the city. Ready to live in the same home her father once grew up in— oh, how she still missed him today. She saw nothing heroic in her own story, but apparently Luke was a hometown hero. Too humble to even talk about it.

"I once had my picture on the front page of the newspaper." Grandma stared out into the field. Her distant words interjected into Katie's thoughts. "Actually, I was sitting on the porch just like we are now, when my younger brother ran up the steps on a somewhat mild Thanksgiving Day and called out, "Grace, Grace! You've got to see this.""

CHAPTER 8

THANKSGIVING DAY 1941

Grace's fingers interlocked with her future groom's hand as she watched her younger brother dash up the three porch steps in one leap to get to his older sister.

"Look, your and Edward's picture is on the front page, right here on the bottom part!" John Jr. jiggled the paper, making it hard to read. At an early age, the family had shortened his full name to J.J. Even though he was the baby of the family, he was not far from passing her in height.

"My word!" She placed her hand to her chest. "It sure is! I thought you said we'd be on page four or five." She gawked between Edward and the announcement.

"I did," Edward confessed and lifted his hands in the air as if pleading his innocence, "but the editor needed another news story, so we got bumped to the bottom on the front page." His eyes shifted to the paper with a look of sincerity and desperation. "And my love, you look stunning! This is the best the front page has looked since I have worked at the newspaper."

She was fine with the picture, but it still caught her off guard. Did everyone need to know they were getting married? Weren't there more important things to discuss? She could only imagine all the little ladies around town sewing together and chattering about her. She scanned the announcement.

She lifted her head and studied her future groom's unsure eyes. It wasn't every day a girl had her picture put in the paper, though. She gave him a large grin.

"Thank you. This is an honor. Now, let's go show my mother and father." J.J. handed her the paper as she clutched Edward's arm and pulled him toward the front door.

J.J. yanked open the front door and sprinted in the house ahead of them. "Mama! Father! Grace is in the paper!"

The couple stepped into the giant nine-foot ceiling foyer. Pale yellow wallpaper covered the walls. A beautiful dark-stained oak entry table and long settee, both made by her great-grandfather, lined the narrow entryway.

The foyer became a hallway separating the bedrooms from the living room, kitchen, and dining area. The square area used for the dining room housed the family's large round oak table. Mahogany fabric with matching lace trim, sewn together by her mother, covered the heirloom.

Grace's family, including grandparents, routinely squished around the table, but for extended family Thanksgivings, the men and women ate separately. As a custom, the men ate first followed by the women and children.

The scent from the Thanksgiving dinner from a few hours earlier still permeated the room—farm-raised turkey with herbs and new potatoes, pickled beets, tomatoes, and corn from their garden, and Mama's special homemade bread. The family favorites.

Grace headed toward the living room knowing Mama and Granny were sitting in there. Her grandmother would be sitting in her favorite wingback chair, her mother on the cream settee.

Her father would be catching a quick nap in his chair, which he rarely did. Farm work never ended, but her father found time to rest on the Lord's Day and on special holidays.

"Mama!" she said just above a whisper as she entered the room, not wanting to wake her father. "I have something to show you!"

Mama casually put down her sewing project for a moment as Grace gave her mother the newspaper. She watched Mama's blue eyes widen as she caught first glance at the paper.

"Look at you two!" She tapped the black and white photo. "On the front page of *The Gatesville Herald*! This will be the talk of Oakmont. Everyone already knows about your engagement, but to see this announcement and such a nice picture of the two of you is such a wonderful sight."

She noticed John Sr. stir in his chair. He glanced at the paper over Mama's shoulder.

"That's a nice picture," her father said, rubbing his square jaw. Dark circles lined the fifty-year-old farmer's eyes. She waited, hoping to soak in any other comments he might happen to release. She squeezed Edward's arm a little tighter as she studied her father reading the article from his chair.

She noticed his blue eyes squinting, as if something wasn't right. He clenched his jaw and concern covered his face as he scanned the rest of the paper.

"Is something wrong, Father?" Grace Katherine asked.

"No, nothing is wrong with your picture," her father replied carefully. "Your picture is lovely. I just noticed the headline above your picture." He pointed to the article emblazoned across the top half of the paper. "The Army has chosen a site for the future Army camp. Looks like it is north of here... in Bosque County. Thankful it is not here, but sorry for those others who will have to deal with it." A look of disgust covered his face as she he shook his head.

"Sir," Edward cleared his throat. "I don't mean to be impolite, but why would you not want to deal with a training camp coming to our area?" Edward's voice rose. "Can you not imagine the economic boost it will bring to the area they have chosen? All the jobs it will provide?"

"No, son," John Sr. stated. He sat up in his chair and turned to face Edward. "I believe the further west the better. Less people affected by all of this."

"A representative out of Waco has had all the county officials coming to him begging and pleading their cases why they think their land is the best. At least that's what I overheard from a friend who works as a reporter in McLennan County. Apparently, the Army leaders are more interested in which area has the terrain best matching that of Europe. I know Mr. Frank Mayborn of Belton has been working hard to get them in Bell County, just south of here," Edward said offering his viewpoint. She knew he'd edited the contents of the article before it went to print since he worked at the newspaper.

"There are always pros and cons to any situation—this one being no different. Two views on one subject. Neither is wrong, but in this case one party will get hurt and one will benefit." Her father's tone stung. She desperately wanted him to bless her engagement and instead her fiancé and father stood arguing about land.

J.J. interrupted the tense moment, bursting his gangly body into the room. This time, he announced the arrival of a guest. "We got ourselves a visitor on Thanksgiving Day and boy is he going fast!" Her brother's eyes were wide with excitement. *Who could be here now?*

All attention turned to the front of the house. Grace ran to the front entryway with Edward behind her. She reached the screen door to the house just in time to see an old Model T burst through the front gate. An involuntary gasp left her mouth. She looked at Edward and he seemed equally surprised. J.J., however, stood in the yard waving and laughing as he cheered on the driver.

She recognized James' auburn hair bouncing up and down in the driver's seat. He spun the steering wheel left and then right and then left again. He couldn't gain control. He missed the smokehouse and the windmill by inches. She stood frozen as her father's thundering boots pounded past her on the wood floor. He ran down the porch steps frantically waving his arms.

Mama, Edward, Ruth, Granny and Grace all gathered on the front porch as they surveyed the old Ford making one last big circle around the yard before running into the horse trough.

Father's face changed to dark red as he barked at James. The young man scrambled out of the car and slammed the door shut. James ignored her father and started jogging for the house.

"Edward, Edward!" James called out.

"James! What in the world do you think you are doing tearing down everything we have worked hard for! I ought to…" Father continued on.

"Mr….Mr. Willis, I…I do apologize sir," James interrupted as he tried to catch his breath. He lifted his palms wide open in a scene of surrender. "My brakes must have gone out. I'm sorry, sir, I will pay for it."

She watched as Father gave him a long stern look. "No, need. Doesn't look like it needs too much fixing. I imagine J.J. could get it fixed rather fast, especially since he was so excited to watch you."

"James, what are you doing driving out here on Thanksgiving Day?" Edward said as he joined the two men in the yard.

"Edward, we got the news about Mr. Mayborn!" James gasped.

"What do you mean, James? What news?"

"I've been trying to call you all morning, but I figured out you must be here so I came to find you myself." James ran his hand through his thick auburn hair. "Mr. Mayborn just gathered together all the judges from Bell, Lampasas, and Coryell Counties and city leaders from Killeen and Gatesville. They are all going to the Army's Eighth Corps Area headquarters at Fort Sam Houston in San Antonio. They left about an hour ago. They are going to be discussing the placement of the new Army camp. This is big-time news!" His words rushed together.

"Do you hear what I am saying, Edward?" James grabbed his friend by his shoulders. "I don't know what all locations they're going to be talking about, but we have to leave now. We have got to get this story before anyone else leaks it out first." James took his hands and pointed directly toward Edward's car urging him to leave.

"Yes, I guess you are right." Edward took a deep breath and ran his hand over his brow.

James hustled toward Edward's car, leaving his own car sitting next to the trough.

Edward headed toward the porch. "Mrs. Willis, thank you for your hospitality. The food was delicious as always," he said.

"And Mr. Willis, thank you for having me out here today." He nodded in the direction of her father. "I will help James in paying for or fixing anything that has been damaged."

Edward grabbed Grace's hand and walked a few steps away from the others. Thanksgiving festivities seemed to be over. He leaned in and gently kissed her on the forehead. "I will come visit you in a few days, darling. I am sorry I have to leave so early. Hopefully, we will get a good story out of this for the paper."

Grace felt a little petulant. *Why does he have to leave so soon, especially for a story?*

"Edward!" shouted James from the car. "We need to go now!"

"I'm coming!" Edward hollered. His hands slipped from Grace's grasp as he took a step back.

"Bye, my love," Edward said and then he turned and jogged toward his car.

"Bye," Grace whispered in return, sad and frustrated to see him leave so early on this holiday.

Edward got in the car and made a rapid turn toward the dirt driveway. A huge cloud of dust bellowed behind the car as the two men raced toward San Antonio.

CHAPTER 9

*E*dward sped toward San Antonio on old country roads and highways, attempting to catch up to the leaders of Coryell and Bell counties. He didn't want them to start their meeting before he got there. It took the young men almost a half a day, but they arrived just as the others had gathered at the Army's Eighth Corps Area headquarters at Fort Sam Houston in San Antonio.

"Well, look at that, James. We all got here at the same time." Edward put the car in park and reached for his notebook.

"Yep! You sure are right! Come on then. Let's try to find a spot before they get started." James grabbed his pen and paper and jogged with Edward to the doorway.

The two men nabbed a couple of spots in the entrance with a good view of the room. This ought to be the perfect spot. And here they come now. Those officials sure had a lot of determination to drive all the way down here thinking General Donovan would change his mind. Edward glanced at the astute Army general sitting at his desk, still looking down at his work, unfazed by the sound of his visitors coming into the building.

One by one the central Texas area leaders entered. The

mastermind of the plan to bring Fort Hood to central Texas, newspaper publisher Frank Mayborn, stepped in first. In his late thirties, Mayborn was also in a sense a powerful political leader. The county judges, mayors, and other officials from Coryell and Bell Counties followed close behind into the office of the commander of the Eighth Corps Area, General Richard Donovan.

General Donovan tilted his chin halfway up and greeted his guests as they entered. As far as Edward knew, General Donovan's decision had already been made as where to put the anti-tank camp. Donovan and other government officials had completed research and decided on Valley Mills, Texas, which was in a neighboring county of Coryell. The space between Edward, Mayborn and Donovan became narrow. It was time to squeeze through before there was nothing to see.

Edward and James shifted through the small crowd and found a space toward the front of the office. They knew this was a clash of two giant figureheads, Mayborn and Donovan. Both men knew what they wanted—and that was the opposite of each other. Mayborn was determined for Coryell County to be the new site. Donovan wanted to keep the location the same. This was going to be a historic moment.

Edward's stomach grumbled as the meeting started. It had been a long time since Thanksgiving lunch, but food had to wait. He watched the young Mayborn stride to the front of General Donovan's huge oak desk as the older commander sat in his plush chair behind the desk.

Those in the small space quieted their voices and turned their focus toward the front of the crowded room. Mayborn waited until he had everyone's attention. He cleared his throat and stepped slightly forward.

"General Donovan, we are all here today to discuss why Valley Mills in Bosque County is not the correct decision for the new anti-tank training camp." Mayborn began his presentation on the negative issues and problems with the Army choosing the small farming community. The high-spirited Mayborn began flailing his arms around. "The pipelines in that area are of much concern as well as not having enough water available for a large Army camp. The water will practically become depleted in the area if you build there."

General Donovan's lips were frozen in a frown while his eyes stared at Mayborn. Edward scribbled down every word as Mayborn debated why Bosque County was not the best possible choice, but rather Coryell and Bell counties. As Mayborn concluded, he stood there silent. Donovan did not look too convinced.

General Donovan looked Mayborn up and down as he inspected him.

General Donovan said, "Young man, you don't think much of the United States Army, do you?"

Tension hung in the ensuing silence, growing more awkward by the moment. Edward stopped scribbling to examine the two men. Their eyes and voices were the only two weapons the men could use.

Donovan studied Mayborn long and hard before asking, "Where are you talking about?"

James and Edward leaned forward. His friend shot him a look of disbelief. *Was he actually considering Mayborn's argument?*

Mayborn then pointed to a location in Coryell County on the general's map.

"Young man, I'll check in to it and have a new inspection of the area."

With that Donovan turned his chair back toward his desk and began sorting through the paperwork dismissing the young businessman and his political acquaintances.

James elbowed Edward in the ribs. Edward glanced over at him with his lips curling into a grin. It was unreal to both young reporters Donovan was considering a different area than had already been announced. Coryell County – which included the Gatesville area - might have a chance at getting the new Army camp.

Edward gazed over his shoulder at the other leaders in the room. A sense of relief settled over the men as they shook hands and patted each other on the back. Edward bent his head down again and furiously began to write notes of the events he witnessed. *Mayborn just might have gotten his way. A new camp for Coryell County.*

CHAPTER 10

DECEMBER 1941

*E*dward traced the detailed thread work on his fiancée's dress with his lanky index finger. It had been over a week since his article debuted in the newspaper. It was now December, and the residents of the central Texas region were still awaiting final word on where the new camp would be located.

Grace reached to her side and stopped his repetitive motion. She weaved her delicate fingers between Edward's and scooted closer on the wooden pew. Her family had worshiped together on this same pew for several generations. This place brought a sense of warmth and love.

She shifted her shoulders and leaned into him as the preacher, a fire-and-brimstone type in his late thirties, neared the end of his sermon in the small Oakmont church. *Having Edward here feels good.* It felt needed on this December 7th Sunday morning. He rarely found time to travel to Oakmont on Sundays, but having him sitting next to her put all the pieces together in her life. He belonged with her. Here and now. And forever.

Grace's mind drifted as she glanced out the window beside their pew. The terrain, brown except for the evergreen live oak and cedar trees, showed it was now winter; however, the warm humid air felt more like fall. She never complained about the hot Texas summers because on days like today she was thankful for mild winters. Her family and others from the church planned to stay after the service to eat together and then watch the men and boys play baseball on the field near the church.

As his sermon neared the end, Reverend Frank led the congregation to stand and sing a final benediction.

Blest be the tie that binds
    our hearts in Christian love;
    the fellowship of kindred minds
    is like to that above.
    Before our Father's throne
    we pour our ardent prayers;
    our fears, our hopes, our aims are one,
    our comforts and our cares.

The stubby pastor raised his hand in victory. His voice billowed through the room as he closed the service. "Amen. Go in peace, brothers and sisters in Christ."

Grace joined Edward and her family in exiting out the only door in the front of the church.

"I'll go to the car and grab the blanket and food. Grace, why don't you and Edward find a spot for us. J.J., you come and help me while your father is talking." Mama instructed as she walked toward the family sedan.

Edward and Grace found a place under the shade of a sprawling live oak tree. Once Mama joined them, they spread on the ground the double wedding ring quilt made with an eclectic array of bright colors. The entire family, including Granny,

Father, Mickey, Ruth, and J.J., all joined together to eat on the lawn.

Mama opened her wicker basket and one by one placed food packets on the heirloom quilt including ham, fresh homemade bread, a jar of spicy pickles and sliced cheese. Her favorite foods. Mama had also spared some of her sugar to make chocolate chip cookies for the entire family.

Grace watched as others in the church family gathered nearby, enjoying the unseasonably warm December day. The farmers in the area had finished harvesting cotton, so all were in good spirits. If a day could be described as perfect, then this would be that day. Church. Sunshine. Family. Homemade bread and a picnic. In this moment, nothing could destroy the day.

"Heya, J.J.!" A young friend from school called out to J.J. from a nearby blanket. "You about finished eating yet, ya slow poke? I'm ready to play some ball," the fifth grader said as he hit his fist into his faded leather glove.

"Yeah! I'm ready!" J.J. said as he stuffed a chocolate chip cookie in his mouth and ran off with his buddy.

"I think I am about ready to go play some ball too!" Edward piped in as he watched the two young boys race toward home base.

Grace caught her throat as she swallowed her spicy pickle. "You are?" She cocked her head to one side. She had never seen him play ball.

"Yes, and why do you look at me like that? You act as if I've never caught a ball before." Edward placed his hand over his chest pretending the comment offended him. "Here, Mickey," he said as he motioned to Grace's twenty-year old brother to toss him a glove and ball.

"You're good with your hands, but I never thought about you playing ball. I guess in the time I've known you, I haven't seen you play." Grace shrugged her shoulders.

"I'm a working man now and I had to pay for that fancy ring

so there is no time to play anymore," Edward joked with her. "But let me tell you," he paused and studied Grace's eyes, "I wouldn't have it any other way."

Waves of brunette hair surrounded her face cascading down just past her shoulders. She pushed it aside and fixed her eyes on Edward. She would not have it any other way either. To be loved and adored by him meant everything to her.

"You are beautiful! You know that, right?" Edward leaned over, grabbed his fiancée's hand, and gently pressed his lips to her warm skin.

Grace could feel her cheeks glowing. This man awakened her heart.

"Come on, Mickey!" Edward called out as he leapt to his feet. "Let's go show these young ones who's in charge!" He turned and sprinted toward the field with his future brother-in-law next to him.

Grace rested her back on the thick bark of the live oak tree as she observed the two men joining the others playing baseball. She stretched her legs on the quilt and absorbed the sights and sounds of her community surrounding her.

Granny and Mama had left the family's blanket and were now visiting with a few other ladies from the church, including Mrs. Miller and Mrs. Carter. Ruth had joined a few high school girls sitting on a bench near the men and boys playing baseball.

Grace scanned the field and realized her father was missing. A group of men gathered near the church building garnered her attention. Father, wearing a pair of dark brown pants and the only white dress shirt he owned, stood in the center. He picked at his teeth and then started chewing on a long piece of chaff. She noticed him shake his head and then scowl at the ground.

A shot of anxiousness jolted through her chest. She *knew* they were talking about the new camp. Every time it was mentioned he became anxious. She really didn't want to ruin her Sunday obsessing about war or the possibility of the Army stationing men nearby. Why couldn't they stay away from the topic? Why did it always have to come up? She wanted things to stay forever the same. Grace shifted her eyes back toward the younger men.

Edward snatched a fly ball at second base and then threw the ball to Mickey, stretching out his long arms at first base as the ball snapped in his glove. In two quick motions, the runner was out before he even touched first base. Grace relaxed and took a deep breath as she watched her brother flip Edward a single thumbs-up before crouching low and beating his glove for a few seconds while the next batter approached home base.

Grace reclined her back against the tree. The gentle breeze soothed her face in the warm afternoon. She brushed away a few loose curls. Tiredness started to consume her. She tried to keep her eyes open as she continued to observe the game from a distance, but they weighed down until they slowly closed.

GRACE NEVER IMAGINED that twenty-four hours later, she would be quieting all the children in the schoolhouse to await an important message being broadcast over the radio on this blustery December 8, Monday afternoon. Even the weather matched the mood of the current situation. Dense clouds enveloped the winter sun and the howling wind roared in from the north through the crack in the front door. The students sat still and motionless. The absence of movement and noise sent a chill through Grace's shoulders to her arms, spiking her hairs. She was sure the children could sense the gravity of the situation even though they were unsure of what had happened.

Others in Oakmont told her the President would be making an urgent address over the radio this afternoon. Electricity had been scarce to find in the small hamlets outside Gatesville until recently. A year ago, the schoolhouse acquired electricity, otherwise she would have had to use a battery-powered radio. She counted her blessings the students could listen to this important message from President Franklin D. Roosevelt at the school.

Grace heard the shallow breathing of the young children behind her as she turned on the radio. Static permeated the soundwaves until an intense, solemn voice filled the room. President Roosevelt was addressing Congress and the entire nation.

"Yesterday, December 7, 1941—a date which will live in infamy—the United States of America was suddenly and deliberately attacked by naval and air forces of the Empire of Japan..."

Grace stared at the radio, soaking in every word. Roosevelt's speech continued for the next seven minutes. He shared over the live broadcast how the Japanese attacked the American Navy at Pearl Harbor in Hawaii. Many lost their lives during this attack on United States' soil.

"With confidence in our armed forces—with the unbounding determination of our people—we will gain the inevitable triumph- so help us God. I ask that the Congress declare that since the unprovoked and dastardly attack by Japan on Sunday, December 7, 1941, a state of war has existed between the United States and the Japanese Empire."

The President's short speech left the room eerily quiet. Grace was unsure of the effects of this speech, but just as swift as the northern wind had changed the temperature outside, she knew more lives would be altered forever.

CHAPTER 11

JUNE 2016

*K*atie glanced one last time in her rearview mirror after she pulled into a parking spot at the Burger Shack. Five minutes early for her lunch appointment, she gave herself props—maybe she could change her bad habit of arriving late after all. Placing her car in park, she took a deep breath and then peeked into the mirror. Despite the hot, humid air, her braid had stayed in place. Finally.

Before she left her grandma's, she'd braided the strands of dark blond hair framing the right side of her face and then gathered the remaining locks into a lower ponytail. The Texas heat made it easy to decide on an up-do; however, choosing what to wear from her modest wardrobe took over an hour.

At last, in despair, she decided on a cyan sleeveless blouse and her favorite white capris. She complimented the outfit with her new brown strappy sandals chosen more for their squishy sole than style and a pair of dangly gold earrings. For her, comfort always won over fashion. She threw her purse over her shoulder and headed for the front door.

"Bye, Grandma!" The older woman faced the TV and was watching the end of *The Price is Right*.

"Young lady…." Grace grabbed the remote. "Wait just a minute."

"You've won a trip to France and a new car!" the announcer shouted on the TV.

"Well, look at that." The older woman turned her full attention back to the end of her show.

"Um, Grandma?" Katie walked toward her. "I said bye. Do you need me?"

"Oh! I'm sorry! I forgot! This is my favorite show." Grandma fiddled with the remote. "Here, let me mute this thing."

Katie double-checked her purse to make sure she had her keys, wallet and phone. Check, check, and check.

"Grandma, I need to go. May I help you?"

"Got it!" The sound disappeared.

The older woman laid the remote on her side table and then turned to inspect her granddaughter.

"My, Katie, you clean up real nice, honey," Grandma teased as she reached out her arms to hug her goodbye. "Are you headed on a date or something? I thought you were grabbing a quick bite to eat with someone?"

"Grandma…" Katie's voice trailed off as she gave her grandma a gentle hug. "Luke and I are just going to lunch," she insisted and rolled her eyes.

"Well, you two have fun and don't get into too much trouble. And be sure and grab that $20 bill on the table by the front door. It can pay for your meal or something else."

"That is sweet of you, but you don't need to give me any money. I am fine."

"Honey, I said there is a $20 and don't forget it. Enjoy!" She turned her attention back to the TV. Katie reached down and unmuted the show.

"I will. Thanks, Grandma." She leaned over and kissed her forehead.

Once she arrived in the pothole-filled parking lot at the local dive, Katie began second-guessing herself as she placed a visor in her front window and then grabbed her purse from the passenger seat. Athletic clothes would have been much better for this hot day, but these capris would do.

She reached for the handle and felt the door move out of her grasp. She jolted back, prepared to kick the intruder. The bellowing hoot resounded on the other side of the door came from Luke.

How did he always have this element of surprise about him? And this time his presence was expected. She joined Luke in laughing at herself, feeling slightly silly for her reaction.

"I apologize, I didn't mean to scare you." His eyes soften and she could tell he did not mean any harm. "I thought you saw me at your window. I wanted to be a gentleman and open your door."

She went from laughing to feeling her cheeks getting hot. It had been a while since a man wanted to put her on a pedestal.

"N-no...I...I'm sorry. I was in deep thought. Trying to solve too many problems at once. Thank you though for thinking of me." Katie accepted Luke's hand as she got out of her car.

"Are you ready to try the best burger in all of Coryell County?" Luke gave her a boyish grin and led her to the entrance. The Burger Shack was a hometown favorite located in the back of a dilapidated gas station.

"Yes, I am ready. I haven't been here since I was twelve or thirteen, but I remember they have great onion rings. I'm sure we would have come here more often, but Grandma didn't like eating out much we when visited her. She preferred to cook for us."

"Your grandma is a great cook! I understand why she didn't enjoy eating out much. She fixed my family several meals throughout the years. She makes the best homemade bread around."

"I agree with you completely." Katie couldn't help the smile that spread across her face. Conversation with Luke was easy.

He opened the front door for her, and they stepped into the burger joint. The aroma of fried foods and a fired-up grill greeted her.

Her stomach rumbled and she put a hand on it. "It smells so delicious in here!"

"I can take the next person in line here!" A young male cashier called. Katie approached the counter and ordered a cheeseburger, onion rings, and a Dr. Pepper.

"Is that all for you, ma'am?" The short, spiky-brown-haired employee's voice was as monotone as his looks were wild.

Before Katie could answer, Luke stepped in and said, "No, I want a double cheeseburger on a toasted bun with jalapenos and bacon, cheesy fries and a Dr. Pepper to drink." He handed money to the cashier before she could say anything. "My treat." Luke gave her a nod.

"I've got a $20," Katie waved the money in the air. "My grandma made me take it."

"Save that bill for another…"

"Hey! You're Mr. Reed!" The cashier interrupted. "I saw your picture in the paper the other day." The bored-monotone young man from a moment ago was now animated and wide-eyed. "You played for Army and I used to watch all your games on TV. And now here you are! I can't wait to play under you. I heard you're one of our new football coaches." The comments rolled one after another. Katie studied her lunch date. There was obviously a lot she didn't know about him.

Luke, for the first time since she met him, appeared perplexed as the student continued treating him like a celebrity.

"Yes, that's right." Luke commented once the young man took a breath.

Seeming to get his focus back, Luke then questioned the boy, "Will you be ready for two-a-days in August?"

"Uh… yeah." The star-struck teen blinked.

"Work on your sprints and weight training now and it will be easier once practice starts." Luke's husky tone was kind yet firm as he leaned over and stared at the skinny kid.

"Yes, sir!" The boy stood tall and straightened his shoulders.

"Good!" Luke smiled. "Now, what was the total?" He nodded toward the money still hanging in the air in the kid's hand.

"Oh right, it will be $16.08. You're order number 124."

Katie observed the scene between the two. Everyone around her knew Luke or something about him. He might not consider himself a celebrity, but it seemed like it to her.

"Let's sit over there." Luke motioned toward a table at the back.

The Burger Shack wouldn't win any awards for cutest or best decorated diner. Disgust filled her head as she glanced at the ceiling tiles stained from a leaky roof. Hopefully they would stay in place until after lunch. The tattered, frayed red seat cushions were a permanent fixture and apparently did not turn away the hometown folks. As long as they served good food, the locals would continue gathering here.

"So… how are you adjusting to Gatesville?" Luke placed a napkin in his lap.

"Pretty good. Much easier than other places I've lived."

A chuckle accompanied Luke's nod. "Can't get lost around here, can you?"

Laughter bubbled up at their easy conversation. "Nope, not really. There's one Walmart, a grocery store, a few shops down-town and some clothing stores. It is a pretty straightforward little town."

"Have you been enjoying your time with your grandma?"

"Oh goodness, yes. I know her memory isn't the same as even a year ago, but she's still full of stories, so I'd say it's going pretty smooth."

"What kind of stories?" He leaned back in his chair and crossed his thick arms.

"She has been living so much in the past lately. I tell her a current story and then she relives one from her past. Most of these stories I've never heard. For instance, at the cemetery the other day, she mentioned an engagement proposal from her past. I have never heard that story before. Another time she shared about Oakmont and the people who lived there. Last night's saga was concerning Pearl Harbor and the start of the war. I guess her memory is good in the sense of what she is able to remember, but I am not sure why she is revealing this to me now."

"My grandpa left Oakmont right after Pearl Harbor happened. FDR announced war on Japan on December 8, 1941 and then Germany on December 11, 1941. My grandpa and his older brother packed their bags on that Thursday night, December 11. By Friday morning, December 12, they headed off to join the Army."

"I'm impressed you know all these dates! I can barely remember Pearl Harbor was on December 7."

"My grandpa's story was engraved in my head as a child. He's the main reason I chose to play for the Army after being recruited by several schools. With Fort Hood residing so close by and idolizing my grandpa, I was destined for military."

"So why did you get out?"

"Two tours are enough for one man. Really one tour is, but I played football for five years—one of those years I was redshirted—and then served in the Army for five years. My contract came up and I decided I was ready to spend time with my family. I had been gone too long. By the time I got home this past spring, I had been away for ten years. I started looking for jobs and one of my high school buddies is the head coach here now, so he offered me a job as an assistant football coach. I might could've found a bigger school or a place that paid more, but it was important for me to be home. I guess that was more than what you were looking for..." Luke's voice trailed off.

"No, no, I love your response. I have been trying to put the puzzle pieces together and figure you out," Katie said and gave a quick laugh. She enjoyed listening to him talk and share. "I knew you played football and you told me you are going to coach in the fall, but I still didn't know why you were back here. Now you have solved that mystery for me!" Katie joked.

"Ticket number 124," the high school cashier's voice cracked as he yelled. "Your order is ready!" He pushed forward a couple of bright red baskets on the counter.

"That's us." Luke glanced at the number on his ticket. "I'll be right back."

She tried not to stare at him as he left to get the food, but he captivated her – even just casually talking to him she kept wanting to learn more about him.

As he started walking back to the table, a cowboy who appeared in his late 70s, wearing dark colored Wranglers and holding a tan hat, grabbed him by his shoulder. Luke jolted and stepped back.

"Luke!" the older cowboy extended his thick tan hand to greet the young man.

The thin lines around Luke's wide eyes crinkled as he smiled in recognition.

"Hey!" Luke set his tray on the small table closest to him. "What are you doing here?" He reached for the man's hand.

"I think the question should be, what are you doing here?" Another older cowboy said as he joined the small reunion. His pearly teeth matched the snap buttons on his light-blue denim shirt as he flashed Luke a grin.

Both cowboys patted Luke on the back as they began talking to him. *Everyone really does love or at least knows Luke,* Katie thought. She wondered how long the conversation was going to last this time. The onion rings just might get a bit soggy before they let him rejoin her. She could almost taste her burger.

"Where are you sitting, son? We can sit right here with you if you want," offered the first cowboy.

Katie felt her cheeks grow warm. Clearly, the men did not see her sitting fifteen feet away.

Luke reached around the men and grabbed the red tray. He motioned toward Katie with his head.

"I'm sitting with my friend, Katie, but you men are welcome to join us."

The empty seats in the dive were quickly being filled.

"Oh now, we don't want to bother you." The elderly cowboy patted Luke on the back again. "But who's the pretty young lady friend you got over there?"

"Why don't you come meet her?" Luke said as he led the way to Katie.

She straightened her clothes as she stood to greet the men.

"Hello, I'm Katie Johnson." She reached her hand out to shake each cowboy's strong, calloused hand.

"Katie, this is Billy and David. These two men have lived in this area for a long time." Luke pointed his thumb toward the guys.

"And Katie recently moved here. She is living with her grandma who lives down the road from my family."

Before Katie realized it, the two men sat beside them and chatted the entire lunch date away. They were enjoyable men to talk to and each had plenty of stories to share, but Katie only listened in to get to know Luke better.

Forty-five minutes later, Katie's phone alarm started beeping. All the men turned in her direction while she fumbled to turn it off.

"That's my cue. I've gotta go pick up my grandma. She's got a 2:00 pm hair appointment."

"Excuse me gentlemen." Luke stood up. "Let me walk my lunch date out to her car and I will be back in."

"Katie, I am so sorry," Luke apologized once they were outside the food joint. He sifted his fingers though his thick dark hair and took a deep breath.

"What are you sorry for?" She shrugged her shoulders. "The men were very nice, and it was enjoyable to visit with them."

"Listen, I want to make it up to you." He opened her car door as she got in. "How about I pick you up sometime on Saturday and maybe we meet up again?"

A tingled pulsed through her heart. Whoa. Slow down.

"Um, yeah. Sounds great." She wasn't quite sure how to handle Luke's possible peaked interest in her. Did he feel sorry that the lunch date was interrupted, or did he really want to spend more time with her?

The last time she'd agreed to let a guy come pick her up was years ago. She rarely had time or energy for the men who pursued her.

"Okay, then." Luke nodded his head. "I'll call you at your grandma's house later this week and we can set a time then."

Katie fumbled with her keys and then found her way into the driver's seat.

"Okay, bye." She shut the car door and started her car with her shaky fingers. She knew she was rushing away from him. She wanted to know him more, but she didn't want to get her hopes up if he only wanted friendship in return.

Luke tilted his head up and tossed a quick wave to her as she backed the car out and then drove toward her grandma's home.

CHAPTER 12

The rest of the afternoon schedule ran as planned for Katie and her grandma. After taking Grandma to get her hair styled, Katie drove them home. She heated up some left-over lasagna and vegetables and they sat at the table.

"Katie." Grandma pushed around the few green beans on her plate. "I noticed you still have your luggage on the floor in your room. Are you planning on leaving soon?"

"Oh no, Grandma." Katie laughed and waved her fork in the air brushing aside her comment. "I'm not planning on leaving you anytime soon. I've only been here a week! The closet and the dresser seemed a little full with some of your keepsakes and I didn't want to disturb them. I'm fine living out of my suitcase. I really don't have that many clothes anyway."

She intentionally failed to mention the overwhelmingly nauseating smell of mothballs that permeated the air space in the small walk-in closet. She didn't want her clothes smelling like an old musty house.

"Nonsense," her grandma replied, setting down her fork and grabbing her cane. "There's plenty of space. I don't need all that junk. Your things are more important, honey." The frail woman's energy renewed as she stood up and used her cane to assist her down the hallway to Katie's room.

"Oh, Grandma. Really. You don't need to bother moving things around," Katie called after the older woman. It was more than likely pointless. She stuffed the last couple bites of lasagna in her mouth and set both plates in the sink.

"No, young lady," Katie heard her determined grandma's faint voice in Katie's room. "You are my guest. I'm so sorry, sweetie, I didn't remember to move things around earlier."

Katie grimaced, regretting she hadn't hidden her suitcase. Grandma had not made space for her, but she also knew her memory was not quite the same. She no longer expected the older woman to do things for her. Roles had changed over the past few years. She'd come to take care of her grandma rather than have her grandma take care of her.

A few moments later, Katie reached the closet. Grandma stood motionless in the middle of the tight space as she stared at the memory boxes and photo albums on the top shelf. The items in the musty closet had remained the same since Katie was a small girl, permanent fixtures. They had never been taken down. There were enough trinkets and other small gadgets to explore in the century-old home that she had never even asked to see them.

"Honey, why don't you reach up there and take down a couple of those boxes and photo albums so you can have space for your belongings." Grandma motioned with her eyes to the shelf. The taller of the two women, Katie reached with ease and grabbed two dust-covered boxes as well as a photo album perched on top.

"Now, just set them over there on the floor next to your bed." This time she motioned with her cane.

Grandma made her way over to the weathered brown rocking chair in the corner to watch Katie as she worked. Strong and able, Katie made a couple of trips back and forth until she exposed the upper portion of one of the closet walls. As she made her last trip, Katie plopped down next to the pile of memories, unsure of where they were going.

"Well, now we have got ourselves a mess." Grandma chuckled. "Oh, dear." She seemed at loss for what to do next.

"How about I just put it under the bed?" Katie suggested as she lifted the white ruffled bed skirt and glanced underneath. Grandma's renewed energy looked to be quickly fading. "I think most everything will fit."

"Yes," Grandma agreed. "Just go ahead and place it under the bed."

Grandma had never mentioned what the memorabilia contained. These items have never been brought down before, so they might contain things Grandma doesn't want to talk about. Maybe they are painful memories. But it was still early in the evening, and Grandma had been talking about the past already since Katie had arrived in town. Besides, once school started Katie might not have the energy to even bring it up. She took a chance in the moment and ventured a few questions.

"Okay, Grandma." She gently placed her hand on the cover of a faded red memory box and caressed the outer edges, wondering what glimpses into the past it possessed. "Would you like to tell me about all these memories before we stash them away?" She hesitantly searched the older woman's light blue eyes.

Grandma adjusted herself and settled back in the seat of the rocker as she drew a deep breath. *Maybe this is too much for her.* "There are just pictures, newspaper clippings and a few other things from before and during the war."

"You mean World War II?" Katie sat up straight. She knew her grandma had lived through World War II, but rarely did she share a story from that time period. Other than going out to the cemetery on Memorial Day weekend she'd never considered her grandma living through the war. Most of the framed pictures in her house were from the 1980s and 1990s. There were pictures from Christmas, and pictures of Grandma's siblings sitting in wheelchairs in their later years of life, and pictures of Katie in grade school, but any pictures of World War II in the house were absent.

"Yes, World War II." Her words became distant.

"Is it okay if I look in here?" Katie's fingers curled the lid of the box. She loved the past, which was one of the main reasons she had become a history teacher. She taught about the history of their country, and always craved to learn more about years gone by—especially when it involved her grandma.

"There's nothing to hide, I guess. And I suppose you will be looking through these one day soon so you might as well open it now while I am here." Grandma relaxed her shoulders in her chair.

'Nothing to hide, I guess...' what is that supposed to mean? Katie thought as she lifted the lid of the first box. Inside, a small squarish black-and-white photo greeted her.

"Aww! Look here! Look at these clothes!" Katie smiled unconsciously as she pulled out the first picture she found. With the photo inches from her face, she soaked in every detail of the image. A young woman in her early twenties with dark curled hair stared at her. She wore a patterned flower dress with a belt exposing her thin waistline. Her thick lips parted in a half smile, but her eyes bore the look of concern and anxiety. Two young men huddled beside the young woman. Their boyish grins made them looked as if they were ready to conquer anything at hand.

"Is this you, Grandma? And who are these two men standing next to you?"

"Yes, that is me, honey." Grandma responded slowly as Katie brought her back to the present from her distant musings. "We were all at a dance in Oakmont in January 1942, a few days after New Year's Day. We were celebrating the start of the New Year and sending off some of our friends to fight in the war. The two men beside me were leaving for war the next day. One is my brother there on the right. There other was my neighbor and friend, James." Grandma crossed her arms over her chest. She looked cold.

Katie flipped over the picture and noticed the scribbled date. January 1942.

"How often did you have a dance in Oakmont?" She turned the photo back over.

"Oh, I'm not sure. Every once in a while, but this picture is from our last dance in Oakmont."

"Your last one? Why?"

Grandma's eyes closed. Tightly. Tremors shook her frail head. Her mouth opened, but nothing came out. A lone tear sneaked down her cheek.

Katie remained quiet. The stories this box held surfaced emotions from long ago. Not knowing what to say or do, she peered into the box and saw a mustard-colored newspaper with the headline *Camp Hood*. "Sorry, Grandma. I know why."

CHAPTER 13

*G*race peered at herself in the vanity mirror. She loved dances, but the floral dress might be too bright and cheery for her current emotions.

Since the President gave his radio address about the attack on Pearl Harbor, the mood of her beloved community had changed. The war that had been far away on distant land was now on U.S. soil. Everyone knew life was about to change if it hadn't already.

After hearing the dreaded Pearl Harbor announcement on December eighth, Grace woke the next morning to her twenty-year-old brother, Mickey, arguing with her parents. His words echoed down the hall like a harsh wind.

"James and the other guys my age are joining. Why can't I? I'm twenty years old. I can decide what I want to do and when I want to do it!"

Mickey's feet pounded on the hardwood floor as he charged out the front door. Even though he was two years younger than her, he always made it a priority to look after her. It made sense for him to want to be one of the first ones to sign up and protect his country.

Almost a month had passed, now here she stood trying to motivate herself to go to the annual Oakmont dance. Grace dreaded tonight, but tomorrow even more. Goodbyes would be said to her brother and one of her best friends. She wished Edward didn't have a news deadline to make so he could be with them all.

"Hey Grace!" Mickey's voice boomed outside her bedroom door. "Are you ready yet? James just pulled up." *Goodness, she was going to miss hearing him.* A tear escaped the corner of her eye.

Grace could hear the familiar honking horn in the distance. She wiped away any evidence of the tear.

"Y-es." She cleared her throat. "Yes. Let me grab my coat."

"Hurry it up, you slow poke. Who ya trying to impress anyway?" He walked away laughing as she heard the front door squeak and the wooden screen door bang closed.

Grace glanced in the mirror again. She lifted her pursed lips, but her eyes still expressed sorrow. "Come on, Grace. You've got to enjoy tonight. For the boys," Grace coached herself out loud. She pasted on her best smile. "There you go. Much better."

She finished putting on her coat and left to join James and Mickey in the car.

Grace let the two guys carry the conversation on the way to the dance. It was better that way. She didn't want any more unwelcome tears to appear. They shifted from talking about the weather to girls and then to mechanics.

"Why are you so stiff and quiet back there, Grace?" James looked over his shoulder.

"I'm not stiff. I'm just listening to you guys jabber. And I am praying back here that your brakes don't go out on us like they did a few months ago." She laughed and reached forward patting James's back.

"I've got good working brakes and a good working horn too!"

James pressed down on the horn as they pulled up to others walking to the dance.

"James!" Grace burst out laughing.

"Good. I'm glad something finally made you happy." James put the car in park.

"Hey, I'm happy. I can't wait to find a sweet girl and dance the evening away." Mickey turned and winked at her.

"Oh, Mickey. Seriously. You two are a handful." She hopped out of the car with the guys.

Once inside the old barn, Grace settled in a corner. Her friends and family danced away the evening while she silently grieved her brother and friend leaving for war. Happiness remained too distant for her even on a fun night like this. Why was it that everyone else could have fun, but she couldn't? It hurt too much.

It seemed as though the laughing and giggling came from the children as they danced with one another on the school room floor. The schoolchildren and Grace had spent the previous day clearing out the room getting it ready for the dance. During the summer months, square dances took place under the tabernacle, but tonight it was too cool to be outside.

Single men and women, young children, families, and even grandparents joined in on one of the most well-attended social events in Oakmont. Many traveled by car to attend the event; a few even rode their horses because it was a shorter distance for them to ride on a horse over the hilltops, as opposed to driving around them on a dirt road in a car.

Those in attendance wore their Sunday best. Some of the young men wore ties. Grace watched as some of the single guys tried to catch the eyes of the pretty single ladies. Several of those single men just like Mickey and James would be leaving the next day to enlist in the Army. Grace wished she could stop the clock for them and let time stand still.

"Grace!" A familiar voice spoke in her ear as the pressure of a male hand gently squeezed her shoulder. She didn't have to turn to see who it was next to her. It could only be James. "Why do you look so gloomy?"

"Yeah, Grace." Mickey joined them from the other side. "Where's that smile?"

"Smile? How can I smile or dance or do anything when I know you two are leaving me tomorrow!" Grace crossed her arms in front of her and gaped at the two young men. She knew she was acting childish, but she didn't care at that moment. Both men were strong and stood well above six feet. They could have been twins except for James' dark auburn hair and Mickey's light brown locks. Her emotions were torn. She wanted to be playful, but to her there was nothing about tomorrow that seemed joyous.

"You'll see us again! It's is not like we're leaving and never coming back! Maybe I'll meet a pretty girl while I am gone, marry her and bring her right back here to good ole Oakmont!" James smiled his flashy grin. He had a way of cheering her up.

"Oh, James! Well, if you meet someone, then why don't you introduce her sister to Mickey here, but make sure she is a good girl. Please!"

"Hey now. I'd like that, too!" Mickey chuckled and playfully struck James' arm.

"You three young 'uns!" Mrs. Carter showed off her shiny new camera. "Look over here for a picture."

In that moment, time slowed down for Grace. *A picture? A picture? I don't want a picture!* Grace's mind screamed. *I just want these two to stay right here by me.*

"Okay, smile on three? One, two, three!" The flash lit the area in front of them before Grace could completely forge a smile for the camera.

"Lovely!" Mrs. Carter commented as she passed on by to the next group.

"I hope that picture turns out and then you can hang it on

your wall forever and think of us every day." Mickey's eyes were dancing as he playfully teased his sister.

"Don't you worry, Mickey." Grace pointed her teacher finger at the two men as she placed her other hand on her hip. "I will treasure that photo forever." Grace teased her brother back. She then wrapped her arms around the thick neck of her childhood friend and her ever-faithful brother. She didn't care if she were going to say goodbye tomorrow. She wanted to get as many hugs as she could now.

A WEEK and half after the dance, life had resumed as normal as possible. It was a cool Thursday afternoon and Grace was looking forward to her walk home. She finished straightening the room and started down the schoolhouse steps when she saw Edward's black sedan stirring up and whirling dust on the town's main road.

Her lips parted as she freely smiled. She had not expected to see him today. Hmm. Maybe he got off early from work.

A few moments later, Edward leaped out of his car and gave her a tender kiss on the forehead as he pulled her into his arms.

"Hi, sweetheart." He brought her closer.

Grace snuggled into his chest. *Don't leave for war, Edward.* He might be forced to join one day, but for now she savored these moments he was here with her.

"What brings you out here, honey?" Grace drew away so she could look him in the eyes.

"A fine young lady who makes my heart flutter," Edward winked at her. He looked as if he wanted to reach down and kiss her again, this time on the lips. He leaned in closer again.

"Edward, really...." Grace could feel her cheeks turning pink. "I'm glad all the schoolchildren are gone," she gently scolded him.

"Why did you really come out here today? I wasn't expecting to see you until the weekend."

"Did you see the paper today?"

"No, I'm just now leaving the schoolhouse for the first time." She shook her head. "What's in it?" Her curiosity was sparked. It must have been something good for him to drive all the way out here.

"I wrote an article about the new anti-tank training camp."

"Oh, the Army camp…I don't want to hear about that again, Edward."

"Grace, everyone in Coryell County is going to have to read this article."

"What do you mean?"

"We got word that the Army will be setting up the new training camp right here in Coryell County. People are going to have to sell their land to the government. A land office is even opening up in a couple days in Gatesville."

"I don't believe it, Edward. They changed the boundary before, they will change it again. No one knows where it is really going to be."

"Grace, listen to me." Edward reached down and gently grabbed her elbow. "I was there that night when Mayborn asked General Donavan to look at Coryell County." His dark brows furrowed closer, and his voice deepened as he became serious. "What happened that night is now coming to pass. We didn't want to report too early on the exact location, but we were told yesterday by an Army spokesperson that part of Coryell County is included in the boundary of this new camp."

His urgency irritated her. "Edward, I already told you I don't want to talk about this. I don't even want to think about the possibility of my family losing their land. So, until my parents receive some kind of official word, please let's talk about something encouraging."

"Are you not even going to read my article then? I wrote a lot about the positive in this move. Can you imagine the kind of economic impact this will have on our area? All the jobs it will bring? Everyone should be elated about bringing in soldiers because it equates to more business. I mean, how many places in the country would love to have a new Army camp?" Edward said.

She covered her ears.

"You can't cover your ears and keep it from coming. Plus, there are so many advantages."

"Stop! You are taking it too far." She threw her arms down. "I don't want to hear any more about economic advantages. My family lives on a self-sufficient farm. We raise our livestock and farm our own fields. We don't need more money. We just need to be able to keep our land. Otherwise, there will be no economic growth for us."

"What about the others who have suffered due to the depression?" He pressed on.

"So now my family might possibly forfeit their land so that other people can benefit?"

"Okay, listen, honey. I was not trying to start an argument."

"Well, you did." She crossed her arms.

"I said I was not trying to. I just wanted you to read the article I wrote." He extended an open palm to her.

She could tell his tone was changed and he was trying to lighten this subject.

"I suppose I can read it later. I mean, the paper is giving you money to write and earn a living." She reached for Edward's hand and gave it a squeeze as he walked her around to the passenger side and opened her door.

She hesitated before getting in and peered into Edward's eyes as thoughts loomed inside her head. "But please, do not bring this up to my father," Grace pleaded. "I don't want him to have any negative thoughts toward you. I know you are not the one bringing in the Army, but I would rather him find out from someone else if he has to move. I can't stand the thought of him not liking you."

Grace gripped her chest. It did not physically hurt, but the possibility of her family losing their land was too much. And she was becoming more troubled that Edward was not in opposition of the Army taking over.

EDWARD DREW Grace into his chest and wrapped his lanky arms around her. He rested his chin on Grace's dark curled locks. He hoped Grace's family would not be included in the land take-over, but he wondered how she could not see the potential for all those unemployed.

A few would lose, but more would gain. Edward believed that to his core.

CHAPTER 14

A brisk chill saturated the air. The entire Willis family stayed busy inside while the cold weather dipped into the low 30s. The thick aroma of sausage and potato soup simmering on the stove wafted through the entire home. Grace gazed out the front window as the sun settled behind the low-lying clouds. She desperately wanted to dream and plan her wedding, but questions about the fate of her parents consumed all her thoughts.

She glanced over her shoulder. Her father had fallen asleep reading the newspaper with the crackle of the fire in the fireplace a few feet away. J.J.'s lanky legs sprawled across the floor as he read one of his favorite magazines, ignoring the constant chattering from Granny next to him.

Mama, Granny, and Ruth huddled over a sewing project. Granny chatted away about the gossip she'd heard at the general store.

"I tell you what, those ladies—all they talk about now is moving. We better not be moving. I've lived here too long. I'm seventy-eight years old—my body is too old to move now. Those ladies at the store are not sure what they are going to do. Where are we supposed to go? Harriet, that brave woman, she said her granddaddy fought for Texas independence, her daddy fought in the Civil War, her son fought in World War I. She could do her part if her country needed her in time of war."

Grace watched her mother nod her head at the appropriate moments.

By now, she was sure the entire Oakmont community had read Edward's article about the grievous possibility of moving, or they had heard about it through the store gossip. She could sense the community's restlessness. The young children she taught in the schoolhouse were naïve of all at hand, but she could tell the news weighed heavily on her older students. They didn't readily answer questions in class. Several of them had forgotten or misplaced their homework over the past few days. They were the ones who probably overheard their parents' late-night conversations anguishing over the possibility of moving. The official word of where the camp would be had not been released yet.

Mrs. Smith had told her there would be a meeting in a few weeks. They didn't want to take any risks and were already searching for another home in the area despite living next door to the store they had owned for the past several decades. Grace was almost certain they would be included in the boundary. With Henry, her oldest son, away at war, Mrs. Smith knew moving would be hard on her husband and three daughters; she wanted to start early. Grace's father, on the other hand, had the opposite reaction of Mrs. Smith and her husband.

She stole a quick glance back at her father, again taking advantage of a late afternoon nap. Such a stubborn man, but how that stubbornness had developed him into a solid farmer. He never surrendered—even though wind, hailstorms, flooding, and drought demolished the majority of his crop numerous times. He would go right back into the field, sometimes even on the same day as the catastrophe, and begin working his field. How often he she watched her father kneel on his back porch with his head bowed and his arms lifted and plead, "Dear Lord, grant me the energy and determination I need to provide for my family. Amen."

Grace had witnessed this intimate prayer to the Lord over the years. She was sure he had already petitioned the Lord during this time of crisis and uncertainty.

She scanned the room. An empty chair sat available next to the couch. She stared a moment longer at the seat. Mickey's seat. What was he doing now? Training? Sleeping? Maybe about to eat dinner. The seat looked cold and painfully out of place without Mickey sitting in it.

There was no sense in thinking about him now. He wouldn't be coming home any sooner. She left the curtains open and plopped down next to her sister on the couch. Better start working on the details of her dress before there was no more time left before the wedding. Plus, Edward was expected soon for supper.

Cold stormy weather had kept him from visiting until today. Over the past week, they had only spoken briefly a few times on the phone about the weather and his upcoming visit. Thankfully, the inevitable subject about the encroaching Army camp hadn't come up in conversation.

"Grace, your wedding dress is coming along so nicely." Mama paused her work. Her father's work pants stretched across her lap as she patched a hole.

"Thanks, Mama." She tried to force a smile. Her mother's words did not lift her spirits.

"Grace." Mama's eyes focused directly on her. "You are thinking about the new camp too, aren't you?"

She paused before she let her chin fall to her chest. Fresh tears blurred her vision.

"Honey, the good Lord is going to take care of us; you don't need to worry." Mama reached over and patted her knee. "We will be fine. Your father has worked long and hard and I am sure the government will give us the money we need to purchase a new house. If we are one of the families who has to move, then we will find another house to make our home. I'm sure there will be plenty of places nearby we will be able to purchase. We all need to do our part during the time of war."

Who was she trying to convince? The thin lines under Mama's eyes had grown darker over the recent days and the slight wrinkles above her hazel eyes now were deep grooves.

"I think the government is foolish trying to take this land here!" Granny's screechy voice startled the quiet. The family matriarch pressed her thick lips together, hiding her yellow stained teeth. She wore her once jet-black hair, now a beautiful shade of snow-white, pulled into a low bun. "I've been living here for over fifty years and I am not going anywhere." She hit the edge of her favorite upholstered chair with her tan frail palm.

Grace knew many in the Oakmont community voiced the same opinion as her granny. They were all torn between desiring to stay on their land and yet still supporting their country.

"I'm not leaving this land. I'm not leaving my church. I'm not leaving my husband buried at the cemetery. I'm not leaving this house. The government is going to have to come get me right out of this chair here and carry me out!" Granny grabbed the blue upholstered arms of her wingback chair.

The beautiful seat with an intricate blue floral pattern had been her deceased grandpa's first gift to Granny in their new home almost fifty years ago. As far as Grace could remember, the chair had never been moved from its current spot next to the fireplace. Her granny sought refuge in her special chair, especially on cold winter days like this evening.

"Granny, shhhh…. you are going to wake John," Mama whispered as the two sisters began to snicker. Grace found it hilarious thinking about Granny being carried out of the house perched upon her chair.

"Goodness, gracious, Georgia! Well, it is true. I'm not leaving!"

"Yes, Granny, I know you do not want to leave. And I don't want to leave either. I don't want to be worried though until I know who has the orders to leave."

"Surely, Mama, if you have to leave, they will give you plenty of time to do so. We have so many things to pack and move. And think about all the animals as well," added seventeen-year-old Ruth. She would be the first one to be concerned about the animals. Always caring for animals and people.

"We are not going anywhere, so I don't want to hear any more talk of it!" Father's voice rumbled from chair where he was sitting.

"Yes, Father." Ruth looked immediately down at her lap and began working on her sewing project.

The only noise in the room came from the popping fire. It remained quiet for a few moments before J.J. ignored the tension and yelled from the floor. "Looks like it's snowing again!" Grace knew J.J.'s outbursts were sometimes unwelcome, but today it came at the perfect time.

Ruth and Grace briskly set down their sewing projects and scrambled for the window.

"Oh wow! Look at it. I can't remember the last time I saw snow." Ruth studied the flakes drifting to the ground.

"I don't think it has ever snowed here!" J.J. stood next to the window at the front door.

"Yes, it did, dear. When you were a baby. We had a good snow. At least a couple of inches." Mama stood as well at one of the living room windows.

"Hey – look here!" J.J. called out. "I think I see Edward's car!"

"I think you're right, J.J." Grace squinted her eyes. The fast-falling snowflakes made it harder to see.

A few minutes later, Edward entered through the front door with his dark jacket exposing the light-colored flakes. The tiny ice crystals disappeared quickly in the warm house.

"Brr! It's cold out there!" Edward shook as he started taking off his coat. "But it sure is a beautiful sight!"

"Welcome, Edward!" Georgia greeted Edward as she took his coat from him. "Dinner will be ready in a few minutes. There's cornbread in the oven and sausage and potato soup on the stove."

"Sounds perfect!"

"Ruth," Georgia motioned. "Please come help me set the dishes on the table."

As the others trailed off to other rooms, Grace helped Edward take off his damp boots and set them aside.

"Why don't you come warm up by the fire?" Grace started walking toward the living room.

"How about not until I first get a hug?" Edward's eyes were gleaming. He grabbed her with one hand and with his other hand he spun her waist toward him. She couldn't help herself. She squealed and sighed as she wrapped her arms around the one she loved and adored. She had missed him.

Edward kissed her on the cheek and then released her.

"Yes, I think a fire would be most excellent! I about froze the entire drive over here, but it was worth it just to see you!"

"Good evening, Edward." John Sr. stood to shake Edward's hand.

"Evening, sir." Edward placed his frigid white hand into his future father-in-law's calloused tan hand.

"Please have a seat." John Sr. motioned to the couch. "How are the roads right now with it snowing outside?"

"They are not slick yet, but I am sure that snow will make it kind of icy tonight. I probably should not stay after dinner just in case." He looked toward her. He had just gotten here and now he would be gone in an hour or two. She released her smile. She knew he might get stuck out here for a couple of days and he could not afford to do so.

"How's the job?" her father questioned again.

She hoped Edward would steer clear of any talk of the Army even though it occupied most of his time.

"I'm not sure my work will be slowing down anytime soon. Another one of our guys in the office is headed off to serve in the military. You two might know him. His name is Jerry. I think he was in the same class as Mickey at Gatesville."

She wasn't sure she wanted to talk about Mickey either, but at least it was better than talking about eminent domain with these two polar-opposite men.

"We got a letter from Mickey yesterday." Father motioned to a small cream-colored paper resting on the end table nearby. "He said he's doing well. They are learning drills and keeping him busy from sun-up to sunset, but he said he is used to that from living here on the farm."

Her father's tense eyebrows relaxed some as he talked a few more minutes about Mickey and working on the farm with him.

"That boy, he is always the first one up, that's for sure. Sometimes, when he was younger, he would beat me downstairs long before sunrise 'cause he was so eager to learn how to plow." Father had so much respect for Mickey.

"We are ready to eat!" Ruth hollered from the dining room door.

"It smells so delicious! Man, I sure am thankful for a warm meal on a cold evening!" Edward praised as the three of them headed for the dining room.

Grace was thankful to eat a warm dinner surrounded by her loved ones in her home with no arguing or discussion of the new camp being mentioned, thankfully. She wasn't sure how many more times she would get to do this seated at this table in this very house.

~

THE WARM MEAL and the sight of his beautiful fiancée hit the spot. His heart wanted to stay longer with Grace, but he couldn't risk getting stranded on a country road. It was too cold tonight.

"I better be leaving." Edward pushed his dessert plate forward. He knew Grace would not be happy. He had only been there an hour.

"Really, Edward? Please stay a little longer. Let's play a quick card game or something."

"Not tonight. It's going to get pretty nasty out there and I've got to work tomorrow. Well, hopefully. I've got several interviews. Everyone is getting ready for the Army coming. Ordering more supplies...."

"Edward, if you are ready, I will walk you to the door." John Sr. stood from his spot at the end of the table.

"Well, okay. Yes, sir. I better get going." Did he really not want to hear about the Army moving here? Or maybe he was just concerned about safety in this winter storm. Edward let out a sigh. Nothing he could do seemed to please this man. He reached over and squeezed Grace's shoulders.

She tucked his hand into her own. She pleaded with her eyes for him to stay.

"Grace, we will talk soon. Love you, dear."

"Bye, Edward. Be safe."

"Don't worry. I will." He glanced at the other end of the table. "Thank you, Mrs. Willis, for a delightful meal as always."

"You are welcome, Edward. We can't wait for you to come again sometime and join us."

He could feel John Sr. becoming impatient as he stood with his arms crossed at the entry way.

"Bye, Edward. And don't let my son-in-law talk to you for too long. He's just anxious," Granny called out.

"Um, sure. Yes, ma'am." He wasn't sure how to respond to her comment. Hopefully, John Sr. did not want to talk to him about the Army. "I'm ready, let me grab my jacket and boots."

John Sr. waited until Edward was ready before opening the door.

The bitter wind attacked him as he stepped out and waited for John Sr.

"Son, are there any details you are keeping from me?"

"Sir, I'm not sure what details you are talking about." Why would he keep anything from his future-father-in-law?

"Do you know the line yet? Is my house going to be included?" He seemed unfazed by the cold air.

"We don't know any of that yet. Sometimes we find out things a day ahead of the community, but what I will tell you is the circle I saw Mr. Mayborn draw on a map back at Thanksgiving…. Well…. I'm pretty sure your property is included." His breath evaporated in the harsh wind.

"But you haven't seen any exact official maps with an exact line?"

"No, sir."

"Are you sure?" The cold wind whipped around them. A crack of thunder sounded in the distance.

Why could the elder man not trust him? He'd only shown honor and loyalty to his family and his daughter. "Sir, I'm sure."

"And son, don't mention your articles about the Army or needing to interview people in my house again."

Granny's words ran through his head. John Sr. was beyond anxious.

CHAPTER 15

FEBRUARY 1942

It did not take long for the ice and snow to melt away. Over the next few weeks, Grace returned to her routine of teaching at the Oakmont school during the weekdays. In the evenings, she occupied her time by grading papers and sewing her wedding dress.

"Grace." Her father's boots pounded on the hard wood floor as he entered the room. She paused hemming the sleeves of her wedding dress. The glowing embers from the fire warmed her feet and cast soft shadows across the room. "Did you hear about this while you were in town today?" Father marched across the living room and handed her a half-sheet of paper with creases down the center.

Grace set aside her needlework and reached for the notice. February 1942. She skimmed the bold lettering of the headline.

"Calling all Landowners! A community meeting will be held tomorrow afternoon at 3 pm at the Tabernacle in Oakmont. A general of the United States Army will be in attendance. Your presence is requested."

Grace's hand quivered as she handed back the crinkled paper to him. "N…n…no."

"Did Edward mention this to you?"

"No, Father." Grace tilted her head. "I mean, he mentioned a few days ago that a general was going around speaking to landowners about the advantage it would provide the Army to have this land. I was hoping, since you had not heard about it, that Oakmont would not be a part of the takeover."

"I'm surprised he hasn't written an article about this yet." Father shook his head. "Well, maybe our land won't be." He crumpled the paper in his thick hand. "This letter only states there will be a meeting. Maybe he will be discussing the boundary and we are on the edge of Oakmont so hopefully we will not be included." He rubbed his forehead as he placed the wad of paper on the end table and headed toward the hallway to his bedroom.

"Father? Are you…are you going to attend the meeting?"

He paused at the doorway and turned to face his oldest daughter. "I have no choice." His dejected eyes gazed upon her. He then forced his lips to curve into a thin and weary smile. "It will be okay, Grace Kathleen." He gave a subtle nod with his head. With those parting words, he headed to bed for the evening.

She grabbed her dress. She wanted to be married here. In her home. Among the sweet smell of bread and within view of the sprawling evergreen live oak trees outside. Where was she going to be married? Would there ever be a place as fitting as this?

GRACE HADN'T ASKED her father's permission to attend the meeting today, but she knew she would not miss it. She planned to let the children out fifteen minutes early. She hoped to have enough time to clean up and walk to the tabernacle, located a short distance from the schoolhouse. The clock ticking on the wall told her she had two minutes until her planned early release time.

"Okay, class." Grace clapped her hands three times to get everyone's attention. "I need you to begin cleaning up for the day. I'm sure it will make all you kids happy—I'm letting you leave a few minutes early today."

In one simultaneous cheer, the kids celebrated being finished for the school day.

"Once you've cleaned up the area around you and straightened up your desk," Grace said from the front of the classroom, "then you are free to grab your coats, bags, and lunch pails and leave for the day."

The kids tidied the room so they could enjoy a few minutes of extra freedom.

"Where ya going, Miss Willis?" Grace felt a gentle tug on her dress as she glanced down to see young Billy Roberts staring straight at her with his inset hazel eyes.

"Billy, what do you mean?" She stared down at him.

"I want to know too, Miss Willis. Are you going to the meeting at the tabernacle? Huh, Miss Willis?" Rebecca Smith joined them.

By this point, several students had stopped to hear her response. She was not planning on telling her father, so why would she tell these children? Then she realized from the look on Billy's face that they all knew. Everyone knew what was going on.

"My daddy says I'm to go straight home and do my chores, but I wanna go to the meet'n real bad, Miss Willis," young Billy continued. On Billy's first day of school a few months earlier, his father had told her he owned about fifty acres on the far of edge town near the tabernacle. He said ever since he was a young child, he had a dream of being a farmer. At the young age of 29, he had scraped every penny he had until he could purchase the land two years ago. "Can I go with you, Miss?" A chill ran down her spine.

"Me, too!" Rebecca grabbed her waist. Several other young students chimed in as well.

"Children, please!" Grace raised her hands to quiet the kids. "Yes. I am going to the meeting." Grace answered their question. "And Billy," Grace leaned down and lifted his chin. "I would take you with me in a heartbeat, but this meeting is for adults only. Your father needs to listen to the general and what he has to say. It's a very important meeting. I'm sure your father would rather you go home and do your chores immediately so when he comes home, he does not have to worry about that as well."

Grace straightened her back and addressed the remaining children in the room, "That goes for all of you as well." She patted several kids' heads who were standing nearby. "Your fathers need you to be responsible and take care of your chores today. They are going to a very crucial meeting and we don't want to cause them any more anxiety. Enjoy your extra fifteen minutes of free play and then go home and finish your household responsibilities."

The children seemed to understand Grace's reasoning as they turned to file out of the room past the empty desks toward the entrance of the schoolhouse.

She breathed a sigh of relief as the students left without an argument. She knew this meeting was not a time for children to be in attendance, but she hoped her father would not mind her presence.

A few minutes later, Grace's arms swung from side to side as she set a quick pace down the front steps and toward the tabernacle, her feet kicking up dust on the road.

The tabernacle housed a large roof but contained no side walls. The community held most of their social gatherings and square dances in the large oak shell during the warmer months and found other places to use during the colder winter months.

Today, however, the sun's warm rays appeared to make the tabernacle an ideal meeting spot.

From a hundred yards away, she could see several horses tied to the posts, along with plenty of old trucks and a few late model sedans. The men in the area were of modest means, but they were hard working farmers and ranchers and landowners. They and their families had all put thousands of hours of sweat, blood and tears into working this Texas terrain. Many of the landowners inherited the land from their fathers who inherited it from their fathers. Over the last one hundred years, generations of landowners had fought off Indians, diseases, harsh weather. They fought for Texas independence from Mexico. They fought for states' rights during the Civil War, they fought for America during the World War and now they were sending their sons to fight for America during a second World War.

Here they gathered together unsure of where the past one hundred years had gotten them and their forefathers. A quiet murmur sifted through the crowd as the men stood side by side. No chairs were needed since this would hopefully be a short meeting.

Grace heard a loud clearing of a man's throat as a strong voice silenced the large crowd and then introduced himself as a general from the United States Army. "Thank you all for joining us today." The voice boomed over the group. Grace shifted her stance. She was not tall enough to see who was talking. She began moving around the back edge of the group until she found an opening. Not a great spot, but this would do.

She could see the demanding voice belong to a man in a pressed Army suit with earned war medals saturating the left side of his chest. He stood rigidly upright with his hat tucked slightly beneath his arm. He was in his late forties, but Grace could tell that the war had worn on this representative of the U.S Army as well.

The general talked with authority as he informed the men in

attendance that war was a time for all of them to come together and be united. After a few more minutes of informing the multi-generational crowd about their patriotic duties, he paused and cleared his throat yet again. The general leaned forward and skimmed the audience looking each man in the face until he garnered their attention.

"We need your land, and we need it soon." His words were crisp and precise. "The United States Army has been scouting the entire country looking for the best place to train our men. We need a large space with plenty of acreage to operate our anti-tank units. We also need an area with tree-covered hills and open valleys very similar to where we are currently fighting in Europe." His eyes fixated on the audience.

"Coryell County, where you live, has been designated one of the best locations in the entire United States of America." The general gestured with his hat to the field located beside the taber-nacle. "Right now, as we speak, men are headed over to Europe to fight for our country. We can better prepare those who are leaving if we have more space where our men can train to operate tanks. "You," he jarred his finger at the motionless crowd, "can help our men in uniform as they prepare to fight this war."

"For those of you who might have issues with turning over your land: our Congress is currently working on a bill that will require you to forfeit your land immediately when requested. The amount you will receive for the acreage that you own will be determined by a firm hired by the United States government. I have not yet released the official boundary map, but Oakmont community is included in this area." With those disturbing words, she could feel tension filling the air.

"An official government document with the United States Army seal will be sent to the affected landowners' homes and a vacancy date will be included in this document. If you have any concerns or questions, please take them to the land office located in downtown Gatesville. Thank you for your patriotic spirit.

Thank you for your time and thank you all for coming today. Good day." The Army general stepped away. He ended the meeting as quickly as he started it.

Grace could tell the harrowing news inflicted invisible pain on the grief-stricken men. No applause. No pats on backs. Her eyes succumbed to tears as she caught a glimpse of her father gripping his well-worn cowboy hat against his chest as the news must have crushed his heart. His eyes slowly closed, and she thought she saw a tear from the man who never cried or gave up. He leaned his head forward slightly and placed his tattered hat on his head. Defeat encroached upon him and the others. As his hand came off his hat, his thumb wiped away the one lone tear.

"Dear God! Have mercy on my daddy!" Grace screamed inside her head. She watched the landowners as they departed the tabernacle with their shoulders lower than when they arrived.

"Oh, Lord, this can't be happening now. These men have worked so hard for this land." Grace silently pleaded to her Heavenly Father as she surveyed the unbelievable scene at hand. Panic, rage, anger, and defeat swelled her chest. Her knees buckled.

As she forced her feet to walk away, young Billy's thick dark hair and red plaid shirt caught her attention. His legs hung several feet in the air as he swung them back and forth while waiting on the oak fence in front of his house. Grace could see Billy's father walking the short distance home from the meeting.

Billy hopped down and raced toward his father. The man had saved every penny and worked long sweat-filled hours for his piece of property. Any dream about securing his land for future generations had been forever dashed a few moments earlier. The man scooped up his young son and embraced him. He rested his jaw on the boy's head and his shoulders began shaking.

Grace resisted the impulse to console the defeated father. The stunned landowner set down his son and staggered through the gate to their home.

CHAPTER 16

MARCH 1942

A few weeks later, on March 6, Grace stood in front of her students as she reviewed history questions from the previous day's lesson. She ignored the dazed eyes of many of her older students. They sat motionless. No one wanted to listen or pay attention. She might as well call it a day.

After the general spoke at the tabernacle, a state of unrest and confusion entered the community. The children, especially the older ones, were aware of the crisis at hand. Grace tapped the blackboard. She watched several heads snap toward her. *There. Finally. A few are were paying attention now.*

"Class, who can answer this last question on the board?"

Grace listened to their breathing and waited for an answer. The younger kids poked their heads into the aisle to look at the older ones. She let uncomfortable silence remain. Several shoulders shrugged around the classroom.

"Well, the answer can be found on page..." Heavy clomping on the steps outside the schoolhouse door could be heard.

She stood there paused in mid-sentence resting her pointer against the board.

The steps grew louder until they stopped. *Who is about to come in?* There were still hours left in the day. The schoolhouse door creaked open, interrupting the melancholy room.

A middle-aged farmer, dressed in a long-sleeve beige shirt tucked into his dirt-smeared denim overalls, stepped into the still room. The wind sucked the door closed, causing a loud unexpected slam. Half the class startled in their chairs.

The man swallowed and peered around the class until his eyes stopped on her.

"Miss Willis," the man spoke with a harsh twang as he removed his hat. "I need my two boys. They'll be leaving the school today and not coming back. Tyne and Junior, stop your staring and get your stuff."

The two boys sat bug-eyed with their mouths open. She could see they were mesmerized by the sight of their father at the schoolhouse early in the day.

"What are you boys doing? Now. Let's go!" The father's voice shook as redness filled his cheeks.

The eleven and twelve-year-old brothers shot up and grabbed their minimal belongings. Without glancing back, the father and son trio exited the building.

Grace's hand remained firmly clutched to the yardstick for a few seconds after they left. The appearance of the father had taken her by such surprise that she hadn't even thought to ask him why the boys were leaving.

What was wrong? Did something happen to their family? Grace stood in front of her entire classroom mulling over the scene, completely forgetting about her class.

"Oh children," Grace gasped. "Please forgive me. Let's go ahead and move on from history to our reading lesson." Grace gave new instructions to the children and tried to forget about the disruption.

Ten minutes later, she stood near the back of the room helping students with their reading.

The hinges on the front door squeaked again as the door pulled open, this time revealing Billy Roberts' father.

"M…Ma'am. I need my boy."

"Yes, sir." She leaned forward and tapped Billy's shoulder.

"Billy, please gather your books for the day. We will see you on Monday."

"Ah…M…Ma'am. I…uh…I…need Billy to gather all of his things. He…he…will not be coming back to school here."

Billy's head immediately went down. He sluggishly grabbed his books, jacket and pail and headed to meet his father.

She was not going to let another father leave with his child without asking some questions.

"Students, I need you to read quietly in your books until I return." Grace instructed to her class. "I am going to step outside for a moment with Billy and his father."

Grace escorted the father and his son out the schoolhouse door and down the steps.

"Sir, please forgive me for inquiring, but did I do something wrong for you to take Billy out of school?" She begged Billy's father with her eyes for an answer.

"Oh no, M…Ma'am!" Astonishment covered the father's face. "Billy sure does like having you for a schoolteacher." The young father sorrowfully peered down at his son and then looked up to her.

"It's just M…Ma'am. We got a letter from the Army delivered to us this morning…." His voice choked over the words.

That one heartbreaking sentence told her everything. They were included in the circle. Inside the boundary. They were feeling the effects of the country's power of eminent domain. They were moving and had no say.

"Do you mind me asking," Grace paused before she uttered her next words.

"How long do you have left on your property?" She hoped the family would have a few months to find more property.

"Three weeks from today." Moisture filled his lower eye lids. "Now, if you will excuse us, M…Ma'am, we have a lot of work to do. Come on, Billy."

The father patted his son on the back as they left the schoolhouse yard.

Grace could not contain the tears streaming down her face. Had her father received the same notice, yet? *Wait. Three weeks for Billy means only three more weeks for this school. Three more weeks for these children to be together. Here.* She slumped over and clutched her stomach. She could barely gain her composure. She'd known this moment would be coming. They'd all known it, but it was easier to believe it would be in the distant future and not a mere three weeks away!

As she stood outside the door, she could not keep her teeth from chattering. It was 70 degrees outside, but it might as well have been 30 degrees. She pushed the tears aside and clenched her jaw as she opened the door. The hinges screeched again.

All eyes peered at her tear-streaked face.

"Class," Grace's teeth chattered again. "We are going to end early for the day." The students turned and gave each other confused looks. "There will be no homework tonight either. Please go home and help your family in any way they might need you today. I will see you all back here on Monday."

The children seemed to sense something was desperately wrong as they grabbed their belongings and shuffled out the only exit.

Grace knew she had one place to be in that moment and she was going to get there as fast as she could.

CHAPTER 17

A minute after the last child left, Grace hurried and gathered her belongings. She raced down the school-house steps two at a time and half-jogged, half-walked home. She had traveled this worn path hundreds of times from the school-house both as a teacher and student, but today her parents' home might as well have been a thousand miles away.

"Mama!" Grace heard Rebecca Smith in the distance running home from school. "Miss Willis let us out early today! What's wrong, Mama!" Helen Smith yelled as the two girls stumbled up the store steps blowing past Mrs. Carter and Mrs. Miller standing on the porch.

Grace locked eyes with the two older women as she approached the general store.

"Mrs. Carter, Mrs. Miller." Grace nodded her head. These women knew. No words were needed. She could still hear the girls' voices.

"Mama! Is it Henry? Did something happen to Henry?" Helen yelled, grasping her side and bending over at the doorway of the store.

Mrs. Smith came out the front door. She extended arms to her two girls as she embraced them both at the same time. "No, Helen," Mrs. Smith said, and she clutched their heads and pressed them into her shoulders. She swayed back and forth. "Henry's fine. Praise the Lord." Her voice came out calm and even, although a desolate expression seemed pasted on her face as she soothed her daughters. "Henry's fine."

Mrs. Smith pulled her two girls tighter and kissed them on their foreheads. She released them and Grace caught her eye as she passed in front of the store. Mrs. Smith half-nodded at Grace before she linked her arms with her daughters and moved inside the store. Mrs. Smith knew, too.

"You made a good decision today," Mrs. Carter said. Grace had forgotten about the two women on the porch. The older woman bit her bottom lip and turned away, looking at the price tags on the water pails.

Grace stopped walking. "I had no other choice. It was a selfish one because I need to be with my family too."

Mrs. Carter lifted her head and looked at Grace. Her pitiful eyes had lost their gleam. She held the woman's gaze for a moment. "How long until you have to move?" Grace nodded her head to include both women.

Mrs. Carter spoke first. "We have three weeks." She tugged her sweater tighter around her chest. The cool spring breeze whipped around the older woman.

"And we only have fifteen days," Mrs. Miller said as she tried to tuck wispy strands of hair behind her ears, safe from the blowing wind. "But that is not the worst part of it," her voice hushed to almost a whisper as she pushed her hair aside. "They only offered us $8 an acre."

The news daggered Grace's heart. She jerked to a stop on the side of the dirt road. "Only eight dollars an acre! That's robbery!" Her mouth remained open. She searched for something else to say. Grace's cold fingers clutched her bag tighter. It hit her in the gut she needed to get home. And fast. "I'm so sorry. I've got to go see my parents."

She left the two women behind. She felt like a small child again, racing home half-walking and half-jogging.

As she passed Mr. Lloyd's familiar homestead, she could see him on his front porch. As usual, if he wasn't at Smith's General Store, he was on his porch whittling the time away like he was today. Grace felt deep sorrow for this widowed man.

Two months ago, he sent his grandson—her childhood friend, James—off to war. Today, she was sure he had received a letter of eviction as well.

"I'm sure it does not matter that Mr. Lloyd's father served in the Republic of Texas or that his grandson is currently serving in the United States Army," Grace murmured. Her words raced off into the wind.

Grace saw Mr. Lloyd lift his head and toss her a brief wave. Her hello would never reach him from this distance, but she said it anyway. He put his head back down and began whittling again.

"It does not matter that he was born on the land or lived here all eighty years of his life. I'm sure there is no exception. I bet every ounce of land here in this community is going to turn into a United States Army training camp," Grace muttered to herself. She kicked a rock out of the path with her foot.

She let out a deep sigh and picked up the pace again. Just before she turned off the road onto the short-cut, Grace noticed a familiar car driving toward her. She shielded her eyes from the afternoon sun.

Is that Edward's car? He probably heard the news and immediately headed toward Oakmont, Grace thought.

"Hey there, beautiful," Edward called to his fiancée as his car came to a stop beside her. Beads of perspiration lined her forehead. "Can I give you a ride home?" he asked.

"Yes." Grace's fingers uncurled their tight grip around her

bag. Her shoulders dropped as she released a thin smile. "I'm glad you are here." Tiredness enveloped her spirit but seeing him brought relief. Edward shifted the car into park and hopped out so he could open Grace's door. Her worn body felt all the strain of the day's news upon her as she settled into the front seat.

Edward closed her door and jogged back around to the driver's side and got in.

"I thought you would still be at the schoolhouse?" Edward questioned first.

Grace slowly shook her head from side to side. "I had two fathers come in and get their children. The Army sent letters to their houses saying they have to move soon." She stared out the front window. "I wasn't sure how many more parents were going to come. Plus, I really want to check in with my family right now…" Her voice faded.

"That's understandable," Edward agreed. They sat in silence for the next minute as they passed by the Springer and White children headed home from school.

Grace's eyes welled up with tears once again as the young children waved. *Stop crying. They are going to be okay. They might not come back to school again, but the children are going to be okay.* She sniffled and took a long deep breath. She clenched her teeth hoping they would not start chattering again.

"Are you crying over there?" Edward glanced at Grace as he maneuvered his car on the dirt road.

She shrugged too afraid tears would stream out if she answered.

"Well, I'll tell you what, Gatesville sure is buzzing with the news everywhere." Edward reached over and grabbed her hand with his own. "With the boundaries being announced today, the townsfolk are ready to start preparing for some new business. Several people are already making their homes ready for soldiers. Just about everyone is excited that the Army is coming soon."

Grace whipped her head and glared straight at Edward.

"You're joking with me, right?" Grace wiped her eyes. "Why are we talking about everyone in Gatesville being excited! The people here in Oakmont are losing their homes and land. I am losing my job, Edward! These poor children will not ever be going to Oakmont school again."

"Darling, all children from Oakmont will eventually go to Gatesville once they reach high school anyway. It will be okay that they are going a few years earlier now."

"You don't get it, do you, Edward?"

"I understand, Grace." He shed his grin. "Your parents are losing their home and their land, but the government will compensate them for it. They will be able to easily buy land again.

"Edward," Grace's cheeks were hot. "Mrs. Miller just told me she and her husband are only getting eight dollars an acre for their land. If this is true, and they are not getting what they rightly deserve for the land, then it is going to be impossible to buy land anywhere near here."

Edward turned the car into the drive toward her parents' home. "You can't believe everything you hear, Grace. Plus, maybe the Miller land isn't as good, so it only deserves $8 an acre."

She knew the Miller's possessed some of the best land in the entire county. They owned both hills and valleys on their 800 acres of land where they farmed and raised cattle as well. She was finished arguing with Edward.

"Listen, Edward. I love you and I don't want to argue with you anymore. I think it's best you don't come inside with me right now. I'll see you on Sunday."

"Grace, don't push me away."

"I said I'll see you on Sunday. I know my father will be upset and I want him to have his space. Meet me at church." Grace repeated herself again and opened her door.

She leaned back and pulled Edward's head closer to her own.

"I love you," she whispered and kissed his cheek. She hopped out of the car and closed the door.

"Bye, Grace." Edward sat waiting until she reached the steps of her house before he shifted the car to drive.

Grace wiped away any remaining tears and smoothed down the hair on the sides of her head. She knew her father was not one to cry so she would try to control her sorrowful emotions.

"Mama!" Her voice echoed in the quiet house. "Papa!" Grace called out again from the living room doorway.

She figured they were in the barn or out in the field. As she turned to leave the room, a tri-folded white paper resting on the end table caught her attention.

Grace knew she should leave it alone. This was not her house or her farm, but the temptation was too great. She walked over to the paper and skimmed the first paragraph.

The words were clearly typed, "You are hereby ordered by the United States of America to evacuate this land by Saturday, March 21."

"Grace, you are home early," a voice spoke up behind her.

In a trance, she someone how failed to hear her mother's footsteps.

"J.J. arrived a few minutes before you pulled up. He said you let the children out early today." Footsteps came toward her from the kitchen. Mama must have come in the back door from the barn.

"Oh, Mama!" Grace turned around. Hearing her sweet mother's voice beckoned the tears even though she tried to hold them back.

"I had a couple of fathers come to the school today and pull their children out early after they heard the news. I had to get home to you and Father." Her words rushed out. She dropped the paper on the table and fell into her mother's chest.

My parents have the huge task of moving, and yet here I am crying, Grace thought.

Mama gingerly stroked her hair as tears fell on off her face onto her mother's arm.

"I know, honey. J.J. explained that to me as well," Mama said.

Her mother stood there holding her in the very home where she'd given birth to her. Grace wasn't sure how she was going to say goodbye to this house and all the memories it stored from her childhood till now.

The two women privately shed tears over the loss of the family farm.

"Where's Father?" Grace asked after she regained her composure.

"He's already started working and organizing tools and farm equipment in the barn."

"Mama!" J.J. yelled from the other side of the screen door. "Daddy needs you!" he hollered.

Mama and Grace made their way from the living room through the kitchen and out the back door.

Seeing her father brought more tears. He hustled around the barn moving around farm equipment as if they were small toys. Three weeks would not be enough time to move all this equipment and all their personal belongings.

"Grace, glad you are home," Father said. A small stream of sweat slid down his nose and dripped off as he tilted his head toward her. "You can help your mother and your grandma in the garden while J.J. and I work together in here. When Ruth gets in from school, she will help wherever needed. Tomorrow, I will head into Gatesville and begin looking for land."

"Yes, Grace." Her mother motioned toward the gardening tools. "We need to go ahead and get as many vegetables as we can today. Tomorrow, we will start canning them."

Grace nodded her head and grabbed an old bonnet and a pair of gloves. She didn't care to change clothes. Every minute was needed to prepare for the big move and right now that place was undetermined. Her father's matter-of-fact voice told her no time should be wasted.

As EDWARD SPED AWAY from the house, he considered Grace's words. Maybe news of people in Gatesville being so happy was a poor idea. But Grace's family would be fine. She had a house and a job, while so many others had lost everything with the Depression.

He wished he could get the right words out for her to under-stand. *Everyone in a society gives a little, gets a little, right? The government provides certain benefits and stability for all the people; in return it expects certain support. Think of all the men who went to fight for this war. They're supporting the country. And now the government needs a piece of land so it can make a place to train those men to be ready for the war effort. It just happens to be this piece. But everyone in the country will benefit from it!*

Why couldn't Grace be impressed by the heroic patriotic opportunity her community had been given? And once all the new soldiers moved to Gatesville, the number of readers for the newspaper would grow, too. She wouldn't even have to work if she'd rather not.

His old car raised a cloud of dust as he flew down the dirt road not caring about his speed. Crooked branches from a couple of hundred-year-old live oaks stretched above the road. The green leaves showed health and life. *That live oak doesn't complain about the weather—hail, wind, or snow. It doesn't shrivel up and die. Heck, its leaves even stay green year-round.*

Grace's community was made of strong people like that. Edward knew in his heart everyone would get through the current hard time, and life would continue. But she couldn't seem to see that. *She's acting as though life is over. Doesn't she under-*

stand we are about to begin our new lives together? We can do whatever we want with it.

He glanced at his watch. Time to get back to the office and finish writing the story from yesterday's interview. Even the woman he interviewed yesterday had made lemonade out of lemons. *And she's making money now. Maybe Grace's family can buy a house in the area and then do the same thing. It would help out the Army and bring in some income, too.*

CHAPTER 18

*a*fter a late dinner, Grace overheard Father talking to Mama in the kitchen. He wanted to have a discussion with his lawyer friend about available land in the Gatesville area. Mama wanted to head to Gatesville too, so she could go to the main general store to purchase more canning supplies and other necessary items for moving. Father decided they would head to Gatesville in the morning and take Ruth and J.J. with them.

An hour later, Father stopped her in the hallway before she went to bed. "Grace, you are welcome to join us or stay here. Whatever helps you most."

"Thanks, I will come along." It would be nice to see Edward again. Especially after not having their conversation end on a positive note. He didn't always work in the office on Saturdays, but maybe he would be there.

The next morning, Grace awoke to the rooster crowing long before daybreak. She rolled over and glanced at her clock. Her arms ached from harvesting vegetables in the garden and moving farm equipment and supplies around in the barn. She got ready, helped with breakfast and the morning chores, and then left with her family two hours later.

As the sun crested the top of the large cedar-covered hill near their home, Grace sat in the backseat of her parents' sedan with her two youngest siblings squeezed in beside her on both sides. Her mother and father sat side by side in the front two seats.

As they traveled the ten-mile trip into Gatesville, Grace glanced behind her. The sun shot rays of dark orange and bright yellow through the clouds in the horizon. A serene and still silence filled the car. Even J.J. stayed quiet almost the entire way.

Most days, Grace loved driving into Gatesville with her family, but the disappointment of yesterday had left her feeling empty.

As they pulled into the town square, the towering Coryell County courthouse came into view. Blocks of limestone lined with red sandstone encompassed this beautiful forty-four-year-old multi-level building. Four Roman-numeral Seth Thomas clocks, each perched atop one side of the building, all struck eight o'clock simultaneously.

As usual, her eyes immediately shot across the town square from the courthouse, over to the building that housed The Gatesville Herald. Many people had today off, but Edward a lot of times worked on Saturday. He seemed to always be working. If a new story came up, he wanted to be the first to cover it.

Once Father parked the car, the men and women headed in different directions. Father and J.J. went to visit with a local lawyer friend, while Grace joined her mother and Ruth for a stroll to the general store.

"Well, look who we have here!" a familiar voice sang inside the Gatesville General Store as the women walked in. The spry sixty-five-year-old woman with a pale pink hat and matching dress sauntered toward the women. "How are you ladies? You girls sure are growing indeed. And look at you, Grace Kathleen, just as beautiful a bride as you can be!"

The short-statured woman clapped her hands together as she managed to wrap her arms around all three women. Her shoulder-length gray-streaked brown hair bobbled up and down in her excitement.

"Thank you, Doris, that's so very kind of you." Grace's pale skin glowed from the compliments. Doris was Georgia's second cousin. It had been Christmas since the last time Grace and her mother had made a special trip into Gatesville.

"Georgia Alabama!" Doris called her younger cousin by first and middle name. "Honey, look at you. What is wrong?" Doris continued to hold onto to Georgia's arms. "Are you sad your oldest daughter is getting married and moving out of your house? Now, honey, she will be living right down the road from you," she gently chastised as she glanced over at Grace. "Aren't you, Grace Kathleen? I heard you and Edward are moving into that old homestead out east of town and you will still be teaching at Oakmont. At least that's what Edward told me a few months ago when I saw him in town." Doris finally stopped to take a breath as the three Willis women stood speechless.

"Um…Yes. Doris," Grace hesitated. "That was mostly all true until yesterday."

"Oh, no. You are still getting married?" the petite woman gasped.

"Doris, we learned some distressing news yesterday," Georgia began in a calm, even voice. She straightened the empty Mason jars beside her and exhaled a deep breath. "Our farm is included in the area that will be taken over by the Army. We have three weeks to find a new place to live, as well as move all our belongings including the farm equipment. As far as Grace's job is concerned, she will not be teaching at Oakmont school." Grace met her mother's sorrowful gaze. "Oakmont school will no longer be in existence. For that matter, Oakmont community will no longer be in existence."

The words pierced Grace's heart. To hear those words audibly spoken had a staggering effect on her. She needed to breathe. She felt the floor closing in on her. Doris shared their sentiments, but it wasn't helping.

"Excuse me, Doris and Mama." Grace interrupted the nonstop apologetic statements of her mother's second cousin. "I think I'm going to see if Edward is at his office. I didn't tell him we were coming this morning, so I want to be sure I catch him if he does go in."

"Yes, Grace." Her mother gave her a slight nod and tenderly patted her shoulder before she turned to leave.

"After we are finished here, we will meet you on the steps of the courthouse or at the newspaper office," Georgia said.

"Thank you, Mama. And Doris, it was good seeing you."

"Yes, Grace Kathleen, it was good seeing you too! And you just hang in there, honey," she waved her floral handkerchief at Grace. "It will all be okay, and you will be alright. I am sure you will be able to find another job as a teacher real fast. Now, tell Edward hello for me."

Grace backed away from the gibberish calling out to her.

Doris has good intentions, but Oakmont is the best school. I want to continue teaching there. Grace quietly closed the door to the store behind her.

She exhaled as she scanned the parking spaces in the town square. Grace still didn't see Edward's car. The office where her father was meeting his lawyer friend was a couple spaces down from Edward's work. She headed across the street to step into that meeting for a few minutes.

Gold lettering covering the front window read, "Charles D. Stone, Lawyer." She twisted the front door handle carefully, trying not to disturb their conversation.

"Now, tell me, John," Stone's deep voice echoed from the back office. "How much did you say the government is paying you for your land?"

"It is right here on this document they gave me yesterday," her father replied. "Look, $17.50 per acre. I've got 200 acres, Charles."

She heard a low whistle from her father's friend. "That's pure robbery," Father's voice intensified in the quiet space. "I should at least be getting double or triple this amount."

"You're right, John, but I've been hearing some farmers are only getting $12 or even as low as $8 per acre." Grace could hear papers being shuffled on the desk.

"That's nonsense!" Father's voice boomed as he pounded his fist on the table.

"John, I know this will upset you more, but I have been searching for available property all over the county since you called me yesterday afternoon. Everyone is looking for land at the same time. I am sorry to tell you, but the price of property has dramatically increased in value. You are better off looking for land in a different county. The government has not put a cap on these prices rising. If you want land here in Coryell County, you are going to have to pay four or five times what you are being paid for your land by the government. Even leasing land will be very pricey."

"Are you telling me there is no land available?" She could hear the exasperation in her father's voice.

"There are a few properties left, but John, at this rate you can only afford fifty acres or less. Farther west, maybe you can get 100 or 150 acres for your money," Stone responded. Silence settled in the room for a moment as both men let the disheartening news settle in. "I don't want to rush you, but you will need to talk with Georgia and give me your answer in the next hour. I'm sure the properties I found yesterday will be gone by noon."

Father will come around the corner any moment. Maybe he won't want to know I heard this. Grace twisted the handle on the front door and exited the building before he could discover her.

Mama just might faint at the news of there being no land available. Farming blood ran strong through Mama and Father;

for there to be no available farmland just might break her. Mama had spent almost her entire life on the farm they still called home. They'd been married there, and Father began farming his part of the deeded land the very next day.

Grace glanced toward the empty parking spaces in front Edward's work. Still no sign of Edward. *Maybe it is best to just leave him a note.* She wasn't sure how long her family would be in Gatesville, but by the sound of it they would probably be leaving soon.

As she stopped outside his building, she noticed several copies of the Gatesville Tribune resting on a bench and waiting to be delivered.

"Gatesville Citizens Opening Homes to the Army Bringing Financial Stability!" blared the headline in dark bold print on the front page. She read Edward's name on the byline and quickly skimmed the paragraphs below the headline. The article informed readers that several commanding officers and their families had already moved to town and were renting space in homes of the nearby residents. One older woman was quoted as "being thankful for an increase in income to help make ends meet." Another middle age couple mentioned "being blessed with this opportunity."

None of this is a blessing. She knew Edward reported the news, but why had he not interviewed her or her family—on anyone in Oakmont? Why did the headline not read, *"Army Evicts Local Families and They Have No Where to Go!"* Fury petrified her veins as she stood motionless.

"Grace!" hollered J.J. "What are you doing just standing there?" J.J. and her father had both just stepped outside the lawyer's office.

She snapped out of her secret thoughts and cleared her throat. "I'm just reading the headlines. Nothing interesting today." She shrugged as she joined them.

"Why don't you hand me a copy? I want to read the headlines." Father held out a hand.

She gulped and handed over a paper. She knew his response before he even saw the bold typed letters.

"Financial stability? Who is getting financial stability from this!" A group of women nearby stopped and turned to look at him. "From what? Hmm…. oh, opening their houses up to Army guys. Who wrote this article anyway?"

He didn't need to say the name out loud. She knew he saw it. He tossed the paper back on the bench.

"He doesn't get it does he? This is affecting us too."

"I don't know. I really don't want to discuss it now. Are you finished with your meeting?" Grace responded.

"For now." His short reply told her he was not ready to discuss any of the meeting with her. "Where are your mother and Ruth?"

"We were supposed to meet at the courthouse steps or here at Edward's office, but I think I see them coming out of the store now."

"Grace, here's a little change." Her father dug some coins out of his pocket. "Why don't you treat yourself, Ruth and J.J. to some ice cream at the drug store? Your mother and I need to discuss a few things."

She knew she had no option but to say yes. The other two could have been sent on alone; they were old enough and didn't need her. She desperately wanted to stay and help her parents discuss available options since there was no land, but she knew it was not her place.

"Yes, Father." She took the money and called out to Ruth to come join her. The three of them left for the drug store and gave their parents some space to figure out where they would be living in less than three short weeks.

CHAPTER 19

The town's courthouse bell resounded nine times as she looked out the drugstore window. Overcast clouds began to eclipse the blue sky. With her long silver spoon, Grace swirled vanilla ice cream in her glass bowl. J.J lifted his bowl to lick the remaining dessert from the bottom of it.

"J.J., stop that. You're not an animal," Ruth playfully chastised the boy and then started laughing at him as he made slurping sounds.

Grace mustered up a laugh. The knots in her stomach made it hard for her to enjoy her family. She glanced out the window.

On the last dong, Grace noticed Edward's familiar sedan shoot into his parking spot. He leapt out and immediately darted inside his office door, oblivious to the eyes watching him from a distance. Grace sat there twisting her diamond ring around her finger.

Why am I so upset at him? He is reporting the news. He didn't bring the Army to my family's land. But he was only sharing one side of the story. Oakmont and its people had a story too, a unique perspective that was also important.

"Hey, is that Edward's car?" J.J. interrupted her internal

debate. He reached his arm across the table and pointed down the street.

"Yes," Grace said clenching her teeth. She knew there was no getting out of seeing him now.

"Why don't you go say hi before Mama and Father get back?" Ruth patted her on the back, seeming to understand her agitated state. "We will be fine." One birthday shy of adulthood, Ruth's perceptiveness reminded her of their brother, Mickey—always watching others and ready to help when needed. The reminder of Mickey being gone to war made Grace want to run far away at that moment.

"Thanks, Ruth. I will be quick." Grace got up from her spot and headed out the door to Edward's office.

Overwhelming emotions raged in her mind. Should she bring up the article? Should she stay silent? He needed to know she disapproved. Their wedding date was so close and yet they stood so divided on the Army coming to town. Grace rotated the worn handle and pushed open the office door. Two bells jingled against the wooden door as she closed it.

"Hello?" Edward's smooth rich voice addressed her from the room nearby. The secretary must be off since today was Saturday.

"Edward?" She moved toward his office.

"Grace?" Edward's puzzled voiced called out as he met her at his doorway. "What are you doing in town today? Is everything okay?" Edward motioned her in his office and hugged her close as he closed the door behind her with one hand. "Darling, come sit down. You are looking pale. Do you have a fever?"

"No." She found herself at a loss. No other words came out. Her mouth felt dry as she sat next to him. She fidgeted with her ring, trying to decide what to say first. "We are here in Gatesville today mainly because my parents need to find land. Apparently, there is no land available for the price they need." Grace's eyes began welling up. "The landowners in Coryell County who are not moving are raising their prices because they know they can make money on these poor farmers and ranchers like my father who have no place to go."

"I know." Edward shook his head. "After I left you yesterday, I met with several men in town who told me the same thing."

She couldn't hold it in any longer. "So why did you write an article about financial stability for the newspaper? There's no financial stability for my family anymore." Grace crossed her arms across her chest.

"Grace," Edward pleaded. "Your family is in a minority. There are, what, maybe three or four hundred families having to move. The majority of Coryell County and Gatesville and a whole lot of Bell County will benefit and are benefiting now from the Army being here. Plus, we need positive stories being written and read about the United States. This is our time to show our support of our government as our men are fighting overseas. We, as a newspaper staff, want to show our patriotism."

"My parents are already showing their patriotism with Mickey fighting overseas. Don't you think that is enough?" Grace wiped the free-flowing tears from her eyes. Mickey probably was in some trench in Europe with bullets blazing past him. She couldn't take it. This war. This change. This move.

"Grace, it was an article in the newspaper that I was assigned to write." Edward grabbed her hands. "Plus, I do agree with it and I think it is a brilliant idea to take advantage of your current situation. Maybe your family could even do the same. They can benefit from all this as well."

The bells jingled at the front door, announcing another visitor.

"Hello?" came a commanding male voice.

Edward jumped to his feet as he opened his office door. "Yes, sir? How can I help you?" Grace listened to his footsteps pattering against the floor as he walked toward the front of the building to greet his next guest.

Grace dabbed her eyes with the hem of her crimson dress. Meeting Edward had not helped in any way. He might have been assigned to write that particular article, but the way he defended it told a different story. Sure, the people were smart to start profiting from the current situation, but he still needed to write a story about the people losing their homes. People like her family. She loved Edward, but their separate opinions widened the gap between them.

"Hold on one minute. Let me finish this conversation with a guest in my office and I will get right back with you." Grace heard Edward's footsteps again on the hardwood floor.

She stood as her fiancé entered the room and pulled the door closed. The two faced each other, not moving. Grace took a deep breath as she twisted the ring on her finger. "Edward, I'm not sure you should come out to the church service tomorrow."

"Grace, I should be there. We haven't spent time together and I want to see you."

"Do you, Edward?" Silence filled the room. "My family and I have patriotism. Maybe you just don't have empathy." She glared at her fiancé and clenched her teeth.

Edward returned her stare at a loss for words. A moment later, she dropped her grief-stricken eyes and stepped around him. "I need to meet my family," she whispered and abandoned Edward in his office as she walked away.

An officer in his early forties, wearing a pressed light-green Army uniform, stood at the front entrance. With his hat in one hand, he opened the front door with his other hand. She didn't care if he saw her with tears streaming down her face.

"Thank you," Grace mumbled as she exited the office in search of her family.

∽

ON THE WAY HOME, her father surprised her and her siblings by turning east two miles early.

"Hey! Where are we going?" J.J. spoke up first.

"Be quiet, J.J.," snapped her father.

"Yes, sir." The twelve-year-old leaned back in his seat and did not ask any more questions.

A short mile later, Father stopped the sedan in front of Mama's second cousin's house, a quaint one-story home with high arches and a porch wrapping around the entire home. Doris and her husband, Samuel, had lived there for forty years. They'd bought the 100-acre property when Doris was in her mid-twenties and Samuel was in his mid-thirties. A white picket fence surrounded the white-painted house.

Grace loved their home with the white paint and white picket fence. Very few homeowners in the area spent money to paint their homes. Grace knew Samuel and Doris had done well in farming since they could afford such a commodity. Samuel had retired from farming the land about five years earlier due to his age and the two of them only had one living son, who moved to Dallas years ago.

Georgia and Doris were cousins through their fathers. Grace heard plenty of stories about Doris; the two cousins saw each other around Christmas and occasional family gatherings.

A smile spread across Grace's lips as she thought about a few hours earlier in the store. It was just like Doris. Words never failed her. She constantly had something to say.

John Sr. slowly pulled off the dirt road and drove up the short driveway next to the weathered white picket fence. She watched her father exit the car. His legs lagged behind him as he hesitantly walked up the steps to the porch. Where was his confidence? He was such a strong man, but he looked like a young child while waiting at the front door.

Grace assumed the older gentleman saw the black dusty sedan because he met John on the front porch shortly after knocking. The men stood talking for a moment. She could not hear them, and her mother did not speak a word from the front seat. Surely, she could say something about what is going on. Grace and her siblings did not ask Mama any questions.

A few minutes later, John rushed back to the car and asked Mama to join him inside.

"I'm getting out. No sense in us sitting in this car, too. Open the door J.J." Grace motioned to the handle.

"You don't have to tell me again! I'm ready to get out. I'm going to see if they still have any horses." J.J. ran across the yard to the barn. *He'll probably stay occupied in there for a while.* Grace chuckled to herself.

"Let's go sit on the porch, Ruth." Grace motioned toward two rocking chairs.

The dark clouds had intensified during their short drive to Doris and Samuel's house. Grace drank in the cool breeze across her face as she closed her eyes. She had no clue why they'd stopped at Doris' house. The clouds continued to gather and swirl as the two young women rocked back and forth on the porch. The smell of rain permeated her nostrils.

"I think we are going to live here," Ruth whispered from the other rocker as she glided back and forth at a steady pace.

Grace opened her eyes, and her eyebrows drew together. "What do you mean live here?" Grace matched her sister's hushed tones.

Ruth continued to rock back and forth unchanged by the news she had shared with her sister.

"I'm not completely sure." The teenager shrugged her slender shoulders. "Doris asked Mama if they could step aside for a moment while we were at the store. All I could hear was Doris saying something about livin' on their property. Mama was all crying and stuff, but she didn't say anything to me after we left."

"Hmmm, that is very thoughtful of Doris." She closed her eyes and felt the wind on her face again. She thought about the words spoken at Mr. Stone's office in town.

There is no land available for my parents so maybe this would be the best place for them, Grace thought.

Twenty minutes passed before her father opened the front door.

"We best be getting' home, Samuel, before it rains." Father turned to shake Samuel's hand. "And thank you again." He clutched Samuel's sunspot covered and wrinkled arm with his other hand.

Samuel nodded, recognizing her father's gratitude. "You're welcome. I'll come out to your place on Monday and get the dimensions of your house. We will make this work, John. Don't worry."

"Grace and Ruth, let's go before it starts raining hard on us." Mama motioned to them as she gathered her dress and hurried down the steps two at a time.

Grace and Ruth gave Samuel a brief hug before they ran to the car. Huge drops of rain pelted them as they rushed to the car.

John Sr. and J.J. joined them in the car moments later. As her father slammed his door closed, a heavy downpour erupted from the skies. The rain poured down on the Willis family car as they drove the three miles home on the mud-covered roads.

"Samuel and Doris have been so gracious to offer us a place to move our home," her mother spoke above the pounding of the rain.

"What do you mean move our home?" J.J. blurted out the same question Grace was thinking.

"Exactly that." Father looked over his shoulder for a moment. "To put it simply, we are going to cut our house in two and roll it over to Samuel and Doris' land. I've made a deal with Samuel to lease some of his land and farm it since he is unable to do it anymore."

"I'm still not understanding how we are going to cut the house in two?" J.J. asked shaking his wet hair back and forth.

"Well, you are going to watch and learn." Grace could see the edges of a thin smile. It was the first time in days—maybe even weeks—since she had seen him with a relaxed attitude. "I helped my father move his house when I was your age. Now you will get the opportunity to do the same thing."

How exactly would this process happen? What about all the fields and fences? It didn't sound like a good plan to her, but then what other options did her parents have?

CHAPTER 20

$\mathcal{T}$he rain continued for the next twenty-four hours keeping her family at home, unable to attend the church service on Sunday. She longed to be in church to see her dear friends. They had very few Sundays remaining as one congregation.

Father feared the creek beds and nearby rivers would overflow their banks, as well as some of the side roads, so she stayed inside. By Sunday evening though, the storm system moved away.

Early Monday morning, she left the house with J.J. to walk their usual route to school. As an energetic almost-teenage boy, J.J. did not usually stay by her side for long.

"Get your energy out before you get to school!" Grace called after him as he ran off. He would probably meet the Springer and White families as usual.

After a mile of praying and then talking out loud to herself about her lessons plans, she jumped when she came around the bend and found her brother standing alone in the middle of the path. "You scared me, J.J.! What are you doing?"

"Where are they, Grace?" her twelve-year old brother stood at the bottom of the trail. His eyes searched in vain for his friends. He pushed away the thick cedar branches blocking his view.

The same routine he'd known for the past six years of his life had suddenly been altered.

"Perhaps they are helping their parents. Why don't you stop by their houses on the way home from school today?"

"I guess," he murmured and sprinted ahead of her to the schoolhouse.

Grace ran her cold hands through her hair as she shook her head. She needed to trudge on. There would be other children in the schoolhouse waiting for school to start. *Get your act together, Miss Willis.*

As she passed by Mr. Lloyd's home, she lifted her hand and acknowledged the older gentleman sitting faithfully on his front porch. Grace's mind wanted to deny that this would be one of the last days she would ever walk this way to school. She watched as Mr. Lloyd paused his whittling and returned her silent gesture. Tears brimmed her eyelids. She tried to focus on the day's tasks, but the moment at hand consumed her.

Grace dug in her purse. She pulled out a pink square piece of cloth and dabbed the edges of her eyes. *The children cannot see these tears.* She cleared her throat and shoved her handkerchief back into her handbag. She then looked up in the direction of her beloved town and with determined steps pressed on toward Oakmont.

Moments later she came in sight of the schoolhouse. At the same time, Rebecca Smith sprinted down the general store steps with her yellow knee-length dress flying in the wind. She grabbed her side, gasping for breath as the black round buttons lining her chest moved up and down. Grace noticed she held two sealed envelopes in her hand.

"Here." Rebecca transferred her deliveries to Grace with one hand as she continued holding her side with her other. Rebecca panted for air again before talking.

"Mama told me that as soon as I saw you, I was to deliver these envelopes to you." Rebecca took a deep breath and pushed her short light brown hair away from her face. "Both of them arrived Saturday during that rainstorm."

"Thank you, Rebecca." She took the envelopes knowing they must have been important if Mrs. Smith wanted them delivered to her before school. "Now, would you like to join me on my walk the rest of the way to the schoolhouse?"

"No, ma'am. I'm not going today." Rebecca dug her toe in the ground with her black boots as she continued breathing hard. Her light stringy hair shifted in front of her face again. Grace tried not to express any shock or emotion in her voice or on her face.

"I'm sure your mama has a lot of work for you to do, especially with Henry away at war."

"Helen is not going to school today either," Rebecca said as her chocolate brown eyes filled with tears. "Mama says we all have to help. The Army said we have to move by this Friday."

"Friday! This week! Surely not." Grace forgot all composure. "The earliest I thought people were moving out is the following Friday."

"No, ma'am. Mama said an Army fellow came by on Friday morning and told her one week."

The shock overwhelmed her entire body as her knees felt weak. "Okay, Rebecca, you head on then and go help your mama." Grace patted the girl's back as she turned to leave.

The young student sprinted back toward her home as Grace resumed briskly walking toward the schoolhouse. She went to the back side of the building to open the letters. She recognized the handwriting on the front of the first envelope as belonging to Mickey. He'd addressed the letter—four brief sentences—to her entire family. She skimmed the words and life came back in her. Mickey and his battalion had been transported overseas, but he was doing well. Nothing else mattered. *Mickey is alive and doing well. This next one hopefully is good news as well.*

Cursive letters written in thick ink on the front of the envelope displayed the name, "Miss Grace Willis." No return address. She tore the end of the envelope and emptied the contents.

The paper had typed letterhead at the top of the brief note.

Miss Willis,

> *Thank you for your time of service at Oakmont school. I must share with you that Oakmont school will conduct its last day this Tuesday. The Army will be converting the schoolhouse into a range shop. They will be providing trucks to assist families moving out of the area to new home sites. Thank you for your understanding. I must add, Gatesville will need more teachers as families move into the area. Please consider applying for one of these open positions. I look forward to hearing from you soon.*

> *Regretfully yours,*
> *Mr. Wright*

Grace stumbled to a large tree stump nearby and sat. The letter beat into her the news she'd already known in her heart. This was the end of Oakmont School.

She'd first entered the Oakmont schoolhouse as a young six-year-old with a short 1920s finger-wave haircut. Inside the school walls, she developed a deep love and devotion for learning. By the time she left with her two long braids in the eighth grade, to go to school in Gatesville, Grace knew she would be a teacher. Her passion intensified and she excelled in both high school and college.

In her last year of college, her former schoolteacher in Oakmont retired and the position came open for her to return to where it all started. She wanted to devote all her passion and energy into teaching and watching her childhood dreams and aspirations come true. Grace was teaching her dream job, but tomorrow it would all stripped away from her. There would not even be another week here to tell the children goodbye. Her heart hurt especially for the little ones. They wouldn't understand what was happening.

She re-read the letter clearly stating her schoolhouse would change into a range shop for the Army very soon. Grace feared children some of the older students might quit school altogether if they moved elsewhere. With prices being outrageously high, families were going to have to settle wherever they could even if that meant another county.

She glanced down at her watch. She knew the children expected her to start class within the next ten minutes. She peeled herself from the stump and headed toward the front door to start her second-to-last day as teacher at Oakmont school. Her children needed her to be strong and dignified in this time of crisis. Grace gathered strength with every step as she planned how to best help the children.

After their morning pledges and school songs outside, Grace escorted the children back inside. She opened the schoolhouse door and walked to the front of the classroom placing the envelopes on the middle of her desk. The chatter in the room extinguished as the children gave Grace their full attention.

"Class," Grace took a deep breath. "I'm sure you all know why I sent you home early on Friday. I, as well, learned that my parents will be moving off the land that has been in my family for many decades." Grace stole a glance at J.J. He sat motionless staring straight down at his desk. The chairs where the two Springer boys sat both in front and behind him were both empty.

"I received a letter as well this morning stating we will no longer have school in Oakmont starting this Wednesday, however..." Grace paused and raised her hands to quiet the whispers across the room. "Let's make the most of both today and tomorrow. First, we will begin by opening your journals. I want you to spend some time thinking and writing down your special memories both at your home and at school. Tomorrow, those of you who want to share your stories will be given time to stand in front of the class and read from your journal."

THE DAY PASSED FASTER than Grace anticipated. There students stayed busy writing in their journals and cleaning out the schoolhouse with very few interruptions. Only a third of her students were in attendance and most of the children lived further north outside of the Oakmont community. Grace learned their families had been given four to five weeks to leave their homes and land versus the ones who lived closer to town who were only given days to move.

After the last child left for the day, Grace prepared to stop by Smith's General Store on her way home. She wanted to thank Mrs. Smith for having Rebecca deliver the letters. As Grace stepped outside the schoolhouse door for the first time since morning, she heard a distant rumbling coming down the main road into the small hamlet.

She paused at the top step and shielded her eyes from the blinding sun. A convoy of large diesel Army trucks rumbled down the road, disrupting the serene Oakmont community. Two trucks halted in front of the general store. Three other trucks swept past Grace and stopped at the three homes closest to the schoolhouse. The fuel burned her nostrils. Several young soldiers hopped out of one of the trucks at the general store and headed inside. A chill streaked through her body.

Grace walked down the schoolhouse steps and cautiously passed by the store on the opposite side of the road.

"Mama! We have got some visitors!" Rebecca yelled from the front porch, waving at her mother to join her.

Grace saw and heard Mrs. Smith join her daughter on the

creaky wooden deck. A young solider took off his hat and spoke in low tones to the store owner.

"Why in the world are you boys here today? I was told we had until Friday," Mrs. Smith questioned.

Grace could hear her hearty voice from across the street. The gray-headed woman stood on her front porch with her hand resting on her thick hip, blocking the entrance to her store.

Grace could not hear the response from the solider. She assumed he was only following orders.

Mrs. Smith was visibly upset by his answer. "Listen here, young man, we are not ready. My paper in my office states we have until Friday. I'm sorry, but three days is not enough time."

"No, sir! We have so much stuff left," Rebecca blurted out before her mother placed her hand over her daughter's mouth.

The solider looked down at Rebecca and replied, "That's why we've been sent here, young lady, to help your family move. It sure is a big task to do it alone."

"Mama!" Rebecca swatted her mother's hand aside. "I'm not ready to move! I don't want us to go anywhere! I want our family to stay here! This is our home!" The twelve-year-old cried in anguish, tears streaming down her face as her mother pulled her inside the store.

Grace turned away from the scene. She felt deep sorrow for her friends, struggling to pack all their belongings as well as move all the items from the store. The words spoken from the child described how they all felt. No one was ready to move, even those given a full three weeks.

She'd intended asking Mrs. Smith where they were moving, but it appeared they would be heading out before she had a chance to visit with the family. The Smith family and their store would never be replaced in her heart.

CHAPTER 21

*A*s the sun rose the next day, Grace pulled the warm covers over her head. The smell of bacon wafted into her bedroom. Normally, one whiff of the flavorful frying pork encouraged her to get out of bed quickly. This morning, however, she wished she had canceled the final day of class. She desired to see the children, but her mind could not get the image of the Smith family out of her head.

A light knock interrupted her sullen thoughts.

"Grace, honey, you are going to be late," Mama said on the other side of the closed door. "Breakfast is ready and J.J. is sitting at the table eating."

Grace groaned. She tossed the blankets off her head. "I'm awake. Thanks, Mama. I'll be there shortly."

She sat up and slung her feet onto the hard floor. She reached her arms toward the ceiling and back down, stretching her sore back and muscles. *Come on—let's make this a great last day for these kids.*

Thirty minutes later, Grace and J.J. went out the front door together on their final trip to the schoolhouse.

As they stepped down the stairs and off the porch, Grace saw

Edward's black sedan coming down the road with dust stirring behind the car. She paused in mid-stride. Why was Edward coming unannounced, so early in the morning?

"J.J., you run ahead. I'm sure whatever reason Edward has for coming is very important."

"Okay." He shrugged his shoulders and sprinted down the driveway. He tossed a thumbs-up as he passed Edward's car and kept running. With long strides, J.J. then cut across the road to a thick batch of cedar trees. He entered the narrow trail, which led him on short-cut to school.

Edward's car continued down the driveway and came to a sudden halt in front of her. "I need you to get in quickly." His voiced sounded strained.

"Edward, I need to get to school. What happened?"

"Just get in. I will tell you on the way."

As she got in the car, she noticed that under his hat his eyes were dark and swollen.

"Edward, did you get in a fight? Did you lose your job? What is it?" her questions tumbled over each other.

Edward turned the car around and headed back down the driveway. "It is not about me." Edward rubbed his forehead.

"Oh, my goodness, Edward. Just tell me."

"I got a phone call this morning from one of James' cousins."

"And…." Grace coaxed him along, dreading the news.

"James fought bravely for the Army…" Edward paused, his voice breaking. "His battalion got a surprise attack and a friend got hit in a firestorm of bullets. James went back to help him…. and…."

"What? What? What, Edward!" She covered her mouth.

"He didn't make it, Grace." The words shattered her heart as everything spun around her.

"What? Oh…oh…oh, my goodness," she stuttered. "No! No. Oh, Edward. Not James!" *This can't be happening, dear God. This can't be true.* She felt numb all over and wanted to curl up into a ball. She released a muted scream as the tears flowed freely.

Edward pulled the car to the side of the road. Tears poured down his cheeks as he reached across the seat and wrapped his long arms around his fiancée. She covered her face and released sobs that shook her entire body. She wept for her friend's family, she wept for herself, and she wept for Edward. He held her as tears continued to stream down his own face, dripping from the stubble on his chin. They mourned the loss of their dear friend together.

After several minutes, Grace lifted her head to wipe the remaining tears away. She tried to remove the unexpected news about James from her head. She needed to get to the schoolhouse.

"Edward, I need you to drive me to my class or I will be late. The children will not know what to think if I am not there when it is time for school to begin."

Edward gently kissed her forehead and shifted the car to drive.

"How did James' family find out the news?" She took a mirror out of her purse and noticed in the reflection wet splotches still on her face.

"A letter was hand-delivered by an Army representative to the family late yesterday evening. James' parents shared the news with Mr. Lloyd, and then called several aunts and uncles. James' cousin knew we used to work together at the paper, so he called me first thing this morning."

"I'm surprised his mother didn't already call my mama." She gazed at the bluebonnets out her window. The native Texas wildflowers had just started appearing all over the countryside. Soon the fields would be covered with these royal-blue-and-white jewels of the land.

"I'm sure it will not be long before the entire community knows. I think the men arrived just before dark to notify the family."

"Ugh. Poor Mr. Lloyd. First his home and now his grandson gone because of this war." Would he still be sitting at his usual spot on his front porch?

"I thought I might stop by his house after I drop you off and visit with him for a few minutes."

"I think that's a good idea. He might need some company."

"Look, there he is now." He did show up. She pointed at the old man whittling on a small piece of wood. "I guess it helps him."

Edward nodded in agreement as he continued driving into Oakmont. As he drove closer, a large Army truck came into view. "What's going on up there?" asked Edward as motioned with his hand.

Tears brimmed Grace's eyes again. Determined not to cry, she blinked several times and cleared her throat before responding. "They are moving the Smith family out earlier than expected. I overheard part of the conversation yesterday between Mrs. Smith and a soldier."

"What do you mean moving them out early?" Edward glanced at her, looking perplexed.

"Rebecca told me they were not supposed to move them out until Friday. Looks like they only got a three-day notice. It is a shame. The family is not even ready to go."

"They should have already been ready to go."

"Edward, please don't start that."

"What?" Edward questioned as he pulled in front of the schoolhouse. "I'm not trying to be mean. They had plenty of notice. I even wrote articles in the newspaper. They should've already been able to find land and a building elsewhere."

"Edward, you know it is not that simple."

"You're right, Grace. It's *not* that simple, but everyone around here has known since I wrote that article at the end of November. Everyone knew this was very likely to happen. James and I went down to San Antonio, and we watched Frank Mayborn and the other political leaders from this area push for the camp to be placed here in Coryell County as well as in Bell County. James and I watched with our own eyes, Mayborn tracing a circle around General Donovan's thumb around this very spot where we are sitting."

"I know that, Edward, but nothing was certain."

"Grace, it's always better to be safe than sorry. I sure hope the Smith family knew where they were going; otherwise, they are going to be kicking themselves."

"Edward, don't be so harsh." Why could he not just understand how deep the roots were for these families. These families have lived on this land for generations, and they were going to pass this land down to their heirs. Some have lived here since the Texas Revolution. They were not moving until they were forced off the land. And that's what it came to.

"Listen, I need to go. Please tell Mr. Lloyd I said hello. I will try to stop by there on my way home," she said trying to change the subject.

"Grace," Edward paused until she faced him. "Let me see your hand." Edward reached for her slender left hand. The ring caught the sun and glistened as her hand rested in his. "Let's not let all the things going on with Oakmont get between us. I love you and I am looking forward to spending the rest of my life with you." He tenderly kissed the back of her hand.

"I'll try not to, Edward. I'm sorry." Grace pasted on a smile as he released her hand. She scooted out of his car and closed the door. She forced her legs to walk up the steps and make this last day for the children one of their best days yet.

CHAPTER 22

*E*mpty desks littered the room as Grace prepared to start her final day as a teacher in the Oakmont schoolhouse. She peered across the room. How many seats would remain vacant today? More children might stay home to help their families. A moment later, J.J. burst through the door with the White and Springer children.

"Their parents said they could come in for the last day!" J.J. exclaimed.

"Hi, Miss Willis," said the children one at a time as they walked to their desks.

"I'm so glad all of you are here today. We missed seeing each one of you yesterday." The children ranged in age from seven to twelve. "And I know J.J. is very glad to have your company again as well." Grace gestured toward her younger brother and gave him a smile.

Several more children entered the schoolhouse before she started the class. The more-than-halfway-full room filled her with thankfulness and gratitude as she began her last day.

The children started their morning routine by walking outside to recite the Pledge of Allegiance.

Grace observed the children one by one placing their hands over their hearts. All eyes gazed upon the flying red-and-white-striped flag.

"I pledge," began Grace as the children joined her, "allegiance to the Flag of the United States of America and to the Republic for which it stands, one nation, under God, indivisible, with liberty and justice for all."

Complete silence filled the air. No Army trucks. No people walking down the street. A lone mockingbird could be heard in the distance. Her hand stayed over her heart a moment longer. The bird seemed to tease them or applaud them. She hoped the latter.

"Students," said Grace as she pointed to the children and then to the waving flag. "Every morning we recite these words. And every morning this pledge is a reminder to us, together, we stand beside each other. This has been one tough year for all of us and today is an especially hard day as we say, 'So long for now' to our friends."

Grace felt a lump forming in her throat as her mind shifted to James for a split second.

"Look at you. We are a part of this great nation and we must embrace our role. Some of us have brothers who are fighting overseas now and some of us are here praying for those defending our freedom. And others of us have been asked to move from our homes to make room for a place for a new Army camp. And that is where you come in. May you always remember, and may our country never forget how you played a huge role in helping fight for freedom, liberty, and justice."

The students stood motionless.

Not sure where her motivational speech had come from, she looked over her shoulder. No more mocking from that bird.

"Come now." Grace clapped twice. "Let's go back inside and begin our day." She led the class toward the front of the school.

The students clambered into their seats as the smell of fresh air and dirt followed them in. Once all the children were inside, Grace tapped her desk with her pointer.

"Children, today we will begin our morning with the older students reading from their journals first. Do we have any volunteers?"

One of the oldest students, J.J.'s thirteen-year-old buddy seated in the back row, glanced around the room before raising his hand.

"Miss Willis, I'll go first," the long-legged boy said.

"Yes, Jack," Grace motioned for him to stand up. His shy personality often kept him from volunteering to stand in front of the class. "I would love for you to start our time today by sharing from your journal."

The teenager wore a white collared shirt covered by light blue overalls streaked with a few dirt stains. He stood to his full five-foot-ten-inch frame.

"My favorite memory is the day before Pearl Harbor. We were playing baseball out here in front of the church on Sunday afternoon. My older brother was still here and not fightin' in the war," Jack coughed, probably to keep the tears at bay. "I hit two home runs and caught several balls at shortstop. That is my favorite memory."

His shoulders slumped over as he slid back into his chair. He rarely showed emotion, but Grace knew he must be hurting inside. For him, he was losing his playmates and lazy days of playing baseball. The effects of adulthood had been forced on Jack very early in life.

An image of Mickey fighting overseas popped up in her mind. Then James. That crazy kid. *What were your last moments like fighting the enemy?* She shook her head trying to dislodge the looming thoughts.

A lump barged into her throat and her eyes grew wet. She swallowed hard and tried again to force the thoughts of her dear friend to go away.

"Thank you, Jack. Would any more of my older students like to go next?" Grace questioned the children seated in the back few rows.

"Miss Willis," the oldest Springer boy raised his hand. "I didn't write anything down since I wasn't here yesterday, but I would like to share something."

"Go ahead, David."

"My favorite memory is swimming in the creek during summer. And I loved surprising J.J. from behind and dunking him in the water!" Laughter erupted from the class as all eyes looked to the feisty young man.

"Heya! You mean I dunked you in the water! Every time!" J.J. called out to the dark-headed boy who was about a head shorter.

"Okay, maybe sometimes," David said, and he started laughing. "But Miss Willis, I really did enjoy swimming in that ole creek. I sure am going to miss it. I wish it was hot enough this week so I could go swimming one last time," David said and sat down. His smile vanished as fast as it appeared.

"Thank you, David. I think we are all going to miss that creek," Grace said.

"And I'm going to miss finding duck eggs and chasing all the ducks back into the water," piped in one of the youngest Springer children.

"Of course, we will miss those pesky ducks and fishing, too," Grace agreed and shared a smile with her.

"Miss Willis, I was not here either yesterday, but I would like to share two of my favorite memories if that is okay," asked the oldest girl in the White family, Betsy. The thirteen-year-old girl had short reddish-blond hair with one side pulled back and tied with a navy ribbon. She wore a matching dark-blue-and-white button-down striped dress.

Grace nodded at the young teenager, giving her permission to speak.

"My first favorite memory," Betsy held out one finger, "is

going to Smith's General Store to get a piece of candy and of course hanging out with my best friend Rebecca," she said with a large grin as she glanced toward the desk where Rebecca used to sit.

"My second favorite memory," the girl extended another finger, "is gettin' all dressed up and going to the dance." Her eyes lit up. "I just loved listening to the fiddle being played, dancing to the music, and of course getting to dance with the older boys that go to the high school." Younger girls in the room giggled at Betsy while several of the boys rolled their eyes.

"Thank you, Betsy, for sharing." Grace motioned her hands for the kids to be quiet again.

"I would like to speak next." Grace heard her young brother's voice call out from the back row. Her eyes open wide. *J.J. wants to share from his journal? He's comical, not personal.* This should be interesting.

"Okay, J.J. go ahead," she told him.

"My favorite memory is being with my father on the farm. I like helping him feed the animals and working next to him in the fields. I like plowing the fresh dirt and watching the rain fall on the soil. And I even like baling hay. It is hard work, and I get real sweaty sometimes, but it's my favorite place to be."

Grace could not keep her tears from falling. He would still have his father, but the farm he loved dearly would soon be gone.

"Thank you, J.J." Grace tried smiling through the tears. J.J. would never inherit his father's land. He might one day be a farmer, but he would never farm in the same exact spot as his grandfather and his father. "I will miss that place, too."

A snaggletooth six-year-old girl sitting in the front row spoke up as well, "I am going to miss my farm too. My daddy said I couldn't take my two baby goats with me or my favorite horse. He said we have to sell them because we have no place for them at our new house in town." The young girl's lips started to quiver.

"I know, sweet girl." She went to hug the little one. "We all have to sell or leave some of our special things behind and it makes us sad, but we always have our memories. No one can take these from you." Grace pointed to the journals. "Always keep these special memories close to your heart and they will make you smile even on the hardest of days."

The class quietly nodded as they seemed to understand the significance of her words.

The rest of the time passed quickly as Grace and the children fully enjoyed spending the day together. More children shared memories out of their journals from both home and school. They smiled, they laughed, and they cried together.

At the end of the day, she closed her time with her students by saying a simple prayer over them all.

"Father, we are heartbroken to leave our friends, but we know you will help us and take care of us. Bless us on our new journeys ahead. Keep us safe and watch out for us. Amen." Grace lifted her head as the students echoed her Amen.

"You are dismissed. I have enjoyed sharing this time with you as your teacher," Grace said as the students quietly gathered their belongings.

Grace wanted to add, *And, if you need me at any time you know where to find me*, but she was not sure where she would be over the next few weeks.

She felt an emptiness in her soul as the students left the classroom slowly. She couldn't control any of it. This bothered her. She wanted to fill this bare spot in her, but nothing could immediately heal it.

The kids continued to talk and share with one another. She knew this might be the last time they would see each other for days, weeks, or maybe even years to come.

"I'll wait for you," her younger brother said as he walked up to Grace's desk.

"Oh, J.J. I will be okay. Why don't you go hang out with your friends? I'm going to call Edward and see if he can come help me pick up the rest of my belongings either on Wednesday or Thursday." Grace motioned to the books and materials boxed up behind her.

"No, I want to walk you home," her younger brother's voice seemed to change as he stood up a little taller. "It will be our last walk home from school and I don't think you should do it alone."

J.J.'s straight shoulders and elongated chin reminded her of Mickey. *He's growing up right before my eyes.*

"Okay," agreed Grace. "How about you carry this bag home for me then?"

"Sure." J.J. reached down and slung the heavy satchel of books on his shoulder.

"I think that is all for now. I will come back tomorrow to make sure the place is ready for the Army," Grace said as she grabbed her sweater off the hook next to the door and led the way outside.

The two strolled past the general store.

"I wonder what is going to happen to the old building?" J.J. asked.

"I'm not sure." Grace shrugged her shoulders. She wondered if the Smith family would try to move their home as well or leave it.

As Grace and J.J. approached Mr. Lloyd's property she thought it best to share about James.

"You know James? Mr. Lloyd's grandson? He used to live over here with his parents, but then moved into Gatesville and started working for the paper with Edward."

"Yeah, I know him," J.J. answered as he swatted a fly away. "Why?"

Grace stopped near the wire fence lining the edge of Mr. Lloyd's property. "Edward came this morning to tell me he died in battle. The news was delivered last night to the family including Mr. Lloyd."

Grace squeezed the boy's shoulder as a few tears streaked down his face.

"I know it is hard to hear. I thought maybe we could stop by and see Mr. Lloyd for a few minutes."

"What about Mickey?" J.J. wiped his eyes with his shoulder.

"What do you mean, J.J.? I don't understand." Grace scanned his face.

"Is Mickey dead too?" he blurted out.

"Oh, no! Not our Mickey!" Grace lifted his chin and stared him square in the eyes. "James and Mickey were not together fighting. They were in two different places."

"How do you know?"

"Mickey would have told us. I'm sure they were not assigned to the same place," Grace said as she started walking on the dirt road again.

"Man, I sure do miss Mickey. How will he even know where we live when he comes home?"

"I'm sure Mama has already written him a letter." Actually, she wasn't so sure that Mama shared the details with Mickey. Mama probably wouldn't want to cause any more stress on her twenty-year-old son. Serving overseas was difficult enough.

"Hey...a...a..., Grace." J.J. came to an abrupt halt at the gate to Mr. Lloyd's property. "Look at Mr. Lloyd. He don't look right."

Grace paused at the metal post. She shielded her eyes from the sun and squinted toward the stretch of property leading to Mr. Lloyd's front porch. She saw the old man leaning over the side of his rocking chair. His two leathery arms hanging stiff. Was he sleeping or did he pass out? "You're right, John, let's go talk to him."

Her heart began beating faster as they approached the motionless man. "Mr. Lloyd! Hello! Mr. Lloyd!" Grace yelled as they drew closer to the gentleman. Panic began consuming her throat. The eighty-year-old man did not look up or move from his rocking chair.

Grace and J.J. sprinted toward the house. "Mr. Lloyd! Are you asleep? Wake up, Mr. Lloyd!" she continued calling. He still did not budge.

As they reached the front porch, Grace saw his whittling tools strewn on the ground. "Mr. Lloyd?" Grace cried as she shook the lifeless man. "J.J., go run and tell James' parents." Grace pointed in the direction of their home.

Her brother barreled across the hay field. She got down on her knees and placed her trembling fingers on the man's bluish neck. She had seen her father do this before to an older woman once when she was a young child. She felt no pulse. Only cold skin and a stiff body.

"Oh, dear Lord!" Grace screamed out to God as she looked up in the sky. She didn't know how long he had been gone, but it had been for a while. "James and now Mr. Lloyd? Why, God? Why?" Grace wept.

As she stood up and pushed the tears away from her face, she noticed a piece of paper still sitting on the man's lap. It was the same letter she saw a few days ago at her parents' home.

Grace picked up the note and skimmed through the words. It was an official letter from the United States Army sharing with Mr. Lloyd his eviction date as well as how much he would be paid for his land.

"Oh, Mr. Lloyd, you poor man," she cried aloud as she gazed upon his lifeless body. "I'm so sorry life's ending was so hard to you."

Grace assumed the man died from a broken heart. The stress must have been too much to bear. She could say or do nothing more at this point. She left the front porch in search of her brother and James' parents. Someone had to tell them the awful news: not only had they lost a son, but a father as well.

CHAPTER 23

As Grace lay in bed later that night, her mind continued to spin despite taking a long warm bath and drinking hot tea. She mused over the day's traumatic events. There were few times in her life where she had experienced such distressing moments so close to each other.

Mr. Lloyd's children did not receive the news well. Mr. Lloyd's son who was also James' father was in his mid-fifties. He collapsed at the sight of his lifeless father. He mumbled in agony, and she realized he had hoped to have spent the rest of his lifetime with his son and at least another decade with his father. Now, he would have to say his earthly goodbyes to both his son and father.

Her partly opened window let in a nippy midnight breeze. A cricket chirped nearby in the yard while a coyote howled in the far distance. She grabbed the covers and turned over in her bed.

She thought of James and their time together as children. Sometimes he wanted to go exploring for coyotes or deer or turkeys. Other days, they would stand for hours at the creek skipping rocks or fishing. Every school day she looked forward to meeting him as they walked the last mile to school together.

He had so much energy, but they were still drawn to each other as friends. He was almost like another brother to her.

A tear trickled down her face and fell on her pillow. She tucked the blanket under her chin. Her mind retraced the events of the past summer. She remembered the hot June day the handsome, auburn-headed, young man had sprinted up the front porch steps, panting for breath. He told her he had been hired at the newspaper and would be working with Edward. She shared with him that she had been appointed as a schoolteacher there in Oakmont.

In the dark room, a smile crept onto Grace's face as she thought about him a few months later. The blaring horn of his old Model T had startled her and Edward shortly after they were engaged. In the still room, she released a quiet laugh. He made sure he was the first to congratulate them. Tears started coming again as her mind drifted to the last time she'd seen James, at the community dance.

"I wonder if Mrs. Carter developed the picture she took of me, Mickey, and James standing together. I'll have to ask her," Grace said out loud.

She shifted her out-loud thoughts to a quick prayer. "Lord," she breathed. "Mickey better make it home to me. I love him too much. I don't want to live the rest of my life without seeing my brother again. Protect him, Lord. Please protect him," she whispered into the night air. *What will it be like when Mickey comes home?* Her mind finally stopped spinning thoughts and she slowly drifted off to sleep.

As the sun's rays peeked over the horizon the next morning, the rooster's crow screeched through the open bedroom window. Grace stirred in her bed. She tried to peel open her eyelids but fell back asleep for a few more minutes. The rooster's raucous voice sounded again. This time she opened her eyes. As she stared at the ceiling, she listened to her parents' hushed voices down the hall.

Grace knew she needed to get out of bed. The smell of beans and pork cooking in the large pot in the fireplace filtered through the entire house. Her mother was going to be feeding a large group of hungry men today. A few distant cousins and family members were coming today to the Willis' farm to assist her father. The relatives were bringing wagons to haul hay as well as other supplies that were currently housed in the barn.

Everything from the farm building would be transferred to Doris and Samuel's barn until her parents' shed could be moved to the family's new property.

She would be helping her family today as well, but first she needed to visit the schoolhouse. Grace called Edward yesterday evening to tell him about Mr. Lloyd and to ask him to help her move her belongings from the schoolhouse. During their brief conversation, they also decided they would live in Edward's current home after they were married. They had planned on living closer to Oakmont, but now that was pointless.

Grace knew Edward would be arriving in a few hours, so she kicked her legs over the side of the bed. She changed into work clothes and went downstairs to help her mother get breakfast ready for the others.

After eating breakfast with her siblings and parents and then helping clean the dishes, she stood in front of the pantry.

"Grace, you look lost. What are you doing, honey?" her mother asked.

"Just scanning the canned jars wondering what kind of dessert I should take to the Lloyd home."

"We have plenty of canned green grapes. Why don't you make a cobbler and one of your famous buttermilk pies? I am sure they will love both of those."

"Sounds like a great idea. Thanks, Mama."

They started gathering the canned grapes and other items needed for the two desserts. She worked at a swift pace mixing all the ingredients together. Soon, the smell of fresh cobbler and pie filled the house.

Grace wrapped the cobbler and pie dishes in two small blankets and went to wait for Edward on the front porch. The slight wind felt good against her flushed cheeks after being in the warm kitchen. She sat down on her favorite wooden rocker and watched the breeze gently move the wildflowers and the smaller branches of the large oak tree near her house.

Bluebonnets were now in full bloom in the field in front of their home. As she observed the blue-and-white flowers wave back and forth, she heard deep bellows of the cows in the pasture and the clucks of the chickens nearby. Her father had decided some of the livestock would be sold and some would move to their new land. The thought of J.J. chasing all the chickens and goats and trying to load them into the back of a truck made her giggle. At least there was some humor to find in the midst of the chaos.

Edward interrupted her thoughts when he pulled into the drive a few minutes later. Grace could see he looked much better than the day before when he delivered the somber news about James. As she got into the sedan, she noted Edward's plaid shirt, dark pants and work boots.

"You are not wearing your office clothes." She settled the dessert dishes in the back seat and sat down in the passenger seat.

"No." A grin spread across his face. "I figured moving all your heavy boxes might be hard work." He winked at her.

"Hey, now. My boxes are not that heavy." Grace smiled back at him. The visit was off to a much better start than yesterday.

As they came within a mile of the small community, she saw thick gray smoke filling the air.

"I wonder what is on fire." Edward pointed in front of them.

"I have no clue." She strained her body forward trying to see its origination. What could be going on now?

"The trees are making it too hard to see, but it looks like

something from the center of Oakmont is burning."

Grace sat there speechless staring straight ahead until she could see what instigated the smoke. As they came around the corner, they passed Mr. Lloyd's homestead and the White and Springer homes. She noticed at least ten Army trucks lining the street.

Several soldiers were pulling down fences and signs and carrying them 100 yards behind the schoolhouse. She followed them with her eyes as they walked down a straight path. Their path headed straight for the fire!

"Edward, stop the car!" She pounded on the dash. "Do you see what they are doing? They are taking the fences to be burned! Are they taking things from the schoolhouse too?"

Edward shifted the car to park a short distance from the schoolhouse. Grace sprinted toward the young men trying to reach them before what they were holding entered the flames. "Stop! Please stop!" Grace yelled, forgetting these were soldiers.

The three men carrying an old wooden sign and the two men carting the white picket fence post from a nearby home all stopped to stare at her.

"Please, tell me—what are you doing?" Grace cried with her palms out as she approached the men.

"Ma'am, we are just following orders," the oldest of the soldiers said first. "We are taking things like fences that are unnecessary for the new Army camp and we're are burning them."

"Good grief! Why in the world would someone tell you to burn them? These are perfectly good wooden fences!" Grace could not control her anger as she felt her cheeks turn a bright red. The wind shifted and unwanted smoke starting filling in the space around them. She started coughing.

"Ma'am, I told you already," the soldier said as he looked down on her, "we are following orders."

Edward walked up to Grace and gently pulled her elbow.

"Grace let's go into the schoolhouse now. Let's leave these men alone."

Grace pulled her arm away. "I don't understand. Why would anyone give orders to burn good fences that can be used elsewhere," she exclaimed, half at Edward and half at the young gentlemen who were heading toward the fire.

She watched in horror as they threw the wood into the fire one piece at a time. "Grace, anything in this area that is left is now Army property and they can do with it what they want." Edward's reasoning didn't make sense to her.

"I don't care whose property it is now. This is inexcusable to burn perfectly good wood! They better not have burned any of the desks, boxes or books in the schoolhouse." She started running toward the front door of the building.

"Excuse me!" Grace said as she barged around a tall lanky soldier coming down the steps.

She clambered up the steps two at a time until she reached the inside of the building. She breathed a sigh of relief as she put her hand over her chest. "Oh, thank you, Lord!"

In the corner behind her desk, the five boxes of books and other belonging sat untouched. Edward joined Grace in the half-empty schoolhouse.

"Come on. Let's pull the car up and go ahead and grab my things before they try to burn them too." Grace spat. "This is all just ridiculous. I am going to let someone high up know about this."

"Really, Grace. I can see why they are doing it. And you shouldn't go out and yell at the soldiers. They are just following orders." Edward chastised Grace as she crossed her arms.

"Edward, are you here to help me or them?" Grace snapped at Edward. *Why is he on their side?*

The couple quickly loaded the car. This was not how Grace imagined her final day in the schoolhouse would end. She only wanted to depart from the sight of wastefulness.

Ten minutes later, Edward moved her final crate into the car. As she glanced back, she noticed the schoolhouse's sign displayed on the front of the building had been painted over. The sign displayed new words. Yesterday, this building stood as a schoolhouse, but less than twenty-four hours later, it had been transformed into an *Army Range Shop*. Grace's shoulders sagged as she climbed into the sedan.

"Edward, would you please drive us down the road toward the tabernacle, the church building, and Billy Roberts' house," Grace said wearily as she pointed down the road. "I want to know if they have been taken over as well."

"We don't need to drive down there. Let's go Grace," Edward replied as he backed the car away from the school building.

"I said—drive down there. If you don't want to drive, then I will walk. You know what? Just let me walk."

"Grace, I'm not going to look like some idiot with you walking. You win. Just stay in the car. I'll drive you down there."

She sat back in her seat and clenched her teeth. *Can't he just be on the same page as me?*

The church and tabernacle both came into view. The two wooden structures still stood untouched. A white paper hung on the front door. "Edward, stop the car. We could not make it to church on Sunday because of the rain. I want to see what the sign says."

Grace removed herself slowly from the car, not sure if she wanted to read the words scrawled on the handwritten note.

"Last church service on Sunday, March 29," the paper read.

Good. At least there would be two more times to worship together. The congregation might decrease in size by that point, but it would be good to see friends again before they all dispersed.

She walked back to the car and closed the door.

"Look," he simply stated as he pointed down the road.

Two Army trucks were parked in front of Billy Roberts'

home. Grace's eyes widened in disbelief as two soldiers started a fire in the home.

"That is ridiculous! What are they doing? This is pure foolishness to burn down houses now!" Grace stared out the car window as the fire consumed the sides of the house.

"I... I... guess they don't need the houses either." Edward appeared at a loss for words.

"This is wastefulness to burn this house! Look, they are putting the fence in it as well. We are supposed to be salvaging metal because of the war and here they are burning it all!" Grace's face felt hot from anger.

"I'm sure the family was unable to move it all. What else is the Army going to do with it? It belongs to them now," Edward reasoned.

Fire engulfed the wood structures as Grace and Edward viewed the scene from a distance.

"I'm going to call someone about this. I don't know who yet, but someone needs to know about this wastefulness." She clenched her fists.

"I don't think calling anyone will help. We are at war, Grace. This doesn't matter."

"Gee. Thanks, Edward. Thanks for the suggestion. You know, you could at least give me a name instead extinguishing my thoughts."

"I really don't think it will do anything, but I guess you could call our state representative. He would probably be the best person to talk to right now."

"Good idea. I think I will give him a call." Grace glanced over at Edward. "Let's go ahead and head to the Lloyd place. I'm not sure how much more of this I can watch."

Edward drove slowly as the two headed back through Oakmont. One month ago, Grace's community sat untouched. Today, it seemed it would all soon be ashes.

CHAPTER 24

The engaged couple pulled up next to the entrance of the Lloyd homestead. Edward shifted the car into park and then turned toward his fiancée. The smell of burning wood mixed with blooming cedar trees seeped in through the cracked windows.

Grace adjusted her gaze to Edward. His eyes fixed on her. "What are you doing?" She cocked her head to the side.

"Do you still want to stop by their house now?" He placed his hand on her shoulder. "I know you are frustrated, and I don't want you to get any more upset. I know it is going to be hard visiting."

"Thank you, Edward, but I am fine."

"Grace, really. I am concerned this might be too much." She could see his eyes soften.

"Yes—I am upset, but I want to see the family, especially after how hard yesterday was for them. I didn't get to see James' mother—only his father." Grace said. She sighed and squeezed Edward's hand hoping to convince him.

He nodded and turned into the driveway. The rocky path bounced them up and down as they passed Mr. Lloyd's home.

Grace lowered her head, not able to bear surveying the area where she'd stood helpless one day earlier.

A few minutes later, they arrived at the home belonging to James' parents. Several cars parked along the drive. Grace and Edward each grabbed a dessert from the back of his car. She could still feel warmth from the homemade dessert. Good. Maybe they would be able to enjoy this soon. She carried in the green grape cobbler while Edward took in the buttermilk pie.

A young black lab with his tongue hanging out and leaving a trail of gooey slobber darted up to them.

"Hey, boy." Edward paused to run his fingers on the dog's short velvety hair.

Grace headed up the steps to the porch of the large unpainted one-story home; its well-kept exterior appeared as a direct opposite of the dog-run cabin and house the elder Mr. Lloyd used to reside in. The porch wrapped around the house, providing a full 180-degree view of the family's property.

"Hello?" Grace called and rapped on the wooden edge of the screen door. Edward and the black lab joined her at the door.

A familiar face appeared behind the hinged door. Mary, one of James' older cousins and Mr. Lloyd's granddaughters—a tall, slender woman in her mid-thirties with fiery red hair—let them in.

"Hello, Grace. It's been a while." The woman clutched a cream handkerchief in one hand and extended a greeting with her other hand.

"Hi, Mary. It's good to see you. I'm sorry it is under such difficult circumstances." She noted a family portrait hanging in the entry hallway. She cleared her throat and shifted her gaze back to Mary.

Mary sniffed and gave a brief nod, her lower lip quivering.

"Um, we brought these desserts. I made a cobbler and a buttermilk pie too." Grace extended her desserts.

"Oh yes, Thank you, Grace. That is so very kind of you," the woman nodded. "You can set them on the dining room table. Let me go with you to make space."

The couple followed the woman to the long oak dining table and placed their two desserts next to other dishes brought by neighbors and friends of the family.

"It looks like several people have already been out here." She attempted to make small talk with the woman, not really knowing what to say.

"Yes, several," a strained smile spread across Mary's face.

"Grace," a woman's voice spoke behind her as she felt a hand on her shoulder. "Oh, Grace." She turned to discover James' mother, Evelyn, a woman in her late fifties standing next to her. "Thank you for..." her voice went hoarse as she started crying. She pushed away the wisps of graying auburn hair that had fallen out of her low bun and covered her face with her hands. She released a long pitiful gut-wrenching cry.

Grace had never experienced this type of grief but had listened to her mother wail in the same way after losing her babies at birth. She scooped her arms around the woman and held her for a solid minute as uncontrollable tears fell from her own eyes.

Grace knew no words were needed. The older woman wrapped her arms around Grace and dug her head into the younger woman's shoulder. Evelyn's body shook as both stood and wept over the loss of two dear loved ones.

The murmur in the house hushed as her cries filled the corridor.

A minute passed before Evelyn stood back and pushed her tears away. She placed her hands on Grace's shoulders.

"Thank you for being a good friend to James. He needed a kind loving friend like you to keep him out of trouble. And thank you for being so observant yesterday. We might not have found my father-in-law until today," Evelyn looked ready to burst into tears again for a brief moment.

"And Edward, James loved working with you at the newspaper. You knew how to keep him in line."

"Mrs. Lloyd, I am so thankful we had James and your father-in-law." Grace smiled as she thought about the auburn-headed young man. What a character and a loyal friend he was at the same time.

"And I am glad I got the chance to know him as well. He was a hard worker and quick learner," stated Edward.

"Now, I just saw you set a dish on the table, but would you two like to stay and eat with us?" Evelyn said as she changed the subject.

"Oh, no, Ma'am," both Edward and Grace responded together.

"We really don't want to be a bother. We just thought we would drop off a few desserts," Grace said.

"You are not a bother. I am so thankful you both stopped by," Evelyn said.

"I need to get back home to help with the move," Grace said as she leaned over and hugged the woman again. "But first before we leave, is Mr. Lloyd's body resting here?"

"Yes, honey, in the front sitting room."

"Thank you, Evelyn. We will see you later."

"You both come back whenever you like."

"Thank you, Ma'am." Edward said and nodded his head.

Edward and Grace headed back down the hallway toward the front door where they met Mary again.

"Is Mr. Lloyd's body in this sitting room?" Grace asked.

"Yes—in this one," Mary said as she motioned to the room closest to the foyer. "I'm not sure when James' body will arrive home."

"Thank you, Mary. We are going to step in for a moment."

"It's a sad thing. His heart giving out. I heard 'bout a man who killed himself yesterday. This move is just too much," Mary stated.

"Killed himself?"

"Yes. Suicide."

"Oh, no." Grace shook her head and walked into the sitting room with Edward behind her. She couldn't take any more.

A few relatives left the space as she gripped Edward's hand and entered the quiet area. The scent of the fresh-cut wood coffin permeated the room.

There in the newly made box, Mr. Lloyd's leathery body rested. He looked much more at peace today than the way she had found him yesterday afternoon. His hands were placed one over another across his waist. His eyes were closed and other than being discolored he almost looked asleep. She had overheard someone say his body would be buried tomorrow at Oakmont Cemetery. The cemetery was the same one her younger siblings who had never lived more than a week were also buried.

"How fitting for him to be buried tomorrow at Oakmont Cemetery," Grace stated while looking down at the body.

"Why's that?" Edward asked.

"Well, Mr. Lloyd's family was one of the first to settle in this area. It seems appropriate for him to be one of the last ones buried in the cemetery."

Grace gazed upon the wrinkles that lined the older man's face. His blueish-gray lips were turned almost in a slight smile. Even though Grace knew his spirit was no longer around she leaned over and whispered in his ear.

"May you be singing praises today in heaven with your Savior, Mr. Lloyd. Please tell your grandson, James, I said hello. And may the two of you rest in peace forever."

With those final words, Grace wiped her tear-streaked face and left the room.

CHAPTER 25

$\mathcal{T}$he early morning sun rays peeked through the gray clouds reflecting on millions of specks of dew covering the field in a bright golden hue. Car and farm-truck tires, wagon wheels, and horses traveled over the wet lawn as they surrounded Grace's family's farm.

Cousins, aunts, uncles and friends from all around the Gatesville area and outside the Fort Hood boundary zone—at least so far—paraded in to assist her family. After observing others move off the land, her father had discovered that anything left behind would more than likely be considered useless. The Army would burn anything remaining including windmills, farm equipment, and even houses. So here they came to help.

Over the previous few intense weeks, Grace watched her father acquire all the necessary permissions needed by neighboring farmers in order to move his house and barn across their properties. The indirect route to the new property required moving the house three miles; however, by cutting across the nearby farms and taking down fences, Father calculated it would be half the distance. The fifty-year-old house, built by her grandfather, needed the most direct route in order to withstand the move.

She greeted her family and friends as they congregated between the house and the barn waiting for instructions.

"Thank you all for coming out," John Willis said to those in attendance as sunbeams flooded the porch steps where he stood. She watched as this fifty-year-old broad-shouldered farmer straightened to his full six-foot frame and gazed over the small crowd.

Dark rings lined his blue sleep-deprived eyes. His light-colored hair had morphed into a shade closer to gray than brown over the past several weeks. He shifted his feet and took a deep breath as his rough voice continued.

"This is a moment in time we never planned on passing through. Thank you for being our friends and family in the good times and in the darkest and hardest of days." Father cleared his throat. She studied his tan face. His jaw trembled as he spoke. "There is a lot of hard work to be done and we wouldn't be able to make it happen without you here." He wiped his forehead with his old red handkerchief as he shifted his stance. He leaned his shoulders forward and she could tell he was trying to fight back tears. He must feel so much grief and despair. After a brief pause, her proud and determined father stuck out his square jaw and adjusted his back again. His land might be taken from him, but his heart and dedication to farming would always remain.

"Now, let's get to business," Father clapped his hands once and then began giving out instructions.

"The smaller items which wouldn't be able to sustain the move have already been removed from our house. We'll need help today loading some of our larger items including our two couches, dining table and chairs, and several bedroom dressers onto your wagons and truck beds. There's not too much left to be loaded so we should be able to finish that part quickly this morning. Once everything has been removed, Leroy and his sons will begin removing the skirting around the house." Her father tilted his head in the direction of his childhood friend and sons.

"Samuel," Father said next as he looked toward Georgia's cousin who had offered the land to move the house to, "you and my brother, Jack, will be in charge of installing the support structure for the ceiling and the roof from inside the house. As you both know, this is necessary for us to do so we will be able to cut the house in half."

All eyes were glued to John Sr. as they gave him their complete attention. Everyone knew he risked his entire home on the efforts of his friends and family. One wrong move and the house might cave in on itself. She recognized he had no other option. His choices were to either trust these men or have no home for his family to live in.

"Outside, I will use J.J.'s assistance." Her younger brother stood against the porch railing with his arms crossed over his chest. He looked proud to be helping his father.

"Walt and his two sons will be with us," he continued, motioning his thick weathered hands toward his cousin—a balding man in his early forties with a thick yellowish beard—and two husky blond-headed older teenage boys. "We will jack up the house so it can be placed on steel beams and axles for the truck to then haul it to the new property. After we have completed all our jobs, then we will work on cutting the house in half. The plan is to move the kitchen and living room first. Now please, remember your safety is most important to me and my family. We ask you to be careful because we don't want anyone hurt. Thank you again for coming here and now let us pray and ask the good Lord for protection before we begin our day." John removed his worn gray hat from the top of his head and tucked his red handkerchief back into his shirt pocket. She watched as the other men in the group followed his lead as all heads bowed in reverence.

"Heavenly Father, we thank you for the generous offerings of our friends and family who are gathered here today. Thank you for their willingness to help our family move in our time of need. Bless them Lord. We ask you for your arms of protection to be over us today. Amen."

Without missing a beat, her father placed his hat back on his head and went into action with the others close behind him.

She witnessed the scene of organized chaos as men of various ages, shapes and sizes trampled down the front porch steps. Some of the men she knew well like her uncle, but others including, her father's childhood friends, she had only been around a handful of times. She watched the rays of sunshine dance in the yard as the men headed toward their stash of tools. A soft glow spread across her face as she placed her hand on her chest. The genuine love and concern displayed by others amazed her.

"Dear Lord, thank you for providing help our way when we were in a time of desperation. Thank you for hope," Grace whispered her prayer as she gazed upon the men sliding on work gloves and picking up tools.

Grace knew Mickey would be frustrated he was not here to assist his father in moving the home. She wasn't even sure if Mickey knew his childhood home was being moved, with the land he knew so well taken over by the Army he served. Mama wrote him a letter last week to give him a few details about the move, but the handwritten note would probably take weeks to get to him. Her mother hadn't mentioned the passing of James. She believed it would be too hard for him to learn the news of his house and of his friend, James.

"Easy! Easy!" the shrill words tumbled out of Granny's mouth as she shadowed the teenagers moving the family's dining room table.

"Now you boys be careful with that piece. It's a beauty. My favorite piece of furniture in the entire house," Granny squawked to the three older boys gently hoisting the heirloom. "My daddy built that table with his own hands almost one hundred years ago when he settled on this land as a young man from Alabama."

"Mama, they are being very careful," Georgia gently scolded the older woman. "No one wants to damage our furniture."

"Well, I want them to know how fragile everything is. Oh, look! My chair! My chair! I think that piece can stay right where it was—next to the fireplace!" Granny waved her arms as one of the young teenagers hauled her blue floral-patterned wingback chair out the door and down the steps. Maybe helping Mama with Granny might be the best job for today. Then again, it might be one of the hardest.

"Mama, let him load it. You do not want it sliding around and possibly getting damaged during the move. Everyone knows how special our furniture is to us," Mama consoled her mother as she patted her weary shoulders.

Mama and Granny stood side by side with forlorn eyes as they observed their beloved home emptied piece by piece. Her mother stood to her full 5'5" frame holding open the screen door for the men as they walked in and out. She wore a light blue button-down dress along with her favorite soft blue-and-white apron and black work boots. Grace could tell she plastered a smile on her face as she thanked the men for their hard work. She might not show it, but this relocation chipped at Mama's heart and soul.

The forced, unplanned move weighed heavily on all the nearby farmers and their families, including Mr. Lloyd's broken heart after hearing the news of his grandson, James, and receiving the letter mandating he leave almost immediately. Over the past week, she spent hours praying over Mickey's safe return as well as an easy transition for her parents to their new property.

"They cannot bear hearing any more bad news, dear Lord," Grace uttered as she left her spot and went to find a place to help.

The next hour passed at a rapid pace as the men emptied the

home and then began working on the different jobs to secure the house for moving. Sweat, dirt, grime and even a little blood covered the hard-working men. The entire process took several hours with only a short break for a lunch of beans and cornbread. Grace, Ruth, and her mother served the hungry crew a hearty meal.

As the men started arriving, Mama's cousin, Doris, joined the women in serving.

"So where is Edward today," Doris inquired as she picked up a bowl and started placing beans in it. "Is he off writing a story?"

"Kind of," Grace shrugged. "He should be here soon. He had a couple of deadlines to make but hoped to be out here by this afternoon. He wants to take pictures of the house cut in two. He said he has never seen anything like this before. And actually, I have never seen a house taken apart and then put back together either."

"I guess desperate times call for desperate measures," the older woman responded as she continued filling bowls.

"I guess you are right," Grace didn't have much else to say to Cousin Doris. Edward really should've volunteered to be here for the entire process of the house move. *He needs to step up. He's almost a son too.* He could grab some tools and at least try to help even if he was not as good at working with his hands. Sure, his job provided an income, but it wasn't helping her family or her father today.

The men ate lunch quickly and got back to work. The next step in the process was to cut the house in two. This part terrified her. She didn't like watching people working in high places. Especially not on a roof.

After cleaning up the dishes, Grace glanced down at her watch and back up toward the road. She pierced her lips together as she squinted down the dirt path. Where is Edward? It was time to take the picture and he couldn't even be on time for that. Her beloved house would not be in its original setting much longer.

The field surrounding her home burst with wildflowers in full bloom. The bluebonnets waved shades of indigo and white in the fields along with patches of brilliant red and orange from the native firewheels and Indian paintbrushes. Other than the thick humidity, she might have called this place paradise. A yearning deep within her wanted to capture this moment in time and take it with her. So many years of memories and special moments had happened here at this home and in this front yard for her and generations past.

In the late 1800s, Grace's granny and grandpa purchased this land from a much larger portion of land belonging to her elderly cousin. Granny arrived on a wagon from the east as a young newlywed sitting alongside her husband, and they built this house with their own hands. They survived the hardships of those beginning years of Texas.

Her grandparents farmed the land and raised livestock, and they survived the rough years with sheer determination and their faith in God. Stories danced through Grace's mind as she remembered her grandma sharing about raising seven children in this house and on this land. Granny watched Mama play in the bluebonnets every spring as a young child. Then Mama watched her play in the same field. Now this serene and peaceful place would be taken from them forever. In a few short days, they would never be able to return to *the fields they called home.*

Regret cut into her, for the present and future generations who would never know this land the way she had been privileged to know it. Her own children and grandchildren would never grow up visiting this farm and playing tag under the shade of the oak trees.

As a young child, she'd listened as her grandfather told her and her siblings stories about Native American tribes using the sprawling hundred-year-old oak tree in their yard as a cool place to rest. He'd pull a beautiful flint arrowhead out of his pocket and let them feel the jagged edges. Grace and Mickey would scour the ground around the tree looking for any remnants of the Comanche and Tonkawa Native American tribes. Mickey's determined spirit always beat hers. Over the years, he acquired twelve arrowheads for his collection while she only had three to show. That could also be because after all her chores were finished Grace spent more time playing pretend school with her two baby dolls seated below the wide trunk of the tree than looking for remnants from the Native Americans.

She exhaled slowly as she tried to take in the final moments before she watched her beloved home cut in two.

"Hey, Edward!" J.J. yelled, a foot away from her.

She jumped and spun to see Edward running toward them with his camera in one hand and his notepad in the other.

"Hey!" he called, breathless as he sprinted toward his fiancée.

"I made it. It looks like just in time," Edward said as stopped next to Grace panting for breath.

"You did. Barely." She glanced at him and then turned back toward the house. "My dad and uncle are just about to put the ladder on the house and head up there."

"Okay, I guess I better start snapping photos," Edward said. He seemed oblivious to her aggravation with him. He re-adjusted his hat on his head and then spent the next five minutes taking pictures of her home before they stood on the roof. Edward moved around the house capturing pictures of Father and Uncle Jack working cautiously side by side as they began cutting the roof and the ceiling inside the house in half.

She saw her father suddenly stand up. "Hey, Walt! Come here a minute."

Walt headed over and her father said something she couldn't quite hear. His cousin ran off and grabbed a tool from his bag. He ran back to her dad.

"Here, just toss it to me," he hollered. She saw her father scoot his feet on the steep roof. He had been in the situation before, but it still made her nervous.

"Okay. You ready?"

"Yeah, ready!" Her father scooted again, but a little too quickly. He lost his footing as he leaned forward to catch the tool. She watched in horror as he fell and slid off the roof.

"Ahh! Father!"

"John!" her mother shrieked from behind her.

He hit a tree stump with the side of his body and then bounced off toward the ground.

She ran to him. She knew she could do nothing for him, but she ran.

"John!" Mama called again as she ran behind her.

Walt and the other men nearby gathered around him first.

Grace reached him to find him conscious. He groaned and rolled back and forth. She could tell her father was in immense pain.

"Leroy, go grab your truck. We need to get to the hospital." Walt yelled.

Father continued groaning as he waited for the truck. Leroy backed up his vehicle to the men and then they quickly loaded her father.

"Everything is going to be fine now, Georgia. You just hop right in there and go with Leroy and his boys. Samuel, Walt, and I will lead out the men. We'll get the job done," her uncle coaxed.

She watched her mother hesitate for a moment and then jump in the cab.

Leroy sped away with her father and Mama. Grace hoped and prayed her father would be able to walk again. She didn't know how they were going to get everything moved and done in time.

The men wasted no time getting back to work. They still had several hours of transporting the house.

"Alright! Let's get back at it, men!" Walt yelled and headed up the ladder to begin working.

Grace found it interesting to watch the house slowly cut in two until finally all sections were separated. When the truck was ready to roll out the kitchen, dining and living room, J.J. and two of his distant teenage cousins, hopped on. The three boys sat in the kitchen and let their long legs hang off the side as the truck began moving out slow and steady across their property.

Edward snapped one final photo as the house progressed across the open terrain. He walked the short distance to his future bride. She could feel the soft dirt beneath her where the front porch steps used to begin. Earthworms squiggled back under ground and crickets scampered away in search of cover. Edward wrapped his arm around her waist as she stared at her beautiful childhood home forever leaving Oakmont community. Her father had been hurt. Her childhood home was being moved. What about her marriage? She hoped it would not have such a bad start.

CHAPTER 26

$\mathcal{A}$ week had passed since the move. With the help of others, her parents managed to move their home, belongings, livestock, farm equipment, and a barn. The windmill and a second older barn used for hay were not structurally sound enough to move. Despite his dramatic fall, John Willis fortunately only suffered a couple of broken ribs. The doctor told him to take it easy, but that did not stop him from working around his new place.

The sounds, smells, and humidity at her home were all the same to Grace, but each morning the different scenery outside her window caught her off guard.

Her favorite live oak tree, field of wildflowers, and her mother's garden were no longer visible or tangible. Different fields and different trees now surrounded the family home. As Grace peered out the window, she could see the edge of Samuel and Doris' house which sat 200 yards behind them.

Grace clutched her stomach as it grumbled. Thank goodness for Doris fixing breakfast every morning this week.

The clock chimed eight times. "Oh, wow. I must have slept in. I better get going," Grace said aloud in the quiet room.

Today, Edward planned to pick her up and drive by several homes. He had been invited by a commanding officer to view and take pictures of the Army moving in and taking over the area. When he mentioned this to her, she asked him if she could tag along. He agreed and told her he would be at her home at 10:00 am.

Grace craved to go back and visit her small community. She wanted to see her longtime friends and check in on their moving progress. Different areas of the new military camp had different deadlines for leaving. Some residents still had several weeks left and some on the outer edges had months; however, there were many others like her family who'd been forced out much sooner.

After getting ready and finding some leftover biscuits and bacon in Doris' kitchen, Grace settled into her favorite rocker on the front porch. She watched as white butterflies fluttered between the pink and yellow primrose wildflowers. The flowers here were beautiful, but not as breathtaking as the bluebonnets and Indian paintbrushes on their old land.

As she thought about the wildflowers, her mind drifted to her upcoming wedding and the wildflowers for her bouquet. Bluebonnets would be out of bloom, but there would be plenty of others to choose from for a beautiful arrangement.

The butterflies continued dancing from plant to plant. Grace rocked back and forth thinking about her beloved church building. She knew it would no longer exist after this coming Sunday. Edward and Grace had agreed her parents' house would be a good substitute for the wedding ceremony. At least they finally agreed on something.

She spun the loose band around her finger as she thought about the remaining two months left until she forever said the words "*I do*." The past few months had been trying on her relationship with Edward. Everything she knew as common in her life had been swept from her in a matter of three weeks—her job, the school children, her friends, and her parents' land. She wanted Edward to tell her he was sorry for her loss; however, he always shifted the conversation to tell her how great the new Army camp would be for Gatesville and for the entire county.

This morning she couldn't feel or see the greatness of the camp. Her restless heart only felt a void. She knew time would heal the deep wound in her soul, but minutes seemed to slow down. Three weeks ago, when she left the schoolhouse for the last time felt like months. Seven days ago, when they'd moved the house, felt like weeks. She wanted time to hurry and pass. She wanted to begin her new job and live in her new home with Edward, but she knew with the passing weeks there would be more and more Army soldiers arriving in Gatesville. Her county would no longer be the same as she had always known.

A few minutes later, Edward promptly arrived at 10:00 am. He hopped out of his black sedan whistling and dancing as he opened Grace's door and bowed.

"Oh, Edward, you sure are in a good mood." Grace scowled at him. He was not the one bringing the Army, but yet she was having a hard time separating her fiancé from the feelings she had toward the recent life-altering changes.

"What? And you are not, my love?" Edward said. "My—look at you." He whistled again. "You are my stunning dark-headed beauty." She wore a cream dress with short sleeves and a thin black belt to accentuate her waist. She'd even taken extra time to style her hair, straightening it and rounding it in a U-shape. A pin kept in place one simple roll above her forehead.

She couldn't make herself smile. Even with his catcalling. A grimace replaced her typical smile. She clutched her simple black wristlet with one hand as she left the comfort of her rocking chair and headed toward her fiancé. She wanted desperately for Edward's cheerful attitude to rub off on her.

"I'm fine. I'm just ready to see if the Carters have moved." She pecked Edward's cheek and sat down in the passenger seat.

He closed the car door and headed around to his side. "Really, you don't seem fine," Edward persisted as he pulled away from the house.

"I'm just tired and dreading all the other changes that will be happening soon." Grace looked down as she straightened her dress.

"Change can be good, Grace," Edward stated seemingly in a cautious way.

"Oh, please, Edward. Why are your eyes so blinded to one side?"

"Grace, I think you are maybe talking to both of us."

"Yes, you are right..." she paused. "I am so incredibly thankful for our government and obviously, you know my family would do anything for this country we love, but this transition has been rough. Not only am I reminded of the new Army camp every morning when I wake up because my parents' house is in a different location, but I know we are about to see more and more soldiers. Every military man is just going to remind me of all that my parents lost as well as knowing Mickey is stationed so far from us."

"War is rough, Grace."

"I don't think you need to tell me that, Edward," she snapped. His eyes flinched at her words. "Just forget it. Let's move on to a different subject."

"Okay..." this time Edward paused. "How is your wedding dress coming along? Have you finished sewing it?"

"Close. Maybe another week or two and I'll be finished." She sat up in her seat. This was a good change of subject. "Hey, looks like we are close to the Miller's house. Why don't we pull up the drive and see their old house before we head over to the Carter place?"

"Sounds like a good plan." Edward turned the car into the narrow drive. A wooden rectangle sign hung over the entrance displaying the family's cattle brand. The Miller family owned 600 acres and their property sat adjacent to her sister's 600 acres of land.

They drove half a mile around a bend of hilly terrain, which opened to a valley of full of brown soil left barren of seed and crops. Grace squinted in search of the familiar two-story house and large barn, which should have been standing 100 yards past the dirt field. She saw nothing. She kept staring down the dirt path. At the end she noticed two heaping piles of burnt wood smoldering.

"Edward! The Miller's home! Do you see that?" Grace frantically cried.

"I see it."

"They have already burned their home as well. Oh, my goodness." She covered her mouth with her hand as she sat stunned.

Edward pulled the car in a circle around the pile of rubbish. The smell of burnt wood seeped in the car.

"Do you want to get out and walk around?"

"No," She forced herself to say.

"I'm going to snap a picture. I'll be back fast." He hopped out of the car and captured a few images before returning.

She continued staring out the window. *Is this real? Did they really burn this house too?* She covered her nose as the scent of charred wood filled the entire car. She'd known homes were going to be burned but seeing and smelling the remains made her weak to her stomach.

"Are you ready to go to the Carter's house now?" He gently touched the back of her shoulder as she continued to look out her window.

"Not really, but I guess you need to go take pictures for the paper," she murmured.

"It would make it much easier since I am already out here." He squeezed her shoulder.

"The sooner we go, then the sooner we get it over with. I'm just hoping their house is still standing. I can't bear to see the ashes left from all the hard work these farmers and ranchers put in over the years. I know the Army needs to do it, but I just don't really want to see the remnants. Then on top of that, these poor landowners only get pennies for their land."

"I don't think the Miller family got pennies for all this land," Edward interrupted.

"You know, what I mean, Edward. Please don't try to start a fight. You know the government is not giving these farmers what they owe them. In fact, many have not yet even gotten a penny. My father is still waiting on a check from the government. How in the world are farmers and ranchers who have very little to nothing saved up supposed to go out and buy more land when haven't even been paid yet for their land that the government is taking," argued Grace. "It is a vicious cycle." Warmth began rising in her cheeks as she crossed her arms. She felt like a petulant child, but someone needed to speak up for all these farmers. They didn't have a voice in any of this.

"The government has a right to any land they want, and they can pay those individuals whatever they deem is fair," he said as he drove the car back down the dusty road.

"You're right, Edward, and in case you are worried, I do understand this new bill and the right to eminent domain and that the government can take any property they desire," Grace huffed. "However, I don't think there is any rhyme or reason to the way the value is being placed on the land out here. Some farmers were paid $8 an acre, some were paid $12 and others were paid $24 an acre. And it sounds like the government is not going to pay any of these hard-working farmers for a while," Grace added before he could speak. "If we didn't have Samuel and Doris, I don't know what my parents would have done. I'm sure my father would have given up his vocation because the government has not yet paid him for his property."

"Listen, I'm on your side." He pushed her hair back behind her ear. "We are sandwiched between backing the government and giving up our livelihoods. I know your family had to give a lot more than other families around here but trust me. America needs this Army camp. I'm sure there will be great things in store for your family. Who knows, maybe better than you or your family would have dreamed."

"I'm not so sure about that, Edward."

"Ruth seems to think the Army coming is a great idea." Edward started chuckling to himself.

"What do you mean, Ruth thinks it is a great idea? She couldn't be more devastated about moving from her house." Grace shook her head. His statement confused her.

"Oh, she might be sad about the house, but I saw her a couple of times this week in town hanging around the same officer. From the looks of it, I think she is smitten with him."

Grace's jaw dropped and she stared at him horrified. "She is only seventeen and she has not said anything to me about meeting a solider," Grace said, perplexed by where the conversation was taking them.

"I don't know....Maybe she is just too scared to tell you, especially since you have been against the Army coming to town." He shrugged his shoulders.

"I'm not against the Army coming to Gatesville and providing jobs and..." Grace knew this conversation was only going to go around in circles again, so she stopped mid-sentence. She turned her body and faced out the side window again letting Edward know she was finished talking about the Army.

She assumed he picked up on her stark signals. He left her alone and drove in silence the remaining short distance. Mrs. Miller and Mrs. Carter's father had been one of the first settlers in this area. The two women told plenty of tales about their father. His land used to spread over 2,000 acres. As he aged, he sold some of his land to others and then divided his remaining land between his children. Mrs. Miller and Mrs. Carter both married men who had a love and passion for farming. The two sisters were each given 600 acres of land.

Edward turned his car down the dusty gravel driveway toward the Carter home. This time Grace could tell from a distance the Carter family had company. Several Army vehicles were parked around the home and soldiers stood nearby as they watched a blaze overtake the house.

"They said they would not start until noon," Edward remarked.

"You knew they were burning the house today." She stared at him in disbelief. Her nostrils flared in fury. She'd told Edward she wanted to come along, but she had not expected this.

"I wasn't sure. They mentioned it might be a possibility," Edward said as they drove closer to the house. The flames stretched high and thick black smoke billowed out of the home.

Grace felt her bacon and biscuits from two hours earlier start to come up. "Stop the car! Stop the car!" she demanded him as she pounded her fist on the dash.

Edward slammed to a stop. Vomit filled her throat. Grace slung the door open as her morning breakfast spewed on the ground below. Seeing this property completely devastated her.

Edward reached over and offered her his handkerchief. She wiped her mouth of the disgusting remnants. So much for eating breakfast. Should've skipped it. She closed the car door and caught her breath, allowing Edward to drive the car down the rest of the way.

As he pulled up, she noticed there were only men in uniform surrounding the area. "I'm guessing the Carters are not here anymore." She felt all her energy being drained from her.

"It doesn't look like it. The officer I spoke to on the phone yesterday told me all families are welcome to watch their homes burn, but I guess the Carter family didn't take him up on his offer."

Grace grimaced in disgust as she gazed out the front window. Why would anyone want to watch his or her life's work crumble to the ground in minutes?

"Do you want to get out or stay in?"

"Get out, I guess," Grace responded sluggishly.

"I'm going to walk around the house and take pictures from several angles. You are welcome to join me or stay near the car. Just don't get too close. I don't want anything burning to collapse near you."

Grace nodded as she pushed open the car door and got out. Her legs froze next to the front fender of the car as the roar of the fire swept past her. She wasn't sure she could move anymore as she watched the fire swallow the entire house.

Edward snapped pictures in front of the house and then moved toward the back. He captured different shots as Grace stood motionless by the car. The fire mesmerized her as it showed its fury and power.

She glanced away for a moment and noticed Edward heading toward the field on the back side of the house. *Where is he going?* She followed him. As she walked past several soldiers and their vehicles, she reached the backside of the house. There she saw Edward standing in the middle of the field taking pictures of a grain thresher in flames.

"What in the world? Why is that being burned!" Grace spoke out loud before she realized it.

Her voice drifted further than she realized. "The owners of the farm said this morning that they couldn't get it moved out in time," the solider standing nearby stated.

"Why would your men burn such a good and valuable piece of equipment?"

"Just following orders ma'am," the soldier responded tipping his hat. "Anything left behind is to be burned."

Grace closed her eyes and shook her head as she turned away from the young man. She slowly opened her eyes and focused on Edward taking pictures of the burning large piece of equipment. Such a shame. They had been taught to save and ration so many things during this time of war and now here was a good solid piece of equipment being burned. Grace crossed her arms over her stomach. She thought she might get sick again. Thankfully, Edward, started jogging toward her.

"Thanks for letting me come out here and take a couple of good shots," Edward called out to the young man next to her.

"Not a problem. You're welcome to join us anytime. Over the next month, we will be clearing out all the houses, barns, fences, and everything in order to make way for the new camp," piped the young fair-skinned solider with a short buzz cut.

Edward reached out to shake his hand as Grace walked away. She knew it was not the young officer's fault. He was following orders, but she was still upset. She clutched her stomach tighter. As she reached the car, she felt everything she had left in her cramping stomach hurl out of her mouth. She opened the car door and stumbled into her seat as she felt the world around her start to spin. Moments later everything became black.

"GRACE! GRACE! LET ME HELP YOU." Edward called out as he jogged toward her.

He watched her wipe her vomit from her face and manage to open the car door. "Grace!"

She shut the door. He reached her door seconds later and swung open the door again.

"Honey, Grace!" No response again. "Grace." He tapped her cheeks begging her to wake up. Why had he pushed her so hard? About the land? Why did he even let her convince him to bring her out here? He knew they might see a couple of burning houses, but he had not expected it to have this kind of effect on her. Still no movement.

"Grace, darling. Wake up."

"Um." Grace uttered quietly.

At that point he realized he had nothing to help her and especially no water. "Hold on, honey. I'll be right back. I'm going to find some water for you."

Edward jogged to the soldiers. "Hey, fellows! Do any of you have a canteen or something with water? My fiancée just passed out. She's waking up now, but I think she is pretty dehydrated."

"Yes, I've got an extra one in the jeep. Let me go grab it." One solider offered and ran off.

"Is she okay? Do you need anything else?" a second solider asked.

"I think she's okay. I'm hoping water will help her."

"How 'bout you go back to her and I will run the water out to you. She probably doesn't need to be alone."

"Thank you." Edward ran back to Grace. *Hopefully, she's waking up by now. There's not a hospital for miles around out here.*

"Grace, I'm back." She stirred slightly. "We got some water coming your way. The boys have an extra canteen. Just hang on."

He heard movement behind him. "Here you go, sir." Edward turned to find the solider there.

"Yah, she doesn't look so good. Looks kinda pale to me. You better get 'er to drink up," the young solider commented.

"Grace sit up. Let me give you a sip of this water." With the soldier's help, he lifted her head slightly and stabilized it. He gave her a capful of water. She slowly started drinking. Her eyes still closed. "Good. Drink the whole thing. Good job." He spoke sweet affirming words helping her get fluids in her depleted body. The solider helped him gently lay her head back on the seat.

"Here you go, buddy." Edward turned to hand the solider the canteen. "Thanks for your help. I'm sure that little bit of water in her will be good enough for now. I'm gonna try to get her home fast and get some more fluids in her."

"You're welcome. Glad we could help ya. Take care. And I hope she gets to feeling better..." He nodded his head at her. "I got one at home just like her. Smart. Pretty. Feisty. Man, I miss her already. You take good care of your girl. For me. I can't be there to take care of mine. And I hope to see mine again. Soon." The solider jogged back to his men.

Edward stared at his dark-headed beauty. Her full lips and cream-colored dress with short sleeves and a thin black belt accentuating her slender waist. She caught the attention of every guy around yet, she rarely noticed. Somehow, he was lucky enough to have her. Pretty. Smart. And yes, feisty. That was a good word to describe her. He wasn't giving up on her, he just wanted the two of them to be on the same page.

Grace slightly shifted her position. "Edward," she spoke in a hoarse voice. "Where am I?"

"Honey, we're in the car right now. I think you passed out. I'm going to get you home now though." He gently kissed her on top of the head.

CHAPTER 27

Grace leaned forward and adjusted the hand-stitched quilt over her feet as the late morning chilly, spring breeze drifted through the cracked window whirling the long lacy white curtains. She leaned back against her pillows again resting her body.

She touched her temples, massaging her soft skin. Her head still throbbed from passing out the day before. She had never blacked out in her short life. She assumed she became dehydrated yesterday after losing her breakfast. When she woke up in the car, Edward stood next to her. She spent the rest of the afternoon in bed and fell asleep before dark. Today, though she felt better, her head still ached.

A gentle rapping sounded on her door. "Grace, can I come in?" Ruth asked.

"Yes." She sat up in bed, shifting her back against the white metal frame.

"How are you feeling?" Ruth poked her head around the door.

"Come on in." Grace motioned to her sister and patted her hand on the bed. "I'm feeling much better. I just need my headache to go away. I don't want to overdo it because I want to be able to see everyone at church tomorrow. I'd hate to wake up in the morning and feel sick again."

"I understand." She sat next to her sister on the quilt. Ruth's naturally wavy dark blond hair cascaded down to her collarbone. Grace and her two brothers both had dark hair like her parents, but Ruth's hair never morphed into dark brown like her siblings. Her hazel eyes matched their mother's and glimmered in the afternoon sun shining through the sheer curtains. The two sisters only differed in age by five years, but Grace often thought of Ruth as much younger even though she transformed into a young woman during Grace's years away at college. Edward's remarks yesterday about Ruth still hung in her head. Should she bring it up now or wait? Why has she not mentioned this guy? Maybe it was supposed to be a secret.

"How's school going for you, Ruth?"

"I've been meaning to talk to you about that."

Grace's back stiffened. Does this have to do with the new solider in town?

"What do you mean, Ruth?" Grace asked as she rubbed her temples trying to soothe out the pain.

"Well, I am completing my junior year, but I have decided to get a full-time job and not finish my senior year."

Grace dropped her hand. Her body tensed up. *Try to remain calm. She's young.* "Ruth, I am confused. Please explain." Her heart raced. It was not unheard of for students not to graduate, but her family believed in education and she fully expected her sister to finish high school.

"I went downtown the other day and I noticed a sign hanging on the door at the Drug Store. It said the Army would be hiring people for all kinds of jobs including dental assistants." Ruth peered down at the quilt, not making eye contact with her sister. She smoothed out a wrinkle in the cover.

"And you want to be a dental assistant?" Grace coaxed. Maybe she could explain her reasoning.

"I was thinking it might be a good paying job," Ruth responded as she made eye contact with her.

"Why not finish your senior year first and then start a job working for the Army?"

"The job is available now. I will be eighteen in September and I am ready to start making an income."

"Does this have anything to do with that boy?" Grace bit her bottom lip. She had not planned on mentioning the young man, but it slipped out before she knew it.

Ruth's hazel eyes stared straight at her sister as she tried to hide a smile. "Edward told you, didn't he?"

"He mentioned he saw you a few times with a young solider."

"He is an officer," Ruth giggled as she corrected Grace. "We almost ran right into Edward one day when we were talking in the Drug Store. I've only talked with him twice, but I feel like I already know him so well. He is living on the back porch at my friend Carol's house."

"He's living on their back porch?" Grace asked puzzled.

"Yes, he is living on their back porch and another solider and his wife are living on their front porch. Since there is not Army housing yet, the soldiers are living with people in Gatesville."

"Oh yes, I did hear that," Grace said as she thought back to the newspaper article she'd read outside of Edward's office few weeks ago. "I thought it was only temporary and these soldiers would have a place to go, but I guess not. Well, you might as well tell me his name," Grace said forcing a smile across her face. She knew she was not going to change her younger sister's mind. But what a mistake she was making forgetting her education for a man.

"His name is Jimmy, oh and he is just the most handsome fellow," Ruth said as she started relaying the story to Grace about how the two of them met a few days ago. Grace laid her tense shoulders onto her pillows as she listened to her sister share about her new possible romance. Mama's voice interrupted them a few minutes later. She could be heard from the kitchen calling for Ruth. The two looked at each other and laughed.

"I guess I have been caught not doing my job in the kitchen. I was supposed to be cutting onions for dinner tonight, but I thought I would come check on you first."

"I'm glad you did." She patted her sister's hand before she stood up to leave. She could eventually get over Ruth not finishing her schooling, but what about this guy? Who was he? Where was he from? Was Ruth really ready for some kind of relationship with a stranger?

"Me too," Ruth said as she gave her sister a knowing grin before she left the room.

CHAPTER 28

*T*he final day for Grace's beloved church to gather together under the same roof came sooner than she desired. She sat scrunched between her two siblings as she rode in her family's sedan. They zipped past familiar trees and terrain as they drove into Oakmont.

Immediately at the first sight of her beloved community, she knew it had transformed into a different place over the past three weeks. As her family passed through, Grace's eyes and jaw opened wide. She couldn't stop staring at the heaping gray piles of ashes and charred wood from the former structures including the cotton gin, the black smith's shop, the post office and the general store.

"Look, Grace! The school is still standing!" hollered J.J as he broke the silence. Large Army trucks were parked in a row outside the schoolhouse.

"Yes, I know, J.J. It is now an Army Range Shop. See the sign?" She pointed to the white board with black stamped letters on the front of the old wooden building. It stung her soul to drive past the schoolhouse, seeing it converted into something other than a place for her to teach her students. She should be in there now, but she wasn't. She didn't belong here anymore.

She peeled her eyes off the building and looked down the road toward the church. She noticed cars parked all over. There were even a few horses tied to the hitching post. So many people had already moved off the land, but from what it looked like everyone wanted to be together at the church. Together for one last time.

Grace studied the cars looking for Edward's sedan. He'd told her he would be coming out this morning. He would probably be late again. She rolled her eyes.

As her father pulled in next to a large oak tree, she caught a glimpse of a bright red and black plaid shirt. Edward. So he actually made it on time today.

Edward stood conversing with the two sisters—Mrs. Miller and Mrs. Carter. She assumed he was relating all the information about their homes from a few days before. She wanted to forget about the other day. The overwhelming sights and smells had been too much for her to take in. She could almost smell the charred wood.

She closed the door and headed toward Edward with Mama and Ruth close behind.

"Hello, ladies. It's good to see you three," Mrs. Carter said as she dabbed her puffy red eyes. Mrs. Miller also wiped the remaining tears from her cheeks, and then she reached over and clasped her arms around her dear friends. These farmers' wives were strong, but they had reached their breaking point. Moving away from their land and homes marked the start of a new era full of challenges and struggles ahead.

After a long pause, the women released their embrace.

"Edward," Mama said, sniffing and wiping her nose with her handkerchief, "it's good to see you here today too. I'm glad you were able to make the last service."

Grace grabbed Edward's hand and briefly squeezed it. It felt good to have his presence nearby.

"Thank you. I brought my camera, too, just in case there is time to take a picture of everyone in front of the church. I thought it might be a good memory for everyone to have one day."

"Yes, maybe one day. Maybe. It is not a good memory right now. I'm not sure we will even be able to convince the men to gather together," the gray-haired Mrs. Miller said. The sage green hat she wore over a low bun matched her solid color sweater and floral dress.

"I'm always up for a picture," Mrs. Carter quipped, dressed in a simple light pink sheer long sleeve dress. "I just wish I had thought of it first." She winked at Edward. "We have a few minutes before the service begins. How about I go tell the preacher and we can start rounding up folks."

"I'll help you," Ruth offered as the two headed toward the steps.

Mrs. Carter lifted two fingers and gave a long sharp whistle.

"Hello everyone!" Her commanding southern voice could be heard from the church's top step. "We are going to take a group picture. I left my camera at home, but Edward, Grace's fiancé, has graciously offered to take one last picture for us," Mrs. Carter addressed the growing crowd. "And Edward, how about you take a picture of all of us folks; then after we've gone inside be sure to take one of the church standing here next to these beautiful old oak trees," Mrs. Carter instructed Edward. "Sound good?"

"Yes, ma'am Mrs. Carter," Edward agreed as he nodded his head.

"Now come on all of you! Don't be shy and don't be too upset." Mrs. Carter motioned for others to join her on the steps. "And don't tell me you don't want to be in a picture either," chided the older woman. "It ain't going to work. I want a picture of everyone in my church family. So come on, y'all. Let's get going."

Men, women, boys and girls gathered on and around the steps of the white-washed church building. Her earliest memories as a child were made at this place of worship. Grace glanced around trying to soak in every minute detail about this place and everything about this moment. On the roof, a slender steeple displayed a simple one-foot metal cross. Beside the old one-story church building stood two great live oaks and several older cedar trees. The church sat at a slightly elevated position on a hill. She could see a few miles in one direction.

"How about we have some taller men in the back. Children, please come to the front. Yes, that is right, some of you can sit on the ground," Edward directed as he pointed to different positions in front of the church steps. Grace found a spot next to her family and watched Edward as he went into action attempting to scoot everyone close enough to take a picture.

She turned to take in the sight of her church family together for one final time. Generations of families stood there before the camera with their faces sagging and their eyes casting dark shadows. The men stooped their shoulders, and the women rested their hands on their children. Some watched their homes burn, while others like Billy Roberts' family left before the sight became too hard to bear—like the Miller and the Carter homes had been for her. A few children displayed their toothless naïve grins in the front row, but the rest stood motionless; the camera would catch on film the raw emotions and feelings of these landowners and their families.

These individuals had been together through births, funerals, weddings, salvations, baptisms, and revivals. They were her life-long friends, brought together under one roof by their belief in God and his son, Jesus. Today, they would be saying goodbye to their beautiful history-filled building, but they would also be disassembling their congregation forever.

"Okay, on the count of three. One, two, three," Edward called to the group. Grace turned to face the camera. Her lips pinched together and her eyes downcast. Edward snapped several pictures. "Thank you all. That should do it." He waved to the group.

"Thank you, Edward," a guttural voice called from the back. Grace heard the man clear his throat. There in the middle row of men Reverend Frank's dark-brown eyes filled with moisture. "Now, let us go into the house of the Lord together. For He is good and merciful. This is the day the Lord has made. We will rejoice and be glad in it." She watched him lead the way inside.

As Grace turned to join the others, an obscure shape caught her eye. *What is that?* She did a double take and looked at the end of the church building. Several boxes stacked one on top of the other, close to the cemetery. *Huh. That's strange.*

The small cemetery sat twenty feet behind the back of the church surrounded by thick cedar brush. A black wrought-iron fence enclosed the small 30' x 30' area. She had many childhood memories of playing around the area. One time, Mickey tried to show off to her and some friends, so he jumped over the fence, but his shirt got caught on the pointed spires on top of the fence. It snagged a large hole in his new birthday shirt and she could still see the sour look of displeasure covering her mama's face.

Grace knew there were several charter members of the congregation as well as a few local families buried there. Many in Oakmont were also buried down the road in the larger Oakmont cemetery. "What are all those wooden boxes doing stacked back here?" Grace jabbed her sister in the side with her elbow and then started walking toward the freshly cut wooden crates.

Ruth turned around. "I don't know."

"Yes, I don't know either," Mrs. Carter said overhearing their conversation. The three made their way toward the back of the building. Just on the inside of the wrought-iron fence rested the mysterious wooden stacks.

"They kind of look like caskets," Ruth mused out loud first.

"Hmmm. I think you might be right, but why would there be so many wooden caskets stacked up right here. We are all getting ready to move. Who's going to be buried here now?" Mrs. Carter asked.

As the three women stepped closer, Grace noticed fresh dirt instead of lush green grass from recent rains sitting in front of the aging headstones. She cocked her head to the side as she read out loud the black scribbling on the side of one of the boxes.

"Mr. Ezekiel Austin, 1835-1898." Her eyes shifted to the box above it. She read the thick black scratch writing on the next box as well, "Mrs. Olivia Baker, 1840-1865."

"Why, these are the bodies of the people in this cemetery!" Mrs. Carter gasped.

"I was wondering why there was so much fresh dirt. I didn't remember anyone being buried here recently," Grace mentioned as she continued silently reading more names on the stacked boxes.

"I don't understand. Why are the remains of the bodies from the cemetery stacked here in these wooden boxes?" Ruth asked. She began walking around counting the number of boxes.

Mrs. Carter stood motionless. Her puffy eyes held tears once again. "They are erasing our heritage on this land."

"I'm still confused," Ruth repeated.

"Not only must they remove and destroy all our possessions on the surface, but they must exhume the bodies of our loved ones and remove all traces and evidence of the people who once lived here."

Grace understood Mrs. Carter's deliberate words.

"This is now an Army camp, Ruth. There is no place for our houses, windmills or fences. There is also no need for cemeteries now. They are moving all of us and therefore they are moving our buried dead with us as well."

"Wouldn't that take a long time? Look at all these graves right here. I can't imagine them taking the time or energy to move them," Ruth pointed to more headstones.

"Well, apparently someone thinks it's necessary," Mrs. Carter retorted as she shook her head.

"Ladies," beckoned Mama from the front of the church. "The service is about to begin."

"Okay, Mama. We are coming," Grace responded for the group.

She turned to Mrs. Carter. This might be the worst thing both of them had seen yet. She reached over and placed her hand around her waist. "Mrs. Carter, you are a strong woman. You are brave and you have survived so many things in your life. This move will not be able to stop you. I know you are such a beautiful woman with great leadership. Please don't let it ruin you." She tried to encourage her older friend as well as herself.

"I don't know, Grace. I just don't know, but thank you for your kind words," Mrs. Carter hugged her young friend.

The only thing certain about the coming days would be no more living life together as a community. Mrs. Carter could not give up. She couldn't let these travesties overtake her. Not now.

The three women walked toward the front of the church together.

"Mama, there are exhumed bodies back there," Ruth said in a hushed voice.

Edward, standing next to Georgia, tilted his head and gave Grace a puzzled face.

"What?" Mama's eyes widened. "Exhumed bodies!" She peered down toward the cemetery.

"Well, they're in caskets. Looks like someone is getting ready to take them somewhere," Grace added.

"I'm guessing these bodies are headed to Gatesville. There's a new cemetery being formed in town for all those who were laid to rest out here. I've been meaning to go out to the new cemetery and do a story sometime. I hear there's a backlog there. Caskets just lined up waiting to be buried," stated Edward.

"I can't hear any more of this. I need to go inside." Mrs. Carter stepped around Mama and headed up to the porch. "Are you all coming?" She stopped on the top step and turned around.

"I'll be glad to join you." Mama followed right behind and motioned for the others to join her.

Edward grabbed the door and the four of them walked in together.

Grace often found herself drawn to this serene, simple chapel with one aisle separating two sections of pews. A thick wooden pulpit rested at the front. Even the same worship service provided a feeling of home. Mrs. Miller pounding at the keys on the piano keeping it in *forte* with the strike of a wrong note every so often.

The order of worship remained the same year after year. A prayer, one hymn, a scripture verse, and then two more hymns. She found comfort in this routine. She knew what to expect. She shuffled into the pew next between her Mama and Edward. Singing these hymns brought such peace and assurance.

What about when the doors open and we have to leave this place, Lord? I'm scared. I'm so sad about not seeing my friends anymore. I'll never be able to meet you here. I know it is not about the place, but so many memories are held here. There are so many mixed emotions inside my head.

She sang louder. She wouldn't forget this little place where she first gave her heart to God. She raised her voice to him in sadness and mourning.

The last note echoed through the building as Reverend Frank motioned with his hands to sit. "Please be seated."

Reverend Frank stood to preach his final sermon from Psalm 23. She watched as the stubby man in his late thirties with a full head of hair combed to one side placed his weathered Bible underneath him and leaned forward. *Offer words of hope, please.*

"The Lord, he is our guide as we go through these difficult days ahead," Reverend Frank's voice bellowed out after reading the passage. He took time to look at each family unit. "Many of you said goodbye to your homes this week. Others of you will say goodbye in the coming weeks and months ahead. Though your hearts ache amidst these trials, remember the Lord is not leaving you on your own. He is here as we go through the darkest valley. I pray you know and feel the Lord's presence and comfort during this time."

She listened for the next twenty minutes wanting desperately to soak in every word in order to saturate her wounded heart. Angst seeped out. Images kept flashing in her mind returning her to James, Mickey, the morose farmers and ranchers, the Smith family, the burning homes, her schoolhouse.

"Please stand as we sing together." Reverend Frank's words jolted her out of her dreary thoughts.

Mrs. Miller for once softly played in the background a familiar tune. The pews squeaked and the floors of the near century old building creaked as the congregation stood.

"This will be our last time to sing this hymn together as an Oakmont church family, but in the coming days remember this will not be your last time to sing prayers and praises to our Heavenly Father. Please grab a hand next to you and join with me in singing, *Blest be the Tie*."

One by one they joined hands and crossed the center aisle clasping hands with one another. She grabbed both Mama and Edward's hands.

> *Blest be the tie that binds*
> *our hearts in Christian love;*
> *the fellowship of kindred minds*
> *is like to that above.*
> *Before our Father's throne*
> *we pour our ardent prayers;*

our fears, our hopes, our aims are one,
our comforts and our cares.

"Amen. Go in peace, brothers and sisters in Christ," Reverend Frank instructed his members one last time.

She filed out of the building behind Edward to the front lawn. There would be no picnic or baseball game today. She watched as many hugged and a few cried.

Thin arms wrapped around Grace's waist and pulled tight.

"Miss Willis," Rebecca said pushing short, light brown, stringy hair to the side. The older girl leaned back and gave Grace a smile across her small face. Not a big grin, but enough to show she was doing okay. Her chocolate brown eyes did not hold any tears today, either. "I have missed you so much!"

"Oh sweet, Rebecca. I have missed seeing you too. Have you started school again?"

"Not yet. My mama says maybe next week." Rebecca looked at her mother a few feet away. Mrs. Smith stood surrounded by several friends and former customers. Trying to make the most of her time with her friends.

"You still have your pretty ring on," Rebecca stated interrupting Grace's thoughts.

Grace focused on the twelve-year old who was only a few inches shorter than her. "My ring?" Grace laughed. "Of course, I do. I am going to get another ring from Mr. Edward soon enough too. On our wedding day!"

"I'm glad you are still getting married. Too many changes going on right now."

"Yes, we are still getting married, Rebecca." She glanced at Edward. To have and to hold. For better. For worse. Edward looked up from his conversation and they met eyes.

We've still got this right, Edward? Get your head on straight, Grace. What are you thinking? Of, course you're going to get married. He's a great guy. Sure, everyone has problems. They just work through them.

"Isn't that right, Miss Willis?" Rebecca asked with Helen standing beside her. She must have walked up.

"Um...what? I'm sorry...Ask me again."

"Oh, I was just telling Helen that we will have to have a reunion. Maybe every year. I don't want to forget all my friends here."

"I think it's a great idea, Rebecca," Helen added.

"Yes. Great idea. And I nominate you to be in charge of the committee." Grace patted Rebecca on the back. "Really, though, I think it is a wonderful plan."

Grace continued the conversation with Rebecca and soon moved on to talk with other friends.

Almost an hour later, she felt her elbow being touched and she looked to find Mama.

"Grace, we are going to go on home to eat lunch." Mama's eyes scanned the dispersing crowd. "I think we have said our goodbyes for now to just about everyone."

"I was thinking about riding back home with Edward." She looked in his direction and back to her mama. "How about I see you all at the house later today."

"Okay, Grace. Take your time. We will see you back home." Mama nodded and walked away with Ruth and J.J. close behind.

Edward turned and started in her direction.

"Grace. You about ready? I parked over here." He pointed toward grove of cedar trees.

"I don't want to go, but I'm ready."

Edward reached her and positioned his hand on the small of her back and guided her toward his car.

"Edward, how about we take one last walk around the church. I am not sure the next time we will ever be able to do it."

"How about we go down this road over here first and walk toward the place where I proposed?"

"Sounds like a plan." She reached for her fiancé's hand.

Edward intertwined his fingers with hers and they strolled

down the gravel road. The mature oak trees stretched across the lane and provided shade from the early afternoon sun. The chit-ter-chattering birds roosting in the trees and the rushing water of the nearby river accompanied them on their stroll.

"How are you doing after Friday? You sure did scare me when I found you motionless in my car."

Grace blushed. "I guess all the sights, sounds and smells were too overwhelming."

"I can understand." Edward squeezed her hand and released.

"I can't believe I didn't faint before church at the sight of all those caskets." A shiver ran down her arms causing her hairs to stand up. "It took a few minutes for us to figure out what they were."

"I've heard people say there is a backload of graves to be dug in Gatesville. Apparently, this new cemetery will keep the remains from other cemeteries all over this area. The wooden caskets are stacked along the edges of the fence there in town."

"That is awful." Grace shook her head. "I'm still not in favor of this Army camp being moved here. Not only do they disturb what is visible, but they also have to go and mess with these graves. I'm not sure how Mrs. Miller or Mrs. Carter or even Mrs. Smith held it together today. I was barely able to contain my tears thinking about today being the last service."

"Grace, there are plenty of great churches around Gatesville. We will be able to join one together as soon as we are married. Plus, think about what this is doing for the economy and all the jobs being created. Ruth told me today she is interested in being a dental assistant. That is amazing for her and will be a jump-start on life."

"Edward, I know there are plenty of great churches, but I am talking about the final service today. The final time these people are going to be together as a church family. Why are you always trying to bring up the good in this situation? I think it is better for Ruth to finish high school. There is no need to start a job early. Sure, she might bring in income now, but she will never have her high school diploma. She will never be able to say I am a high school graduate. Please don't bring my sister into this situation." She tossed away Edward's hand.

Why does he keep trying to argue about the new Army camp? It seems the fighting and arguing keeps escalating. She scowled and crossed her arms.

"Grace, I only brought up your sister because she is making the most of the situation. You haven't even applied yet for a job at the school."

"It has only been one week since we have moved! I'm going to do it—just stop pestering me, Edward."

"Pestering you?" Edward coughed. "We are going to be married soon! I think I have the right to mention applying for jobs!" Edward paused as he tried to gain his composure. "Grace, you seem to be depressed about everything that is happening right now, from not teaching to your parents moving. Then to top it off, you passed out while watching the fire. I am worried about you."

"Don't be Edward," Grace cut him off. She twisted the ring around with her thumb. "If you didn't agitate me then I wouldn't get so irritated."

Edward stared at her with his mouth open. "Agitate you?" He threw both hands in the air. "Well, then why are we getting married if I agitate you so much?"

"I don't know, Edward!" Grace yelled back at him. She didn't care if anyone was nearby to hear. Grace noticed the bushes behind Edward. The same bushes Rebecca Smith and the other children were hiding in when Edward proposed to her. And they kept giggling. Those sweet giggles would not ever sound again in Oakmont. The memory of Edward on one knee lifting the ring toward her seemed years ago.

"I don't know, Edward." She twisted the ring off her finger.

"Grace, what are you doing?" Edward's eyes widened. He seemed to be pleading her not to do it.

"We have grown apart, Edward. I need a break. I need some time to think. I...shouldn't k....keep...this ring." She placed the ring in her palm and lifted it toward him.

"Grace, it is your ring. It is my gift to you." Fury and sadness mixed together enveloped his voice. "I never want it back," he growled as he turned his back on her and stormed down the road to his car parked at the church.

Tears streamed down Grace's cheeks and cascaded off her jaw as she fell to her knees on the wildflowers below. She lifted her hands and covered her face as gut-wrenching sobs consumed her.

"What in the world have I done?" she cried out in the silence as Edward was almost to his car. "Edward, please come back." She knew he could not hear her.

Tears continued to streak down her face. A few moments later, she realized she was completely alone. *The ring. It's still here.* She opened her palm and there the ring sat. Through blurry eyes she stared at Oakmont cemetery a short distance in front of her and then she stared down at the simple gold band with its beautiful square diamond. In the sunlight, the radiating diamond boasted all shades of the rainbow. She stood. She was unsure about tomorrow, but what she was sure about was she did not want to keep Edward's ring in her possession.

EDWARD KNEW a few people were still around.

Someone else can give her a ride back home; I can't stand to be in her presence. He picked up the closest rock, took a few steps running start, and hurled it out in the field. *Maybe she will change her mind and maybe she won't, but I can't be with her now.* He kicked the dirt.

He marched all the way to his car and slammed the door shut. *There are plenty of positive things about the Army coming. Why can't she realize them? Why can't she just stop being so sad? The newspaper will probably even pick up more business too.*

He circled around the dirt lot and sped down the hill. *At least Reverend Frank is still here. He can give her a ride home.* He sped down the hill. Past the creek. Past the looming oak trees. Past her old schoolhouse. Past Mr. Lloyd's old homestead.

No, Oakmont would not be here again, but everyone had to give and take a little during the time of war. Maybe she would realize that one day. Maybe she wouldn't. For now, it seemed better to be apart from her.

CHAPTER 29

JUNE 2016

"Grandma? Grandma?" Katie whispered as she tapped the frail woman's shoulder.

Grandma had fallen asleep mid-sentence. Katie found a pale-blue-and-white crocheted blanket and placed it on the older woman, covering her waist and feet.

She glanced at the clock on the dresser. Its green numbers blinked 10:00 pm. It was still early for her, but she knew it was an hour past her grandma's bedtime. *No wonder she passed out while telling her story. She must be wiped out from waking up so early this morning, too.*

She turned on the seventies-style brass lamp and then clicked off the bedroom light switch. As she gathered her brush and pajamas, she noticed the familiar picture of her grandma and grandpa facing directly at her. Her grandparents were in their late sixties in this picture. Grandma often told her she had such a big smile because a few hours earlier they'd found out they were going to be grandparents again. Her mother's surprise fourth pregnancy caught everyone off guard including her parents and grandparents. Her mother, Mary, had miscarried three times before giving birth to Katie.

Her grandpa, often called D.J. by friends, passed away six years after this picture was taken. As Katie grew older, her memories of her grandpa became increasingly fuzzy. At thirty years old, she could only recall vague moments with him. She often remembered his silvery voice encouraging her to cast her rod further when they went fishing at the pond. He'd also taught her how to write her name, when he pulled a gold-plated pen from his white shirt pocket and wrote out the letters "K-a-t-i-e." He placed his strong, leathery hands on her fair-skinned child hands and taught her how to trace over the letters.

Looking at his picture, she recalled the thick, intriguing cologne she'd catch whiffs of as he would tickle her and then give her a giant bear hug. But she'd only had five years; she wished she had more special memories. But Grandma had lost more. She had lived another twenty-five years—prime years, full of living—alone, without Grandpa by her side.

She peered at Grace Kathleen as her head rested on the back of the chair where she slept. A soft snore came from her slightly open mouth. The name Edward didn't make sense. If Grandpa's name was D.J., then who was Edward? What did the initials D.J. mean? The questions flooded Katie's mind as she tried to put the puzzle pieces together.

Asking those questions now could be a risk, especially if Edward was someone other than her grandpa; maybe it would be upsetting. However, Katie's curiosity was burning, and she did not want to rest the subject.

THE NEXT MORNING, Katie woke to the smell of bacon frying in Grandma's faithful countertop grill. This was the one and only cooking appliance her grandma was allowed to use. As Katie inhaled the greasy goodness, she thought she heard a male voice.

Who in the world would be in Grandma's house this early in the morning? She rolled over to look at the alarm clock. It blinked 9:30. Katie groaned.

"How did I sleep in so late? Well, I know she is not watching the *Price is Right* since it is too early for that show, so I guess someone really is in the kitchen. I better get dressed and go see," Katie said to herself.

Hopefully the person down the hall was a neighbor and not a stranger. Grandma was not afraid to talk to strangers or let them in her home.

Katie threw on a pair of teal athletic shorts and a matching hot pink and teal shirt. She brushed her hair and teeth and scanned herself briefly in the bathroom mirror. Good enough. She wandered down the hallway in her white ankle high socks.

As she passed through the main entry hallway and entered the living room, the thick Texas accent sounded familiar. Still groggy from sleep, she could not quite place who the voice belonged to before both her grandma and the visitor spotted her.

"Good mornin', sleepy head," Grandma sang. "We were just wondering when you would wake up. You slept so long I thought I would fix our visitor some bacon and coffee."

Katie stood motionless and wide-eyed as she stared at her handsome visitor. His broad shoulders and muscular arms fit well in his black athletic shirt. He wore matching black athletic shorts. A bold neon green stripe running down the side of both made his legs appear long and strong. Luke sat up straight with a huge smirk across his face.

"Mornin', Sunshine," Luke smiled.

"I thought I was dreaming when I heard your voice, but then I realized I was awake, and I'd better come check on Grandma and see who was in her kitchen."

"You were dreaming about me, huh?" Luke's eyebrows perked up and he started laughing.

"Dreaming of...you...you?" She was unsure how to back herself out of her mistake. "I said... thought."

"Maybe next time I will be lucky enough to make it into your dreams." Luke winked at her as she turned a bright red and headed for the kitchen cabinet to pull out a mug for herself.

"Your grandma has already thought of it, Katie," Luke said. Her face remained red as she turned around to face him.

"Huh?"

"Your mug. It's sitting right here."

"Oh. Thanks," Katie mumbled as she grabbed the mug off the table and poured herself a cup of coffee. She'd expected to see Luke again, but his unexpected presence startled her this morning. She would have put on lip gloss or mascara or something. Thankfully, she'd at least taken an extra minute to brush her hair.

"Katie, honey, would you like some bacon?" Grandma asked as she picked up each slice with a fork and placed it on a paper towel-lined plate.

"Yes, please, Grandma."

"Luke, dear, would you like some too?"

"Of course. I would love some." Luke stood to help Grandma bring the hot bacon to the table. His sprawling hands reached in front of Katie as he placed the blue-and-white-patterned china plate on the old farm table.

Katie sat down and peered into her coffee. She could not think of anything to say right after waking up, especially to a surprise visitor. She glanced over at his coffee mug on the table. At that moment mortification hit her full on.

Luke wrapped his hand around a huge photo sprawled across the mug. A fifteen-year-old Katie with a huge gaping smile and gray metal braces stared at her. Other smaller photos of Katie throughout her teenage years surrounded the larger photo. Fifteen years ago, Katie's mother gave the mug as a Christmas gift to her grandma. Katie had always wanted to accidentally drop or break the mug but knew Grandma enjoyed the present too much. Hopefully, Luke had not noticed the mug he was using, but she knew better.

"Are you looking at my one-of-a-kind mug?" Katie muttered in embarrassment. "It's more like a mug shot."

Luke picked up the Christmas gift and turned it around, admiring each teenage photo of her.

"Oh, I don't know about that," he drawled. "I'm thinking… this is my favorite one." His thick square jaw gave way to a boyish grin as he pointed it out. She was wearing white feathery angel wings in the church's Christmas musical.

"Oh, geez. Can we put the mug in the sink or something!" Katie slapped her forehead, still mortified by the old photos.

"I'm enjoying using it. If your grandma likes it, then I like it, too." He placed the mug on the table and stared at Katie.

"That's why I like you, Luke," interrupted Grandma. "You know a good thing when you see it."

Katie laughed out loud. She was not sure what to think of these two. "So why are you here so early in the morning?" She picked up a piece of bacon.

"This is not early in Texas. It's already 85 degrees outside. I heard we are supposed to get close to 98 today and it is only June. I can't imagine what the heat will be like in July." Luke pointed outside. "Anyway, I was out running. I crossed in front of your grandma's place and thought I would stop and say hi. Little did I know that there would be at least one sleepy head. Did you girls have a slumber party or something last night?"

"Ha! Sort of. Grandma doesn't remember though. She passed out while she was telling me about her family and all they went through when Fort Hood came to town."

"I fell asleep while I was talking. I don't remember that."

"Exactly." Katie met eyes with Luke and they both started laughing.

At that moment, a knock on the kitchen screen door interrupted them.

"Good morning," called Betty, Grandma's home health care worker. Today, she wore pale rose-pink scrubs and white tennis shoes. Her thick short bleach-blond hair was pulled up into a half-ponytail. "Oh, good morning, Luke. I haven't seen you in a while. I heard you got a coaching job and are settled back in town now."

"Yes, ma'am. It's good to be back." Luke stood up to greet the woman.

"Now, Ms. Grace. Why don't you join me in the living room so we can take your blood pressure and make sure you have already taken all your medicines for the morning," Betty said leading the older woman to the next room where her blood pressure machine sat on an old wooden end table. Grandma sat down on her grandmother's blue wingback chair while Betty helped her elderly patient with putting on the blood pressure cuff.

"Hey, would you like to join me on a trip around the area?" Luke playfully pushed her arm.

"Umm, I'm not really into running or exercising of any kind this early in the morning." Katie wrinkled her nose.

Luke laughed. "No, I mean just a ride in the truck. Sometimes, I like to go driving on the country roads around here. And you are new here so it would be fun to show you around."

"I guess." Katie shrugged.

"You don't have to go; it was a thought."

"Oh, no. I mean...I ...would love to, I'm just kind of slow getting going in the morning." She pushed her wispy dark blond hair out of her eyes. It would be kind of fun to get out of the house. "How about I go grab my shoes and tell my grandma I will be back before Betty leaves today. I will meet you outside."

She half-trotted down the hallway to her bedroom. She grabbed her bright pink tennis shoes, quickly put on some mascara and lip gloss and returned to the living room.

"Hey, Grandma," Katie rested her hand on the antique wing-back chair. "Luke and I are going to head out and drive around a little. He thought it might be fun to show me the area."

"Mmm." Betty smirked as she surveyed her morning "to do" list for Grandma.

"Okay, honey. You two have fun. We will be fine here. I'll see you in a little while." Grandma patted Katie's back as she reached down to give her grandma a hug.

She walked out the kitchen door and down the steps where she found Luke standing next to her car. His truck was nowhere in sight.

"I thought we would take your car since I ran here." Luke shrugged his shoulders and raised his eyebrows laughing at himself. "I guess I wasn't thinking when I asked you if you wanted to drive around."

Katie joined him in laughter. "Apparently, my brain wasn't working either. I completely forgot about you running here," she said. "Okay, let me grab my keys." She dashed inside the house and grabbed her car keys on the kitchen counter and headed back outside.

"I hope you are okay with a tight squeeze." She sized up Luke as she joined him. Hopefully, his long legs would fit in the car. "Sorry, my seats don't adjust very far."

"That's okay, I'm used to cramped quarters. Most cars are not made for 6'4 guys with long legs."

"Wow, 6'4! You really are tall." Katie didn't know what else to say as she peered up at him.

"It is good for reaching on the top shelf of kitchen cabinets and playing sports, but not so much for riding in compact cars," Luke teased as he clambered in the small red car.

Katie laughed again. He sure had a way of keeping a smile on her face. "So where to first?" She started the car.

"How about we turn left, and I can show you where my

parents live and my grandparents used to live." Luke motioned his hands, showing her which way to go.

"Okay, that sounds like a great start."

Katie drove her red Corolla down the dirt driveway onto the main highway and then turned left again two miles later onto a black paved driveway.

She surveyed the area ahead as they came in view of several structures. Several large oak trees sprawled across the manicured lawn. It looked like a picture out of a magazine. The cedar trees and stray brush had been cleared, making the area wide and spacious. The two homes on the property sat about a fourth of a mile apart. There was one large metal barn between the two houses. Katie guessed the first home they passed was built in the 1940s. The second home looked like it was built in the late '70s.

She circled around the driveway as Luke started talking about the first home.

"As you know, my great-grandparents lived in Oakmont community," said Luke. "They owned several hundred acres of land. I believe it was 600 acres. They hopped place to place until around 1945, when this property became available. My great-grandparents were in their late sixties by this point and didn't want to start over with farming and ranching again, but they wanted some land to spread out. They found this piece of land with several large oak trees and with a scenic view of the smaller hills and valleys which reminded them of their original homestead."

Katie's eyes stayed mesmerized by the gorgeous scenery—a huge garden, a shaded lawn, hanging flower baskets every twenty feet or so, and an old rustic barn with the Texas flag painted on the aging roof.

"They purchased 100 acres of land. Their old house was destroyed on Fort Hood property, but they decided to build a similar home. From what I remember, the home is half the size. We can get out and look at it if you would like; no one lives in this house now. My grandparents built the rock home over there in the late 1960s. My parents have since remodeled it and live it now. I would introduce you, but they are in Austin today shopping for an upcoming vacation.

"I would love to get out and walk around." Katie shifted to park and the two got out of the car. "Your family's land is so peaceful. And look!" She placed her hand over her chest. "An old oak tree with a tire swing hanging from it! That was always a childhood dream."

"What, to have a tree swing?" Luke snickered as he grabbed the rope of the tire swing. The century old tree's thick branches hovered above them.

"Of course! Who wouldn't want a tire swing!"

"Why don't you sit down and try it out?" Luke coaxed. "I'll push you."

"Ha! I said it was a childhood dream. I don't want to break it," Katie joked.

"Just sit down." Luke patted the tire.

Katie gave in. She cautiously placed one leg and then her other leg through the gaping hole and then rested her weight onto the worn tire. The old white-washed homestead sat behind her. This was the most picturesque scenery ever.

Luke began to push her. For the first time since she met Luke, her face did not turn various shades of pink. Swinging brought a sense of freedom and peace as the wind swept past her. As a child, she'd begged her mom constantly to go to the park just to swing.

"This place is beautiful! And the swing is like a cherry on top! I feel like I can see for miles."

"If you look directly in front of you, which is to the south, you can see the old part of Fort Hood." Luke motioned with his hands.

"Fort Hood expanded over here as well?" questioned Katie. "I never realized the land so close to my grandma's house is Fort Hood property."

"Originally, Fort Hood stretched over the area in front of us - which was known as Fort Gates. The old fort was established in 1849 to protect the first settlers in the area from Native Americans," explained Luke.

"Wow. You know your history," Katie commented as Luke pushed her higher.

"I am good at remembering stories, or maybe I have read the historical marker almost every time I passed it while jogging around the area." He gave her that boyish grin again.

Katie shook her head at him and rolled her eyes.

"My grandpa used to tell me though about how the Army built a hospital and even had POWs from Africa housed over here during World War II. The land directly in front of us was eventually bought back by civilians, but the last range you can see in the distance is still owned and operated by Fort Hood."

"How much land does Fort Hood own today?"

"A little over 200,000 acres. It is one of the largest bases in the world now."

"It is still almost unbelievable how hundreds of families were forced to move from their homes and land so the Army could establish a base here. My grandma was reliving the story last night. She shared things with me I never knew. I'm starting to realize I just never asked her—or maybe she never choose to tell me." Luke began to slow the swing.

"Let's walk around the house," Luke suggested as he helped Katie off the tire. "So why did she start telling you her story last night?"

"We were moving some items out of the closet. I didn't care to, but she really wanted to make space for me." They strolled toward the front porch. "I pulled down several memory boxes and photo albums. I asked her if I could look in them. Then she responded she had nothing to hide. The first picture I came across was from a dance in Oakmont. I didn't even know my grandma knew how to dance!" She let out a chuckle. "Grandma described the move from Oakmont and cutting the house in half. I had no clue the house she lives in was cut in half! I mean how does that even happen?"

"Amazing, isn't it? I guess sheer determination and survival will allow people to do things we think are impossible. My great-grandparents' home was one of the many destroyed," added Luke. "Well, what else did she share with you?"

"She told me more about Edward, her fiancé, and how they broke up. I am so confused. I thought Edward was maybe my grandpa somehow, but I am not sure at all. I'm guessing my grandma was engaged to some guy before she met my grandpa. I never really thought to ask her how they met. What I do know is when I was growing up my grandpa went by the initials D.J. And of course, my grandma had to fall asleep before she told me the ending," Katie climbed the steps and sat down on the front porch. "I will say though, one of the most interesting things I didn't realize about the move is the price of land. I think she mentioned her dad got $17 an acre. I always wondered how my grandparents ended up on the land where she is still living today. Apparently, there was no land available and so some distant cousins offered to let them live on their property and lease out the land until they were paid by the government."

"I actually have heard stories about the price of land." Luke joined her on porch. His long legs hung off the front of the pier and beam house. "It seems to be something that continues to come up around here. I mean, everyone is thankful for the Army and all the jobs the base provided, just a little disappointed in what happened with the price per acre."

"I know so little about them being forced off that land. I wished I had asked her and my grandpa more when I was younger. What do you know? Did you ever talk to your grandparents about it?" Katie crossed her legs together as she waited for his answer.

"This is one area my grandpa stayed sore about for years and years. He never would have shared his feelings outside our family though for fear others might think him disloyal to the United States. My great-grandparents, Henry and Ida Carter, fought to get the price of land raised. They were essentially only given a small increase in the price per acre by a Waco judge."

JUNE 1942

The wooden railing on the front porch creaked as Grace leaned her slender waist against it on this blistery June afternoon. The intense heat from the sun about melted her as she stood in her dark navy-blue dress. She listened as Mrs. Carter shared the latest news with her father and mama. On her way home, the older woman had stopped by to pay the family a visit.

"My husband and I will be headed to Waco tomorrow. We are still waiting on payment from the government." The older woman's eyes had lost their shimmer and love for life. "We are able to afford another home, but so many farmers are in such a financial difficulty," Mrs. Carter said as she shook her head. "I have heard from many others that the banks in town are not willing to give them credit until they receive their money from the government. These banks are requiring collateral and the only thing these poor farmers had to give the banks was taken from them."

"I'm sure we would have been in the same situation as many of these farmers if Doris and Samuel had not stepped in and allowed us to live on their property. I can't even imagine how we would be able to survive right now..." Mama's voice left her, and her eyes began welling up. Grace knew her mama felt sorry for her friends who were put in such desperate situations.

"Have you received your payment from the government yet?" Mrs. Carter pointedly asked the couple.

"No, we are still waiting as well." Father wiped the sweat from his brow.

"Henry and I have decided we are not going to accept our $8 an acre from the government, which is why we are headed to Waco tomorrow. We will be going to federal court to ask for a higher compensation. You might want to think about going to court as well."

"We wouldn't have the money to pay all the court fees. We were fortunate and did get $17 an acre. I know the price per acre should be at least $80, but we are going to have to be thankful for it and move forward," Father stated.

"I can't possibly be thankful for $8 an acre," Mrs. Carter shook her head. "Others in town who were not forced to move are saying we should be satisfied, but I feel like I am being cheated. I have learned to keep my mouth closed and talk about other subjects with these individuals. I don't want anyone to think I am being disloyal to the government. For goodness sake, *two* of my sons are off fighting the war just like your Mickey! I love the United States, but I am requesting from them what I rightfully deserve." Mrs. Carter stated with her hand on her hip.

"We are in agreement with you, Ida, and we believe you should do what you feel is best. If we were in your financial position, I'm sure we would be handling things differently than we are now," Mama agreed.

"Well, thank you, Georgia. It is nice to be supported. Well, I'd best be going." Mrs. Carter gave Mama a hug and headed to her car.

"Mrs. Carter," Grace interjected. "Do you mind if I catch a ride with you and your husband tomorrow to Waco? I've not been in a while and there are a couple of shops I would like to visit downtown while you are at the courthouse."

"Grace, we would love to have you join us, but please know we might be gone all day."

"That's fine with me. It'll be nice to get away for a while." She forced a smile. Her heart still grieved turning away from Edward.

~

THE NEXT DAY, Henry and Ida Carter picked up Grace early in the morning and headed the thirty miles to Waco. Once they reach the federal courthouse, Grace noticed two families from Oakmont as well as other families from surrounding communities taken over by the Army as well.

"I guess you will not be alone in presenting your case." Grace motioned toward the front of the courthouse where the families were entering the building.

"You're right. Looks like there are others here that we know. Grace, I'm not sure how long we will take. How about you stop back here at lunch time? I sure hope we will be finished by then," Mrs. Carter said as Mr. Carter parked the car in front of the ornate courthouse decorated with tall columns.

"That sounds like a plan to me."

Grace paused and then placed her left hand on Mrs. Carter's shoulder, noticing the diamond ring missing from her finger. She pushed her sad thoughts away. "Um, Mrs. Carter, I really do hope things go in your favor. And if they don't, well, know I admire you for trying."

"Thank you, my dear. That means a lot." The older women patted Grace's hand and gave her a weak smile.

Grace left the couple and perused the downtown shops for two hours. She drifted in and out of the buildings until she found a store filled with beautiful material. She chose enough fabric to sew a new dress. An hour later she found the perfect matching hat in a different shop. With her new purchases in her hands, she headed toward the courthouse to check on the status of the Carter's case.

Grace glanced up the lengthy outdoor steps before taking them two by two toward the multi-story beige brick building. She found the courtroom nearby and noticed a sign in front of the door warning her court was in session. With only the soft tapping of her shoes on the hard floor, she quietly entered the room and found a place in the back. She shifted in her seat until she saw Mr. and Mrs. Carter at the front of the room at the same time as the harsh tone of the judge echoed through the still courtroom.

"You two are wasting my time and the federal court's time by coming here today," lectured the federal judge. "We have more important things to cover and you are requesting more money for your land? Mr. and Mrs. Carter, I wonder if you are unpatriotic. Your country demands the utmost support and respect from you. This is your patriotic duty." The judge's voice continued to grow louder.

It almost seemed as if he formed his opinion before they even entered the courtroom. His words were so harsh and unfair. The judge continued to pelt them with jarring and unexpected words.

"I believe $8.00 an acre is a fair share; however," he took a long pause and squinted his eyes at the worn couple, inspecting them one last time. "I am willing to raise the value of your land to $22 an acre. I believe this is a fair and suitable price." The judge pounded his gavel.

Mr. Carter's head immediately fell forward. His wife squeezed her husband's firm hand and they turned to gather their items. Grace watched the couple with their heads hanging low as they walked down the aisle toward the back door. She jumped up from her seat and joined them as they left the courtroom. She felt horrible for them having to go through that situation. She wanted to wipe away all their injustices, worries, and hardships. She reached for Mrs. Carter's arm and clung to it.

"I am so sorry, Mrs. Carter. I am so sorry," Grace whispered as she rested her head on the woman's shoulder. Mrs. Carter reached over and stroked Grace's hair.

"Honey, don't be sorry for us. We will make it through. Be sorry for others who listened to that harsh judge for him to only grant them pennies more for their land." She cast a sorrowful look toward the courtroom doors. "How many more people will suffer because of lost land?"

CHAPTER 30

JUNE 2016

"Unpatriotic!" Katie exclaimed. "The judge said they were being unpatriotic?" She raised her hands in the air as she stared at Luke. "They deserved the money for their hard-earned land. Obviously, the judge wasn't forced off his own land. How could he call them unpatriotic? They were trying to survive."

"Do you understand now why my grandpa and others stayed quiet about the entire situation? Many of those same people started working for the Army and the government soon after. They were afraid to speak out against it for fear of being labeled unpatriotic to their country, but in essence, they were some of the most patriotic in the entire country. They gave up every-thing." Luke looked in the direction of Fort Hood. "Some lost not only their land, but their sons as well. My grandpa's older brother never made it back home from the War."

"I'm so sorry." She sat there quiet, unsure of what other condolences to offer him.

"My grandpa told me there were several young men from this area who left soon after the announcement of Pearl Harbor."

"My grandma mentioned her younger brother, Mickey, served in the Army as well."

Katie and Luke continued visiting for the next hour. They strolled alongside each other across his family's property while he introduced her to several of the family's pets and animals.

"I know I should be used to this Texas heat, but I'm going have to find some shade." She wiped the sweat off her forehead.

"I told you it would be hot today! How about we go get a soft drink or lemonade or something in town?"

"That sounds good to me, but I'll probably need to head back to my grandma's house soon. My mom is supposed to call us today around noon, so it looks like we have about forty-five minutes."

"It's a deal. And since you are driving how about I buy." Luke stuck out his hand to shake on it.

"Okay, I agree." Katie gave him her hand. Tingles ricocheted from her slender arm to her fluttering heart, causing it to beat faster.

"Umm, maybe...maybe we should go get that drink now." Katie started walking toward her car.

"Well, you are my driver, so if you say so." Luke winked at her.

Forty-five minutes later, Katie dropped Luke off at his house before she headed back to her grandma's place.

"By the way, I will be gone for three weeks—family vacation with my parents and siblings, and then coaching school—but when I get back, we will have to see each other again. I'm sorry my schedule is so full.

"Oh, don't be. I'll be busy as well. Actually, the week of July 4th I am heading home and taking my grandma with me. My mom lives just outside the city limits and her neighborhood always has one of the greatest fireworks shows around."

"I enjoyed my day with you, Katie," Luke said as he gazed in her eyes for a brief moment before looking away. "We'll be in touch." He tapped the side of her car twice and walked away.

A MONTH PASSED without Katie mentioning the unfinished story of Edward and Oakmont to her grandma. Grandma did not bring up the past again, so Katie left the subject untouched. She still wondered though if D.J. and Edward were the same man, as well as what happened to all the people whose lives were drastically changed when they were forced to move.

Katie and Grandma returned from the Dallas area a few nights after July 4th. She would have loved to stay there longer, but she knew her grandma missed sleeping in her own bed as well as her daily routine in her own house. Even on the two-hour trip to Dallas and then back home to Gatesville, Katie stayed away from asking Grandma about her past.

A few nights after returning home, the two women were watching the evening news. Katie sat curled up on the soft brown leather couch eating some leftover pizza while Grandma rested in her favorite blue wingback chair holding a glass of tea. The frizzy hair news anchor on the local TV channel reported on the huge turn-out for the local fireworks show from July 4th and how successful the event had been for the city. Fireworks flashed on the screen as the anchor continued talking.

"I sat alone on the 4th of July watching the town's fireworks," Grace mumbled.

"Grandma, you didn't sit alone. We all sat together watching the fireworks. We were in Dallas. Remember?" Katie took another bite of pizza and went back to watching tv.

"I sat alone on the 4th of July watching the town's fireworks," Grandma murmured again. "I sat on Mama's red, white, and blue checkered quilt. Mama, Father, and Granny were down by the creek. J.J. was playing with friends. Mickey was away at war. And

Ruth stood by the large oak tree holding her new Army boyfriend's hand. I was surrounded by people, but, yet, I sat alone watching the fireworks," Grandma said as she stared at the TV.

The news turned to a commercial. Katie sat up and fumbled with the remote, trying to turn down the volume on the TV. She had been waiting weeks for her grandma to start sharing the story again. Finally, a time to discuss it without upsetting her.

"Why were you alone, Grandma; where was Edward?" She knew Grandma had ended the engagement but thought she would ask anyway.

"Oh, no, honey. I cut off the engagement and regretted almost every minute of it. I waited weeks before I went to find him at work. I was afraid he would be too mad at me to even want to talk or look at me."

∾

JUNE 1942

Grace seldom drove her family's car, but her mama didn't know how to operate a vehicle and Father was working in the field. Ruth needed a ride into Gatesville so she could interview for her dental assistant position. She pestered her older sister all morning until Grace grudgingly agreed to drive her into town.

"Okay, you win. I'll take you."

Grace managed to avoid taking trips into Gatesville for fear she would run into Edward. She wanted to see him, but she thought he would be too upset with her. Had he moved past her and their relationship? Had he found someone else? The questions stung her heart. She assumed after the way she had treated him, he would never want to talk to her again.

As she drove Ruth to town, she noticed the spring wildflowers had been replaced. Now the late June wildflowers with various shades of yellow and red were popping out of the tall green grass.

"Are you going to the fireworks show next week, Grace?" Ruth asked.

"I'm not sure. What fireworks show?" She really didn't want to small talk or visit.

"Jimmy told me there was going to be a huge show downtown especially since all the Army guys are reporting for duty." Ruth said.

Grace took a quick glance at Ruth. *Why does she have to go and mention her boyfriend's name now too?* Grace rolled her eyes. She didn't care if her sister saw her. Ruth and Jimmy had now been dating for almost a month. The two met each other downtown at the Drug Store. Jimmy was the main reason Ruth quit school and decided to apply for the dental assistant position at Camp Hood. Jimmy was an officer in the Army. He stood six foot even and was four years older than Ruth, but neither seemed to mind.

"I'm sure you and Jimmy will have a nice time together." She kept her eyes fixed on the dirt road. "Being with two love birds doesn't sound appealing to me."

"Oh, Grace! You need to get out. Maybe you can meet an Army fellow, too?" Ruth seemed to be trying to cheer her up, but it wasn't working. "Jimmy says he there are lots of guys lining up just waiting to meet you."

"Don't be foolish, Ruth," Grace jabbed.

"I'm serious," Ruth adjusted in her seat to face her sister. "I told Jimmy you are a dark-headed beauty with stunning hazel eyes and you are an amazing dancer and great with children."

"I bet there are plenty of men wanting to go on a date with me after hearing that description," Grace spouted sarcastically.

"Well, if you are interested in meeting any one of them then let me know," Ruth turned her body away facing forward again.

Grace did not desire to be with an Army fellow. She only longed for Edward, but her fear consumed her and kept her from reaching out to him. Maybe she shouldn't let fear keep her from Edward. Maybe she should at least walk by the newspaper office. And maybe if she saw his car, she would have enough courage to talk to him.

Once they reached the square in downtown Gatesville, Ruth hopped out and walked directly to the Army office in town. Great, an hour to waste. Maybe something was happening downtown around the square. She spent twenty minutes perusing the new clothing catalogues in the general store. Still no sign of Ruth. Maybe a soda would be nice. She headed in the direction of the Drug Store.

Her eyes desperately wanted to glance in the direction of the newspaper office to see if she could find Edward's car in front of the building. Maybe one quick peek wouldn't hurt. Just before she went into the shop, she stole a quick look toward the direction of his usual place to park. The spot sat empty. Relief washed over her right before regret stepped in. She sighed. She had such mixed emotions.

After paying the cashier for a bottled drink, Grace strolled toward Edward's office. She hesitated but decided to step in and ask his assistant if he would be in today. Her hands trembled as she turned the golden doorknob. The bells attached to the front door jingled announcing her presence. She paused. Maybe this wasn't a good idea. She started to turn around. Grace began to turn to go back out the door when she heard a nasal voice from behind the front desk.

"Hello, Grace. How can I help you today?" She had been caught.

"Oh, hi, Susan," Grace stopped to greet a woman in her mid-thirties with short jet-black hair and thick wire rim glasses. "I guess it has been a while since we've seen each other."

"Yes, it has." She peered at Grace through her glasses. She seemed to be waiting for her to continue the conversation.

"Well, I was wondering if Edward would be in today?" Did she really just say his name out loud. Her heart beat faster.

"Edward?" Susan cocked her head to the side. "You're looking for Edward?" Her face still seemed puzzled.

"Um...yes. Is he here today, and I just missed seeing his car?"

"Sweetie, he's been gone for a few weeks. His number got called up and he was deployed."

"What?" Grace felt her chest drop to the floor as the ground started to spin.

"Yes, he didn't call to tell you?"

Grace shook her head. No words came out.

"I'm sorry, sweetie. We've not heard from him since the day he packed up his office and left. Isn't it crazy how life can change so suddenly?" Susan rambled on as Grace began grasping for the doorknob again. She couldn't open it fast enough.

"Thank you, Susan," Grace whispered. The door slammed behind her.

She sprinted to her car, blinded to the strangers who stopped to stare at her. She could not believe Edward would leave without calling to tell her goodbye. They weren't together anymore, but still. She wasn't supposed to care about him anymore, but she did. Tears spewed from her eyes as she wiped them aside.

"I am the one who pushed Edward away. Why would he call me?" she chided herself.

Grace reached for her handkerchief in her purse and rubbed her swollen eyes. She had never dreamed he would be drafted before she could speak to him again. He might return with eyes for another girl, or worse, he might not ever return.

"He didn't care to even talk to me. Why should I even spend my time thinking about him. I'm sure he has moved on." Grace released one last sob before she raised her head. "I must move on too. I can't spend the rest of my life wondering about Edward."

She dabbed the last of the tears from her face as Ruth opened the door to the Army office. Grace watch in horror as she pointed toward their family's car and spoke to a young man dressed in beige Army attire.

"Yes, my sister is over there. I'm sure she would love to be a dental assistant too, but she is a teacher. Well, she was a teacher before the Army moved in and took over the school where she taught. She is going to apply to be a teacher again though.

Grace rolled her eyes as she watched the conversation. Her sister was a great listener, but today it looked like she would be good at gabbing with a stranger.

"Okay, thank you sir! Yes, I will see you around." Ruth bounced down the steps with a proud and dazzling smile. Her hair glimmered in the morning sun.

Grace greeted her sister with puffy, red-lined eyes.

"Grace, what happened to you?" Ruth's eyebrows arched up.

"Edward is gone." She thought she might burst in to tears again.

"What do you mean gone? Did he get another job?"

"No, he was drafted." Grace couldn't say anymore. Ruth gasped in the silent car and clutched her hand over her mouth.

"Oh, Grace. I'm so sorry. How did you find out?"

"Edward's former assistant, Susan, told me when I walked in the newspaper office and inquired about him."

"And he didn't call you either before he left? How long has he been gone?"

"A few weeks."

"I'm so sorry." Ruth leaned over and wrapped her arms around her broken sister. "Come on. Let me treat you to a soda at the Drug Store." She started to open the car door.

"I already bought one." Grace lifted her bottle, "But why don't we get you one? It looks like you have a reason to celebrate. Did you get the job?"

"Yes!" Ruth burst out. "They said I will start in a few weeks. They also said they will have plenty more jobs. They are expecting almost 50,000 soldiers to report to Camp Hood by the end of this year. And that doesn't even include all their families! Can you image what this small town of only a few thousand people will look like in a few months, Grace?" she squealed.

"No, Ruth, I can't." She didn't look amused. "Come on let's go."

The two women got out of the car and began walking to the Drug Store. A white paper sign with printed words rested in the front window.

"Need money? We need housing! Housing needed for Army soldiers and their families! Please contact your local Army office."

"Grace, do you see this?" Ruth pointed to the ad. "I wonder if Mama and Father would be willing to open their house. We have Mickey's old room available."

"That's a good idea. I actually remember reading an article Edward wrote several months ago about an Army soldier taking space on the front porch of a house. I'll mentioned it to Mama and Father. I know they have not received their check for the land from the government yet so I am sure something like this could be helpful. Good eye, Ruth!" She gave her a slight smile.

"Thanks." Ruth released a large grin across her face.

CHAPTER 31

JUNE 1942

*F*ather and Mama at first refused to consider renting out their porches to soldiers, but the more they heard about others doing it, the more they contemplated it as option for an increase in income. After taking Ruth to interview for a job, Grace felt ready to apply for teaching positions. She'd had enough time sulking about her broken engagement and lost community. She applied for a job in late June 1942. A few days later she got a phone call asking her for an interview. She came home in the afternoon on July 2 to tell her family about her new job as a 3rd grade elementary teacher in Gatesville for the upcoming school year.

As Grace pulled the family's sedan into the driveway, two other vehicles she had never seen before greeted her. As soon as she shifted to park, Grace watched J.J. run around to the driver's window and smash his nose right on the glass.

"What are you doing J.J.? I can't understand you." Grace

laughed at her brother as he tried to mouth words to her through the glass.

"Hold on." She grabbed her purse and binder from the passenger seat.

J.J. impatiently tapped on the car's door as he waited for Grace.

She opened the car door and stood next to her now teenage brother. J.J. had celebrated his thirteenth birthday a few days earlier. "Okay, now try to tell me this time."

"We have guests!"

"I can tell. Who's here?"

"I thought you knew about them. Mama and Father tell you everything. I always get left out of knowing the exciting stuff. Are you telling me I actually know something before you?" J.J. smirked as he started to sprint toward the house.

"Hey, J.J. that's not fair. Come back and tell me. Do I really have to go inside and find out who's here? Really, J.J.?"

She took the front porch steps two at a time. She slowly pulled opened the front screen door as she listened for voices. In the living room. A female voice. Now a male voice. They didn't seem familiar. She then overheard her father discussing the rules of the house. Grace crept into the entry hallway trying to veer away from the squeaky planks. *Creeaakk.* Her father's voice paused.

"Grace is that you? J.J. said you were here," her father called her.

"Yes, sir." She stepped into the living room not knowing who she would see. She glanced around and saw Granny perched in the blue wingback chair, and J.J. and Ruth both standing next to the kitchen doorway. Next to the fireplace sat Mama and Father. And there, in the middle of the room, lounged three guests.

"This is Grace, my oldest daughter. She lives here with us as well," her father explained as he introduced her to the small group sitting on the couch. The man and woman looked no more than twenty and the other male visitor looked to be few years older than her. "Grace, this is Floyd and Anna. They've been married three months and are originally from Oklahoma City. They will be living in Mickey's room." House guests. Father and Mama had finally decided to earn more income.

The couple leapt from their seats and shook her hand several times. "It is nice to meet you."

Anna, who had slightly crooked front teeth forming into a pleasant and warm smile, wore a solid pale-yellow dress with her strawberry blond hair pinned straight up, leaving soft curls on top. Floyd wore a pressed beige shirt and gray slacks. His light brown hair was buzzed all the way around his head. He flashed her a smile with his straight white teeth. They appeared harmless and pleasant enough.

"And this is Dean. He's from Lubbock, Texas." Her father motioned to the other man seated on the couch.

Dean briefly stood and reached out his thick calloused hand. She locked eyes with the dark headed stranger and matched his firm shake. He had a sleek crew cut with dark brown hair and a five o'clock shadow to match. Her stomach fluttered. She turned her head. She felt utterly ashamed. She was supposed to love Edward—not have some kind of feelings for another man. No matter how small.

"Dean will be living on our back porch." Her father rose from his position. "Now, since I have already shared the boarding guidelines for our house, Mrs. Willis and I would like to welcome you to Gatesville as well as our home."

Grace withdrew from the group and made her way toward the kitchen.

"Grace, what are you doing leaving? You just got here," Granny croaked. "Why don't you get to know these new guys and gal? They need friends too, you know."

Granny was right. Nothing like being alone in a new town.

She fixed a smile on her lips and forced herself to act chipper in front of their new house guests.

TWO DAYS LATER, on the evening of the fourth of July, she squished in the cramped sedan with her entire family, including Granny, to go watch the fireworks in downtown Gatesville. Floyd, Anna, and Dean all said they would be at the park too.

Fireworks usually brought squeals of excitement and joyous laughter, but tonight Grace only wanted to stay secluded at home. At the park, she went through the motions of helping Mama and Granny place the quilt on the ground. Ruth had already found Jimmy and was walking with him along the banks of the creek bed. A fiddle played in the distance as families gathered around for an entertaining evening.

Mama and Father left to stroll along the creek banks. J.J. scurried off with a football looking for his friends and Granny stood near the pie table chattering away with old acquaintances. *Might as well sit down and enjoy the sights*. Grace smoothed the wrinkles on the checkered red, white, and blue patterned quilt. Maybe it would have been better to bring a book to read or something to do. Loneliness wrapped around her as friends and family shared laughs and stories with one another all around her. An early firework went off causing the crowds to erupt in cheers.

They had all been though a lot, living in America. Her family had been through several wars and then the forced move. A few older men were seated nearby on one of the long picnic benches. Those three men who sat there, each had fought in the Civil War. There were also other men around the park this evening who had fought in the first World War. Yet, somehow, America had gotten through it all. In the good times and in the bad times, she had stuck it out.

"A penny for your thoughts?" interrupted Dean as he joined her on the blanket.

Grace inspected the soldier. Was he just trying to make small talk? "Why do you want to know?"

His dark eyes studied her. "You look like you have just solved some sort of problem in your head. You seemed to have relaxed for a brief moment."

"Oh." She hadn't realized she appeared so tense. "I'm just thinking about how much America has been through and how far she has come and yet she still manages to stay together."

"Those are good thoughts to have on the fourth of July. I couldn't agree with you more." He yanked a yellow dandelion from the ground.

"I'm not sure if my parents have told you, but the only reason you are boarding in their home is because money is tight," she turned to face the handsome dark-haired solider.

"That was my assumption. How does that have to do with America and the 4th of July?" his forehead crinkled.

"I have been so blind to think my family and those who lived in the area south of Gatesville were the only ones who have suffered for America. Their land was taken at a moment's notice and they had to relocate. It's been pretty hard for everyone. Yet look at those men who fought during World War I. And here I am sitting next to a solider from West Texas who left everything and is now going to fight in this terrible War," Grace said revealing her full thoughts. "We all have to give and take for this great nation to survive. Edward was right. He was just so blunt in how he shared his feelings."

"Edward? Who is Edward?" Dean leaned back on his elbows.

"I'm sorry, Dean, I was rambling. I have been trying to figure life out lately."

"Me too, which is partly why I am here today." He reached for a long piece of buffalo grass and stuck the end in his mouth.

"Why's that?"

"I got scared and ran away."

"You don't look like the type to get scared." She gave him a grin. With his dark eyes and manly appearance, he didn't look the type to be afraid.

Dean shrugged his shoulders and sat up. "We all struggle with something. Money, relationships, expectations. I was afraid of my life as a farmer following in the footsteps of my daddy. I watched him struggle to make ends meet during the Depression. I was scared to live his life repeated. I wanted to travel the world and the Army was the first opportunity that came my way." He twisted the grass in his fingers.

"You are not alone. I got scared too. I'm still scared."

"I'm guessing it is concerning this guy, Edward, huh? You sure are a pretty girl, but loneliness is written all over your face. Why don't you go find him?"

Grace felt odd sharing her feelings with this man she barely knew. "I can't."

Dean raised his eyebrows. He didn't seem to believe her short response.

"I tried, but he got drafted." Grace turned, afraid the tears would start to come.

"If he loves you—he'll come back. I've heard war changes a man. I guess I will experience for myself soon enough."

"Thanks, Dean." She noticed his eyes shifted to the crowd of young women gathering near the band.

"Yep, now it looks like I've got some dancing to do." He hopped up and tossed the piece of grass on the ground and headed toward the women.

She wasn't so sure she completely believed Dean. She wanted to. She watched Dean extend his hand to a single lady as the sun settled below the horizon and they sky faded into dark hues exposing several blinking stars. An older man in denim overalls announced the fireworks would be starting soon.

The weight of her broken engagement rested heavy upon her.

Even America stayed together in good times and bad. She had said yes to marrying Edward and staying with him for life. Yet she knew she ultimately initiated the break-up. The first firework exploded in the night sky, casting out sparks of vibrant red and yellow hues. Was Edward out there somewhere watching fireworks? Or was he asleep in the barracks? She wondered if he missed her as much as she longed for him.

CHAPTER 32

FALL 1942

*S*everal months passed after Grace's night viewing the fireworks alone on her mama's blanket. The hot summer days turned into mild fall afternoons. The young couple living in Mickey's room moved into the first available Army housing and Dean deployed overseas. J.J. started school as a teenager at Gatesville Junior High. Ruth accepted Jimmy's marriage proposal and they planned to be wed after his safe return home. Mickey still remained at war. He wrote Grace and the rest of the family often and they returned his letters. And somewhere in that mix, Father, Mama and Granny all began to accept their new routines on the new plot of land.

Grace's strong desire to be with Edward took a back seat as she plodded into new territory as a 3rd grade teacher. She waited anxiously for a letter or postcard to greet her when she arrived at home from teaching, yet every day rejection met her. *He didn't say goodbye or send a note before he left, so why would he send one now?*

She knew she needed to move on, but the thought of Edward always seemed to stay close on her mind.

Three weeks before Thanksgiving, Grace shut the car door and covered her head with her scarf. Leaves fell all around in the cool crisp November air. A brisk north wind had moved in, but she still checked the mail before going inside to enjoy some warm dinner. The mailbox greeted her empty yet again. Why was she waiting for a letter that she knew would never come? She was the one who'd broken their engagement. Grace shivered and headed inside. Maybe the blazing fireplace could ease the chill from her heart.

The scent of tomato-basil soup greeted her as she opened the front door.

"Grace, is that you?" her mother called from the kitchen table.

"Yes, Mama." Grace discarded her royal-blue scarf and matching coat, placing both on the hall tree in the front entry.

"I need to see you in the kitchen, please. We received a telegram from the Army today."

"A telegram?" *Did something happen to Mickey or Edward? No, it wouldn't be Edward. The military wouldn't even know to send that information here.* She shook her head. Her hands began to tremble, and her teeth chattered as she waited to hear the news.

"What is it, Mama. Who got hurt?" she tried to not let her voice seem panicked as she sat at the kitchen table with her mother and Granny who were preparing rolls for the evening dinner.

Mama paused from rolling out the dough to look at her. The Army only sent telegrams about dead soldiers, missing soldiers, or injured soldiers—none of those were things a family wanted to hear. The dreaded receipt of a telegram couldn't be good news.

"I know these things, Mama. I know the Army will inform us when someone dies or gets hurt," she responded. "Is it Mickey?

How bad is he?" She grasped her queasy stomach waiting for the response.

"You're right." Her mama searched her eyes. She seemed to not want to scare her. "Mickey was hurt. The good news is he will be able to recover. He had surgery, but we do not know the extent of his injury. However, we do know he is coming home."

Relief swept over Grace's face as she released her stomach. "They didn't tell you what kind of surgery?" she asked.

"No. The telegram was brief and to the point. It was delivered about two hours before you arrived." She wiped her hands on her floral apron and reached for the telegram on the kitchen counter behind her and handed it to Grace.

"Where is J.J.? Is he home from the bus? Or is Ruth home from work? Do they know, yet?" Grace began to skim the official government paper.

"No, J.J. is spending the night with a friend in Gatesville and Ruth told me this morning she would be working late tonight." Mama began rolling the dough again. She seemed so calm.

"You're right, Mama. No explanation of what happened to him." Grace turned the paper over and looked on the back.

"I guess all we can do is hope the best but fear the worst." Granny's blunt words voiced what they all were probably thinking. "I remember my sister getting the same telegraph about your cousin, Herbert, Georgia. No one knew what to expect. Was he blind? Was he crippled? Could he hear? Those were the worst weeks waiting until he came home."

Geez, Granny. That's not helping the situation. "Then we will pray and hope for the best. No matter what injury or surgery he has had, I am so ready to see Mickey. It has been too long. Almost eleven months." Grace stood up and gave her mother a hug. "He is fine, Mama. I just know it." Grace squeezed her mother's shoulders.

She felt Mama freeze. Large, thick tears flowed down her

mama's cheeks. Grace stood holding her mother as silent sobs shook her entire body.

~

TIME CREPT by as they waited on Mickey's arrival. Mama freshened his sheets and prepared his bedroom. Grace continued to go about her daily routines, but the thought of seeing Mickey soon stayed on her mind.

One day, J.J. blurted out, "How's he going to know where our home is? Do you think he got lost?"

Grace laughed out loud at her younger brother, but deep inside she wondered how the placement of their childhood home in a new location would affect Mickey. So much change since Mickey had been here last. Would he even be able to find their new location?

The evening before Thanksgiving, aromas of nutmeg and cinnamon filled the entire home as she helped her Mama and Granny prepare for the next day's feast. Ruth assisted Granny with pies and desserts and Grace helped Mama with cornbread dressing and green bean casserole. She could hardly wait to sneak a bite of the roast turkey. The house flooded with familiar holiday smells. She glanced at Father and J.J. They stayed hunched over the side table in the living room as they whittled away on a new woodworking project.

She had really hoped Mickey would join them for Thanksgiving, but now everyone assumed he would not be home until closer to Christmas. At least his letter from earlier this week eased everyone's minds.

My dearest family,

My lower left leg was struck by shrapnel. I thought I might lose my leg, but the surgery went better than expected and the doctors were able to save it. I consider my injury nothing compared to others in my battalion. Not sure when I will make it home. Maybe by Christmas. I am currently writing this letter from my hospital bed. Thanks for all your notes. They have kept me going.

Mickey

She crumbled the cornbread in her hands and let it release on the cooked vegetables below. One year ago today, Mickey was home. It was before Pearl Harbor. Before Camp Hood. Before the move. Before Edward left. She stared at her left hand as she grabbed another piece of cornbread. The blaring omission of the ring on her finger for over half a year pierced her heart each time she dwelled on it.

And one year ago, the front page of the Gatesville paper showcased her engagement picture. By that evening, Edward learned the first details about the possibility of a new Army camp. She released a long sigh. She needed to let go of all her thoughts about Edward. It was time, but for some reason she couldn't force them away.

"Someone's here!" hollered J.J. from the living room. "Hey, we got ourselves a visitor!"

"Who is it? Doris or Samuel here with some food?" Mama questioned from the kitchen.

"Georgia, why don't you go to the front door and see," Father called from the living room window.

She watched her Mama's eyes widen as she set down the dish she was holding. They were both curious now. Father rarely gave such blunt instructions to Mama. A tinge of excitement seeped out of his deep voice. Mama led the way to the living room. They peered out the front window. A military vehicle sat idling in front of their home. Two men wearing Army uniforms assisted a third man on crutches. His lowered head stayed down as he concentrated on carefully watching his step below.

Mama rushed to the front door and threw it open as the Grace, Ruth, and J.J. crowded behind her eager to get closer to the man hobbling in their yard.

"Mickey! Oh Mickey! Oh, my baby boy!" Tears streamed

down Mama's weary face as she flung her arms wide and bolted down the porch steps. Mickey's head shot up as he paused and gave his family the familiar boyish grin they all knew and cherished. The two other Army officials stepped aside as Grace's entire family gathered close behind Georgia and welcomed Mickey home at last.

CHAPTER 33

THANKSGIVING DAY 1942

*M*ickey scooped up his fourth helping of mashed potatoes. He seemed to enjoy all the sights and sounds of home and Thanksgiving Day. His once muscular face now exposed thinning cheek and jaw bones. War had obviously taken more of a toll on Mickey than he led them to believe in his letters. Maybe his letters were short and hopeful because he didn't want Mama or any of us to fear. He had failed to mention all the details of his injury. The shrapnel had done significant nerve damage to his left leg. He would be able to walk again without assistance but would always be left with a limp.

"These are the best mashed potatoes!" Mickey stuffed another bite in his mouth.

Grace and the others laughed. "This is what I missed the most. Home cooking," Mickey blurted. "And of course, all you as well." Mickey winked and shoved more food in.

"I'm glad you're home," Georgia said.

"I'm glad to be home too, Mama, but it sure is confusing

looking out my bedroom window and not seeing the barn and the live oak tree. I'm not sure how all of you've adjusted to our house being in a different place. And I'm still amazed, Father, at how you were able to move this house and put it back together again!"

"It's not all the way back together. Look up." Father pointed to a large crack.

"It looks good to me." Mickey scraped his plate and finished his mashed potatoes.

"I'm not sure this house will ever be the same as it was before we moved, but it's home and it'll work for now." Her father grimaced.

"Well, you did an amazing job. Simply amazing. And it still seems like home to me." Mickey looked around the room.

"Here let me take your plate, Mickey, unless you are not finished yet." Mama stood up.

"Oh no, Mama, I'm finished. Four helpings are enough!" He pushed his plate forward and lifted his hands in surrender. Grace and the others around the table laughed.

Granny, Doris, Mama, and Ruth began clearing the table to make room for pie. Each took a stack of dishes into the kitchen. Samuel, Father, and John Jr. stepped outside for a moment so Cousin Samuel could show him a new blacksmith project he was working on. Grace paused a moment longer at the table before helping with the dishes.

"Tell me, Grace, why didn't you write me about your wedding being canceled?"

"Oh, Mickey, please don't bring it up."

"Grace, I'm serious. You never told me you were not getting married."

"And you didn't tell us you just how injured you really are." She felt bad for chastising her younger brother. Doris stepped back in the dining room and grabbed a few more plates. Grace waited until they were alone again. "How was I supposed to write in a letter that I broke up with Edward?"

"Seems that would've been simple enough. Mama was the one who told me you were not getting married and that Edward was drafted. Did you ever write Edward and try to stay in touch with him?"

Grace slightly moved her dark head of hair side to side.

"The letters I received from you, Mama, and the others," Mickey paused for a moment. She watched as tears formed in his eyes. "Grace, those letters are what got me through. It's why I had a deep desire within me to make it back home. When I was laying there not sure if the doctors were going to be able to save my leg.... I thought I knew so much when I joined the Army. I wanted to change the world. Instead, I was met with the brutality of war. It was hard, Grace." His eyes turned glassy. "I cannot describe all I went through out there. It's too much. I know you will not like hearing this coming from your brother, but Edward needs to hear from you."

Grace turned her head hoping to avoid tears forming in her eyes. She didn't want her sadness and pity to ruin this day of thankfulness for everyone else. Hearing Edward's name spoken out loud stung her heart. She wasn't sure if it was pride or fear keeping her from writing Edward.

"Who's ready for some pie?" exclaimed Doris from the entryway of the kitchen. The petite gray-headed woman carried one pie on each arm. "Now where did those men run off to?"

"I think they went outside to look at something Samuel is making. I'll get them." She started to stand up.

"Don't bother, Grace. I'm sure once I say the word 'pie' they will all come running." The bubbly woman smiled as she headed across the wood floor of the living room toward the front door.

"Pie is ready!" Doris yelled as she held open the front screen. Within seconds J.J. scrambled inside and took his place at the dining table.

"I'm sure not missing out on the best part of the meal!" teased her youngest sibling as Samuel and Father walked through the door.

Everyone laughed at J.J. as they joined together once again around the dining table. Surrounded by a mountain of pies, fellowship of family, and her younger brother home from the war, Grace's heart still ached for something—or rather someone —more.

A few evenings later, Grace sat alone in her bedroom at her desk writing lesson plans for the coming week. Edward's face kept popping up in her mind. She pulled opened the top drawer of her work desk and rummaged around until she found a thin worn envelope. She emptied the contents. A love note from Edward and their first picture together as a couple. It was a cold December evening when Edward spotted a photo booth. He'd grabbed her by the waist and led her into the tight space. Seconds later, the camera snapped their first picture together and then the candid photo developed a minute later. A week later, Edward placed the photo booth picture and a short note in an envelope and had it delivered to her college mailbox.

My dearest Grace,

These have been the sweetest weeks of my life. Every moment I am not around you I can't wait until we are together again. You are beautiful both inside and outside. I'm so glad you are my girl. I'm excited to take you out Friday night. Do well on your test today.

I love you.

Edward

Grace folded the note and placed the black and white image and the creased paper back in the envelope. The letter was the first time he'd written the words "I love you" to her. She closed her eyes trying to imagine being with him two years ago as a new couple and then a year ago as an engaged couple. She envisioned Edward picking her up and spinning her around moments after she said yes to marrying him. Her dark hair loose in the wind.

She heard the laughter and squeals of the children in the bushes nearby.

Grace's mind skipped forward to six months later. She saw herself removing the ring from her finger and trying to give it to him. Oh, how she wished she could take back those fleeting minutes. Her heart hurt. She remembered surveying the cemetery in front of her and approaching the area with her ring clutched in her hand.

A cold tingling sensation traveled up her spine. She shuddered and opened her eyes. She found the closest pen and paper and began to write with everything she had in her. She knew the government would censor her letter, but she wrote with passion and determination to not let Edward fight alone on the battlefield without knowing her love for him. She missed the peace within her soul while holding his hand; she missed gazing intently into his dark handsome eyes; she missed listening to him talk passionately about his job. She missed his presence.

Marriage means staying together in the good times and in the bad times. Her parents stayed devoted to each other through the loss of several infant babies, through catastrophic drought and flood on the farm, and even the permanent loss of their land by the government. They never wavered in their love and passion for one another. Edward had a different opinion, but he was truthful with her. He continued to love and support her despite her having a different opinion from him. He supported her through the passing of her friend, losing her teaching job, going to the last church service, and saying goodbye to her parents' land. All the emotions and feelings she felt about not seeing him over the past six months she wrapped into a long love letter.

She might not ever know if Edward would forgive her, but she knew she could not live her life without trying to seek reconciliation with him.

CHAPTER 34

FEBRUARY 1943

*D*ays drifted into months. Grace waited patiently for a return letter from Edward. Every day she would check the mailbox before entering her parents' home after long hours working at school. Most of the time, a letter addressed from Jimmy to Ruth greeted her. Once or twice a week, Mickey would receive letters from young women he'd met while stationed at various places across the country before being deployed.

Despite never receiving any mail, Grace stayed determined to keep her routine of checking the box. One Friday, at the beginning of February, she opened the mailbox to find four letters. The first envelope addressed to Ruth, the next two letters to Mickey and the third addressed to her.

Grace stood motionless as the wind beat against her thick coat. She read the scribbled return address. No name, only an address was scrawled across the top left. She hurried inside the house. Did Edward finally write her? She tossed down her bag and the other three letters on the entryway table. She went straight to her room without saying hello to anyone.

Still wearing her thick coat and scarf, Grace's pale thin hands trembled as she grabbed her letter opener to disclose the contents of the envelope.

Dear Grace,

How are you doing? Swell, I hope. I'm sitting here trying to pass the hours away. Thought I would write you. I enjoyed my time getting to know you. I wished I could be by your side right now. Maybe watching fireworks or drinking a soda water. How's your family doing?

I would love to hear from you. Please write soon.

Dean

"Oh, Dean! You sure made me think I was getting a letter from Edward. Poor guy! You must be getting homesick," Grace said out loud to the letter.

She forced herself to write the tall dark cowboy from Lubbock a return letter even though disappointment racked her heart.

Dear Dean,

Good to hear from you! My family is well. Mickey returned home in November and we are all happy and complete again as a family. I'm glad you lived with us even for a short time. Maybe one day you can meet my brother, Mickey. Swell guy. I would enjoy drinking a soda water with you too. Maybe someday when you return.

Love, Grace

Grace continued the correspondence with Dean each time she received a letter from him over the next several weeks. She even began to look forward to opening the box and finding an envelope with her name on the front. Writing to Dean helped her pass the time. Her mind still drifted to Edward, but as time passed, she became less hopeful of reuniting with him. The one-year anniversary of the last day she saw him was no longer months away, but now days.

MARCH 1943

One year earlier on March 29, Grace reveled in the fullness of a future with her soon-to-be husband. On this Monday, three hundred sixty-five days later, she went through the motions of getting ready, driving to work, teaching school, and returning home.

Today, she had a pounding headache as she pulled into the driveway that she had not been able to relieve. The pain felt almost too overwhelming to get out of the car and walk to the house. Rather than follow her usual route to the mailbox, Grace slung her bag on her shoulder and headed up the porch steps to her bedroom.

"Grace is that you?" she heard Granny shout from the kitchen.

"Yes, Granny. I'm headed to my room. I've got a horrible headache." She felt like she was in a tunnel. She released a deep yawn as she opened the door to her room.

Grace escaped into her bedroom and pushed the door closed. She flung her bag on her desk chair and sprawled out on her bed. Birds sang songs of springtime joy outside her window as her curtains gently flowed back and forth in the warm afternoon breeze. Grace usually savored good weather days like this, but today her head and her heart were in agony. Suddenly, she felt cold. She pulled her blanket over her body as sleep overcame her.

"Grace? Grace, honey? Do you feel okay?" Mama asked in a hushed tone outside her door. The setting sun cast long shadows across her room.

"Should you wake her, Mama? I know she is going to want to see the letter." Grace distantly heard Ruth's muffled voice before she passed out again.

The next morning, the rooster crowed as usual long before daybreak. Grace wiped the drool from her mouth. She stretched her arms and legs out on her bed and looked down to discover the same clothes on her from the day before. She shook her head trying to remember how she ended up in her bed. Her swelling headache. That's how.

Grace perched herself on the edge of her mattress as she reached her arms toward the ceiling. How did she manage to sleep through the entire evening and all through the night? Thank goodness she felt much better today.

Grace dragged herself to the kitchen. Her headache had disappeared, but now her stomach felt like an empty pit. Sizzling bacon on the stovetop made her stomach growl.

"Good morning, sleepy head. I'm not sure you got enough rest last night," said Granny from the kitchen table. Her smile filled with sarcasm.

"Hi, Grace!" Mama closed the door on their new electric fridge. They might've lost the farm, but they at least kept electricity moving in closer to town. One of many perks she had discovered with the move. "I'm glad to see you this morning. I sure was worried about you last night." Mama left her spot and met her at the entryway.

"I had this raging headache all day, and then when I got in my bed I fell asleep immediately. I barely remember anything after that point," Grace said. "I'm feeling much better this morning though. Can I help you with the eggs or biscuits?"

"Oh no. Why don't you sit down? I already have some eggs and bacon ready. Biscuits will be done any minute. Can I get you some gravy as well?" Mama began spinning in motion as she started filling Grace's plate.

"Gravy sounds amazing. Thanks, Mama." Grace joined Granny at the kitchen table. The older woman slowly sipped on her steaming cup of coffee.

The pitter-patter of footsteps approaching the cozy kitchen. "Grace! Good morning! I was wondering when you were going to wake up! I've been waiting since last night," said an exasperated Ruth. "Mama, did you tell her about the letter yet?" Ruth gave her mother a quick hug and stole a piece of bacon off the plate on the counter.

"What letter?" asked Grace, confused. Maybe Dean had mailed another letter.

"This one," Granny simply stated with a glint of light in her aging hazel eyes. She pointed her crooked index finger toward the middle of the kitchen table. There sitting next to an old mason jar filled with striking bluebonnets and blazing Indian paintbrushes from their yard, a small plain envelope rested.

Grace noticed her name scrawled on the front. She squinted but wasn't able to make out the return address. The room went silent as she reached for the weathered envelope. One simple word caught her attention on the top left corner, "Edward." Grace's mouth dropped open.

The room caved in as she thought she might pass out. Grace grabbed the table and steadied herself. Ruth, Granny and Mama watched her rigid motions as she picked up the envelope.

This might be best to open alone. She wanted to excuse herself but felt too weak to move. She carefully tore open the envelope with one finger. A white piece of paper was crisply folded three times. She swallowed hard. The words folded in this letter would tell her what she had been longing to know for months. Did he still want her? With trembling hands, Grace unfolded the note. She could feel her heart beating in her throat. All the words were written on one side. She closed her eyes and took a deep slow breath before she allowed herself to encompass the words written before her.

"*My dearest Grace,*" she paused at his first three words and silently re-read them. Tears instantly welled up in her eyes and began pouring down her face clouding her view.

Words cannot describe how I felt when I received your letter. I've written you several letters over the year, but I was too afraid they would be received unwanted, so I never mailed them. This war has taken a toll on me. I am a changed man. Please forgive me if I was ever harsh to you. I wish I had written you a letter before I left Gatesville. I have missed you so much. I long to hold you in my arms. My love for you still remains. I would love to hear from you again.

Yours forever, Edward.

P.S. I noticed the postmark date—Your letter must have gotten lost. It took several months to find me. Hope this gets to you soon.

Grace dropped the letter as she covered her face. Sobs of relief overcame her entire body. She had rejected this man, yet he still loved her through all the trials.

"Well, Grace, what did he say?" Granny impatiently reached over and snatched the letter on the table. Emotion overcame her as she sat with her hand over her mouth. Unable to say anything.

"Well, my goodness. He says he loves her!" shouted Granny. Mama and Ruth immediately embraced Grace with joy and delight.

Grace allowed the tears to fall as she savored the moment.

∼

JUNE 1944

A little more than one year later, in June 1944, a black sedan pulled into the Willis' driveway. The Army camp, a few miles down the road, had developed into a bustling and busy area also known as Fort Hood; however, the driver of this car was looking for this particular house that used to be located on the Fort Hood grounds.

The twenty-six-year-old American soldier was in pursuit of a dark headed beauty with hazel eyes and tender lips. Grace Kathleen. He ached to grasp this slender woman in all her glory with his calloused hands. His once lean frame was replaced with a hard body ready to take on any condition. He proudly wore his Army uniform and the medals he received from serving overseas. *Will she even recognize me?* He glanced in the rearview mirror.

He'd spent time away from the one he loved most, but it had been time to serve his country during its greatest crisis. He had dreamed about this moment for the past two years. Had she changed? He didn't care. He just wanted to hold her. The only reason he survived combat was knowing she waited patiently for his return. As he closed the car door and came to attention in front of the familiar home, his eyes locked on the one his heart desired.

GRACE CAUGHT her breath as she took in every detail of the man standing before her. The clean-shaven face still bore Edward's features, but his jaw and neck were thick and strong. Every step he took toward her exuded determination and resilience. She clutched the small gold band in the palm of her left hand and with all her energy rushed down the old creaky steps toward her lover. Thankfully, she'd decided against throwing her engagement ring into the cemetery two years earlier. She had contemplated it, but never went through with it. She ran toward the man who meant the world to her.

Edward caught Grace as her blue-and-white striped dress swirled around her. She could feel him embracing her with all the passion he had within him. She buried her head into his chest. The chest she had desired to hold and touch for years.

After a few minutes he released her, and she brought the small gold ring with its sparkling square diamond to his attention. *Is this real? Is he really here?* He took the ring from her slender hand and went down on one knee.

"Grace Kathleen, my heart has missed you all these years. I have missed touching you, looking into your beautiful eyes, seeing your infectious smile, and hearing your sweet voice. I love you and I will love you forever. I do not want to go another day without calling you my own. Will you marry me.... today?" Her lover proposed as he gazed straight into her eyes.

"I will," Grace said, and he placed the ring on her slender finger. She then wrapped her arms around Edward's neck and kissed him passionately on the lips she had missed for years. Her fiancé soon-to-be husband in a few hours stood up and she held tightly to him as he spun her around.

Edward set Grace back down as a smile of joy lit up her face. "Edward, I will marry you today and love you always." The soon to be bride embraced her love once again.

CHAPTER 35

JULY 2016

*G*randma took several weeks to share the parts of her story which had never been exposed to her grand-daughter. Katie waited patiently and little by little she put the pieces together.

Katie and Grandma rested in the wooden rockers on the front porch at the family homestead on a peaceful July evening. The familiar singing of the cicadas could be heard in the distance. The in-service at school would be starting in a few short weeks. She tried to cherish every evening with her grandma before the long days would begin. The glaring rays of the Texas sun would soon drift below the horizon and hopefully offer some relief from the record hot day.

"Okay, I love this picture of you in your striped dress. And you said it was a bright red belt and matching red high heels," Katie delicately held the seventy-year-old black-and-white photo as she examined it. "Nice job, Grandma. You had great taste in clothes. Were you married in this dress?"

"I knew he was coming home soon. He called me as soon as he stepped foot on United States' soil. Nothing I had looked appropriate for his long-awaited homecoming so I went out and bought the most patriotic and stunning dress I could find. And of course, I had to have matching shoes. I needed to look good for my future husband." Smile wrinkles stretched across Grandma's face as the glistening sun shone on her.

"Well, you looked absolutely stunning. I'm sure he was ready to fall over when he saw what he had been missing. You are gorgeous." Katie sat mesmerized by the photo of the woman with flowing dark, wavy hair and glowing skin.

"Grandma?" Katie asked a moment later.

"Yes, honey?" The rocker squeaked as Grandma gently rocked back and forth against the hardwood porch.

"I am still confused about one thing."

"Go ahead. Maybe I can remember and answer your question." Grandma began chuckling at herself. She seemed like she was trying to stay lighthearted about her forgetfulness.

"You kept telling me about a guy named Edward, but I only know Grandpa as D.J. or Papa D. You have always called Grandpa, D.J. and his friends called him D.J., but you just told me you married an Edward."

"Hmmm. I did," nodded the woman.

"Yes, you did and...." Katie said trying to encourage her grandma. Hopefully she wouldn't forget about who was whom.

"I called him Edward. Hmmm. That is funny," Grace continued looking in the distance.

"Yes, you said Edward proposed to you and then you married a guy named Edward. So are D.J. and Edward the same?" Katie pushed.

"I haven't called him Edward in years," Grace Kathleen turned to gaze at her granddaughter. "I wonder why I used that name?" She quietly laughed at herself again.

Katie rubbed her hands over her face. Clearly, she was not

going to get a straight answer from this woman suffering with the beginning stages of dementia. What if Edward was Grandma's first husband? What if Grandma and Edward had kids and those kids were out there somewhere? Her mind continued rolling on thinking of all the crazy possibilities.

"I called him Edward when we were dating, but during the war he changed his name to his middle and last initials. He served in the same battalion as two other guys named Edward. My Edward wanted a life change. We were recently broken up and he was ready for something different. The guys called him D from his middle initial and J from his last name.

Katie's mouth dropped open at her words. Lifting her eyebrows, she asked again, "So my grandpa is the same as Edward?"

"Yes." Grandma's eyes stayed focused on the road near the house; her chair continued to click the hardwood porch as she rocked it back again.

"What a beautiful story, Grandma." She gently placed her hand on her grandma's worn and tan wrinkled hand with dark sunspots. "You two overcame so many things and in the end you reunited. I never knew your engagement story. I'm sorry I never asked. You hold such valuable knowledge about life and history. I had no clue all the things that happened to Oakmont and all the other surrounding families and communities either. I knew you all had to leave, but I didn't realize how it happened."

"Over 400 families were displaced." Grandma looked down and noticed Katie's hand on her own. She gingerly touched her granddaughter's hand. Grandma seemed thankful to share time with her. "But those families survived. They figured out a way to make it despite being in the worst of circumstances. Homes, farms, barns, fences, and acres of land all gone within a matter of weeks. Small farming communities were erased from the maps as if they never existed. But the people of this area loved America and made it work."

"You never told me what happened to the Smith family who owned the general store. Did you ever see their youngest daughter, Rebecca, again? And what about the pastor? Did your church ever meet again?"

"We never came together under the same church roof again. Some churches in the area were able to move their structures, but ours would have had too far to go to get out of Fort Hood's property," explained Grandma. "Also, too many of our members left the area. Some moved to Evant just thirty minutes west, and others to Jonesboro northwest of here. Still others relocated even further away in order to find land they could afford. Reverend Frank eventually found a place to preach again in a small community fifteen miles outside of Waco. He passed away several years ago, but his youngest son, who was just a young 'un at the time of the move, leads our annual gathering at the cemetery each year. I think he is around seventy-eight or so now."

"The old guy who spoke and gave a prayer at the beginning of the service?" Katie asked still trying to put faces with names.

"Yes, his name is Paul. He followed in his dad's footsteps. He's a retired preacher."

"Oh." Katie nodded. "After all these years, even Paul still attends the ceremony, wow."

"The Smith family though," Grandma shook her head as she pulled the sides of her light blue cardigan together and rested her hands over her petite waist. Katie noticed her grandma felt cool as usual on the shaded porch, despite it still being ninety-five degrees outside. "Their story ended much different. Our family was very fortunate to have land provided for us nearby, but the Smith family as well as many other farmers suffered for years." She paused and took a deep breath.

"The government took up to two years to pay many of the families for their properties. If a landowner did not have money saved up, his or her life was devastated. Most farmers hopped around from place to place as tenants. Many of them gave up and found small rentals until they received their checks from the government. Even those rentals almost maxed out these families. The Smith family, even though they owned a store, were not exempt from becoming almost like nomads. Mr. Smith died of a heart attack less than a year later leaving Mrs. Smith and her two daughters to figure out how to generate an income on their own. The Smith family moved at least three or four times in two years."

"Where did they move to?" Katie asked as she straightened her back against the smooth rocking chair.

"They hopped around from small town to small town here in Coryell County. Once they finally received their government check, Mrs. Smith opened a laundromat in Gatesville since there were so many new soldiers in town. However, their business never took off. Mrs. Smith retired shortly after both girls graduated from high school and left home; thankfully, the children fared better than their parents.

"Henry, the oldest son, came back from war several years later and married his fiancé. He became a mechanic in town. Helen married a solider and moved to Kansas where her husband called home. And Rebecca. Oh my, how that girl sure did change." Grandma chuckled again to herself. "Rebecca ended up marrying one of her classmates from Oakmont. The two of them still live in Gatesville today. I didn't see them at the cemetery this year. They must have been out of town visiting their grandchildren or great-grandchildren."

Katie tried to envision a twelve-year old Rebecca with stringy light brown hair and dark chocolate eyes as a great-grandma and covered in wrinkles with white poofy hair.

"What an incredible story. It seems Rebecca Smith's future inevitably was altered along with all the other families who lived where present-day Fort Hood currently resides; however, these families survived. And it seems many of them were never able to fully recover from all their losses, but they survived."

"You're right, Katie. And they taught their children and grandchildren to be loyal and patriotic even when their own country took their most valuable possession and gave them pennies for it."

Katie never heard the people and former residents of these smaller communities gripe about their country. At the cemetery, they only shared praises and offered prayers for the United States. The past took a difficult toil on these families, yet they continued to support their country throughout the war and into the next several decades. They showed true patriotism.

Katie had never understood the full gravity of the situation until listening to her grandma over the summer. She had only known her grandma as a hard-working, God-fearing, Bible believing, law abiding woman. She now had one more title to add to her grandma's list of attributes—patriotic.

Katie heard a buzz on the table next to her. Looking down she noticed her phone light up with a message. Luke. She hadn't seen him in several weeks. They kept missing each other.

Katie. I just got back in town from our football coaching school. I've got a coach's meeting in the morning, but I want to see you. Can I pick you up in 20 minutes and take you for a short drive or maybe to go get ice cream?

Her heart leaped. She didn't hesitate to reply.

Sure. I'm just sitting on the porch with my grandma. I'll look for you. Glad you are back home.

Was that too much? She was more excited for him to be home, but she didn't want to overdo it. Oh well. The message was already sent.

"Grandma, Luke is going to stop by in a few minutes and pick me up. I won't be gone long. Let me run inside and grab my purse before he gets here."

She kissed grandma on the forehead and then dashed inside, letting the screen door slam behind her.

"Katie, don't rush back for me. Take all the time you need." Grandma called from her rocker.

Oh, Grandma. Definitely playing a matchmaker. Was she ready to be in a real relationship, though, or was Luke still just wanting to be friends? He did want to see her, but maybe it was to tell her that they needed to go separate directions or maybe....

Katie needed to stop. She had waited weeks for Luke to return home and now he wanted to see her the day he returned home.

She took a brief look in the mirror and brushed her hair. Her forehead showed signs of sweat, but nothing she could do about that with it still being hot outside. Even the sleeveless shirt and shorts she had on didn't help much with the heat. She put on a smidge of lip-gloss and then grabbed her purse, putting the strap over her shoulder and across her chest.

Grandma had moved inside and sat in front of the TV with the volume way too loud.

"Grandma, I told Luke I would be waiting on the porch for him. I'm going to head back outside."

"Sure, honey. But be sure and grab that $20 on the counter in case you go get food or something."

"Oh, Grandma. I don't need your money, but I'll take it just in case."

Katie didn't want to have a disagreement with her grandma about the money. "Love you, Grandma." She grabbed the cash and started heading out.

"Love you too, Katie. Oh, and Katie—just remember—I too have waited for my soon-to-be husband on that porch."

"Grandma!" Katie hoped Luke had not appeared at the front door without her knowing. She felt warmth rising in her cheeks. Grandma sure thought highly of Luke.

"Love you, Grandma. Bye!" Katie pushed open the screen door then closed the wooden door. Firmly. She didn't want any more unfiltered statements to come out with Luke around.

Grandma's statement was true though. She had waited on this very porch for her loved one to come home. Katie had only gone a few weeks without seeing Luke. She couldn't imagine going several years due to war, but thankfully her grandparents finally found each other.

Katie let out a deep sigh. Standing on this porch brought so much peace. More than she had ever known. She had raced away from this place after her dad died years ago but returning here she found peace. The time with her grandma refreshed her soul. All the hours they had spent over the summer sitting on the front porch reconnecting—not to mention the stories grandma had unlocked from her past, revealing even more about Grace's true character and perseverance.

Katie heard the roar of a diesel engine on the road. The familiar white truck pulled onto the dirt path in front of her. This time she knew the driver. It had been less than two months since she met Luke for the first time when she had a flat tire, but so many things had changed. Including how much she liked the man driving that truck.

Luke hopped out of the truck and headed to the passenger side as Katie joined him. His skin was now a dark tan from the sun and his shoulders seemingly broader than the last time she saw him. His rugged good looks made her heart skip a beat.

"Hi." No other words came from her mouth. Her mind went blank. She had so much to say to him yet in that moment she couldn't think of anything else. Luke's sturdy arms reached for the door handle.

"Hi. I'm glad you could meet me. I got out of my meetings earlier than I thought I would today, and I raced home. Made it just in time." Luke motioned toward the setting sun. "At least we will get a spectacular show with all those colors in the sky right now."

Katie climbed in the seat. "Yes, you are right." She had been so lost in her thoughts that she hadn't even noticed the radiant sunset. She watched Luke jog back to his side of the truck and get in.

Luke put the truck in drive, and they headed away from Grandma's house. This was her first time inside his truck. Her heart began beating super-fast.

"Would you like to go get some ice cream? Sorry—it won't be super fancy, but the Ice Cream House is still open."

"That sounds great." Katie still could not think of anything else to say as a commercial on the radio ended in the background and a country song started to play.

"Before we head there, I want to take you somewhere else first. I think we have just enough time." Luke turned away from Gatesville and the ice cream shop. He then turned a sharp right on a dirt road and then headed up a steep hill. She had not been on this road before.

At the top of the hill there was a lookout area. Luke pulled over and turned off the truck. The color from the sunset mesmerized her. The handsome man once again went to her side and opened the door.

"Let me help you down." Katie reached for Luke's hand to help her down as she slid out of her seat and joined him. His eyes softened as he gazed at her. He continued to hold her hand as they began walking. She felt a tingle through her arm. His strong, calloused hand felt good to her. It felt right.

She followed him to the edge of the lookout. Luke continued to hold her hand as they watched the sun go below the horizon. No words spoken. Just a peaceful silence as a warm breeze gently blew past them. Luke squeezed her hand and then let go, sliding his arm around her waist.

"Katie, I know we haven't seen each other a lot the past few weeks, but you have stayed constantly on my mind. Even while I was on vacation with my family, I was ready to be back with you."

Did he really just say those words? He wanted to be with her.

He let go of her waist and reached for her hand, turning to look at her. "I'm glad I have a job and I was able to go to coaching school for football with all the other coaches, but again I just couldn't wait to be done so I could be with you."

"Luke, you haven't been far from my mind either. I've loved being with my grandma, but I was ready for you to be back in Gatesville. You have really made me feel at home here." Her stomach, heart, and mind all raced at once. She was falling for this guy. He held her heart.

"I'm going to be busy again from now until the end of fall with coaching football, but I want to see you as much as possible. Even if that means evening drives to see the sunset like this. I've really enjoyed getting to know you, Katie. And I want to get to know you more."

"I would like that very much, Luke."

His hand reached up and gently lifted her chin as he leaned down and kissed her. A gentle, calm wave went through her body. She kissed him back for a few moments before they both pulled away to watch the remaining moments of the sunset. His arm again wrapped around her waist.

For Katie, this was the best place to be in all of Texas and the panoramic view of the radiating sunset could have been a description of her heart at that moment. Full. Peaceful. Loved.

CHAPTER 36

*I*n-service days in August flew by and made way for Katie's first day of teaching U.S. history at Gatesville High School. The several-decades-old building bustled with teenage students slamming their bright yellow lockers and heading to class. As Katie's classroom desks began to fill with students, she headed for the front of the square room with bright white washed walls. The musty smell of the older school permeated her room.

As the first bell sounded through the speaker, Katie turned her back on her classroom and opened her black dry erase marker. She lifted the marker and slowly and steadily began writing in cursive across the white board, *"Describe the word patriot and what it means to you."*

Three more students filed in, filling all twenty-five desks in front of Katie. The boys and girls stared at her with bleak and uninterested looks. *This might be a long year if their expressions don't change.* After the second bell sounded a few moments later, the class noise drifted to a murmur as she took her place in front of her students with her waist high podium nearby.

"Welcome to United States History. My name is Miss Johnson. We have a few class rules as well as a class syllabus to discuss; however, first I would like you to all take out a pen and notepad." Katie paused as she waited for the rustling of paper and folders to subside. "I want you to write the short essay question written behind me in your spiral. Then I would like you to spend the next fifteen to twenty minutes of class time dissecting the word '*Patriot*' as well as its meaning. This evening, you are welcome to make any changes or add to your one-to-two-page essay. Tomorrow, we will go over our answers before we dive into our history books the following day. You may begin now." Katie walked around her podium and sat on her stool waiting for the students to work on their first assignment on the first day of school.

She peered around the classroom as young teenage heads bobbled up and down thinking and writing about the word *patriot*. She had spent the past several weeks planning and preparing for the first week of school. *Maybe somehow this will leave a lasting first impression on their minds about history. Many probably think history is in the past and in no way affects them. Maybe they can understand the importance of remembering and recalling history.*

Her first goal was to allow the students to reflect and understand the word *patriot*. As her lesson plans starting forming a week ago, an idea popped into her head about having someone who was living history speak to her students.

Later that the evening after the first day of school, Katie and Grandma were finishing up tomato soup and grilled cheese sandwiches. The conversation revolved around her first day of school and all the different personalities she encountered.

"Okay, Grandma, are you ready to tackle the halls of

Gatesville High School once again even though it's a different building?"

"Oh honey, I imagine they have rebuilt and remodeled several times since I graduated from there more than seventy years ago." Grandma snickered. "But I'm ready. I even wrote down a couple of phrases to remind myself what I am supposed to talk about. My handwriting is so shaky, but I think I will be able to read it. I don't want to bore your students by chasing rabbits." Grandma chuckled again.

"If they are bored by you then they definitely do not know how to appreciate the finer people of this life." Katie grinned as she reached over and squeezed her grandma's bony shoulders. "I am looking forward to you sharing." Katie smiled. Her only concern and nervousness remained how the students would respond and respect her grandma. Hopefully there would be no sleeping or unnecessary whispering during classes tomorrow morning.

THE FIRST PERIOD BELL RANG, summoning students to her classroom. Katie's petite grandma wore a vibrant red calf-length dress and sat next to her on a brown leather chair in the front of the classroom. Grandma changed her hair appointment to the day before so her large silvery-white curls would be fresh and tight across the top of her head. Delicate gold shapes dangled from her ears, and a matching necklace rested across her collar bone. On her chest, an American flag thumb-size pin shimmered as it reflected the florescent light. Today, Grandma would be sharing with Katie's U.S. history classes her story of trial, love, and patriotism.

A second after the tardy bell rang, Katie studied her notes at the podium for a moment and then scanned the faces of her students. "Students, welcome. Today, we will be sharing our personal essays describing the word '*patriot*.' However, first I would like to introduce you to our special guest. This is my grandma, Mrs. Grace Kathleen Johnson." She caught Grandma's eye and smiled.

"Mrs. Johnson will be telling us a story today. I'm sure some of you know the story of Fort Hood, but most of you probably have never heard details describing this specific event in U.S. history concerning the government's right to eminent domain. In 1941, the Unites States Army knew they needed to expand. After searching across the entire United States, their focus shifted toward the area just southeast of where we are today. Over 400 families lived, worked and worshiped on the land. Some had even lived there almost ninety years when suddenly they were expected to move everything they owned to a new place."

"Grandma." She glanced toward her beautiful elderly grandma seated at her desk. "Why don't you finish the rest of the story?"

"I would love to," Grandma responded as her eyes shone softly. She seemed ready to relive history once again.

A couple of the kids smirked, and a few arched their eyebrows. *At least this has captured their attention. They are listening now.*

Grandma shared for the next twenty minutes her memoir of the placement of Camp Hood from the perspective of a civilian. She relayed the suddenness of the announcement, the burning and destroying of homes and farm equipment left on the land, the price they received per acre, and the rise of real estate in the rest of the county outside the Fort Hood boundary zone.

Katie listened as grandma shared her pride in the boys leaving for war and the heartache for those who never returned. She told about the moving of her parents' house as well as the final worship service of her home church. Then she discussed the economic development and jobs provided to individuals like her sister, Ruth, and many others. Some students gasped as she told of the soldiers and their spouses living on the front and back porches of the homes belonging to complete strangers because there was not enough housing. Her grandma sat up straight as she spoke with pride, reliving her past once again.

"Everyone had to help and was willing to assist each other during the war. I guess some of us made bigger sacrifices than others, but it was still a sacrifice. My father and mama never fully recovered financially after the loss of their farm, but everyone chipped in and gave during the war efforts. We did not completely realize the effects until years later as we watched Fort Hood grow into the massive Army base it is today." Grandma folded her hands in her lap as she finished speaking.

The students sat motionless. All eyes were locked on the elderly woman sitting before them. A student with spiky blond hair near the front of the class timidly raised his hand.

"Yes, Colton?"

"Miss Johnson, the word patriot is written right above your grandma's head. I guess she is a patriot."

Another student on the second row with braces and long dark wavy hair raised her dark-skinned hand.

"Yes, Maddie?" Katie asked. *The kids are actually interested in continuing the conversation. This is a good start.*

"We often think of soldiers and people wearing red, white, and blue as patriots. Or at least that's what I wrote down." She gave a toothy smile and skimmed over her at her paper. "But your Grandma is a patriot without even realizing it. Not because she wears the right colors. Not because she went and fought overseas, but instead, she stayed on the home front right here on U.S. soil."

Another student raised his hand from the back row to join the discussion. He tossed his dark hair out of his eyebrows toward the side of his head.

"Yes, Austin? What would you like to add?" She pointed to the lanky teenager.

He sat up for a brief moment from his slouched position. "They were silent patriots." He scooted down again.

"Silent patriots? Hmmm. I have never thought about it that way. Please explain. I would love for you to expand on that thought."

The teenager tossed his hair aside once more and straightened in his chair. "You know," he shrugged his shoulders. "Your grandma said they didn't have a choice. Which means they had to be silent as the government took over their land. But here your grandma is today, and she is still supporting her country."

The simple words from her student spoke profound meaning to her heart. "I follow you, Austin." She nodded her head affirming him.

"Well, Grandma. I think the students and I are all in agreement. Whether we call you a patriot or a silent patriot, you and your family sacrificed for our country. As students of history, we have so much to learn from you and your generation. Thank you for sharing."

Katie heard a set of hands come together in a loud clap. Then more claps joined in throughout the entire classroom. Grace Kathleen beamed as she gazed across the room looking at the students.

"Thank you," she whispered as she raised her withered hand and waved to the group.

Katie noticed at the door a familiar head looking in. Luke. *What's he up to?* As soon as she saw his head, he disappeared again. Her heart sank, wishing she could have at least said hello.

"Okay, class, thank you all for listening so well. Grandma you can stay here or move back to my chair. Let's turn to page ten in your history books." Maybe it would work out later today for her to run into Luke again. He had either stayed gone or busy most of the summer and now he was always coaching football. But maybe. Just maybe there would be a chance to say hello later today.

CHAPTER 37

"I heard your Grandma was at school this week," Luke said as he caught Katie walking to her car on Thursday afternoon. "There is even a rumor the kids are wanting to throw a big homecoming party for all the people who had to leave Oakmont and the other communities."

"Yes." She couldn't contain her excitement both with the new idea and the opportunity to see Luke. She released a huge beaming smile. "I have already had several students approach me saying their great-aunt or great-great uncle or grandpa had to move off the land. One of the kids in my 5th period came up with the idea of having a 75th anniversary party." She shook her head in disbelief. She thought they would fall asleep, but instead they took ownership. "This student started adding up the years in his head and then mentioned why don't we have a homecoming for all these patriots. Seriously, I have some amazing students."

"I would agree with you. They were thinking outside of the box, but you helped encourage them to do it. I've never heard of a teacher asking his or her grandma to come speak to a group of high schoolers, but this history lesson sure did connect with these students. Let me know if I can help you in any way."

"I think the first thing I need to do is figure out how to promote this, and I also want to see if my grandma has any friends still living who would be interested in coming."

"A great place for you to start is to go to that place you dread most in town," Luke said with a glint in his eyes.

"What place?"

"The Burger Shack!"

"The Burger Shack? Why would I go there?" She cocked her head sideways, lifting her lips in disgust.

"It is the place where all the old people gather and go drink coffee. They sit around the table for hours."

"Are you being serious? I don't want to go there and find out it was just a ploy to get me to eat at that place again." She playfully shook her finger at him. Going with Luke might be fun again, but definitely not alone.

"Ha! No, really I'm serious." Luke raised his hands to his chest in surrender. "No kidding here. When my grandpa was alive, he used to go there and hang out for hours with those guys. I bet they could tell you plenty of stories. Really."

"Well then, okay. Thanks for the advice. I will go there sometime and meet these old fellows. Thanks, Luke."

"Not a problem. Now I've got to run to practice. We are starting here any minute. I'll call you later." He glanced at his watch and started jogging toward the field house.

"Okay, talk to you later." Katie said, but her words got lost in the wind as he headed toward the football team. She already missed talking to him.

~

OCTOBER 2016

Two months later, plans were moving along to set up a 75th reunion for all those who had to move because of Fort Hood.

Katie finally decided to take the plunge and head toward the Burger Shack.

She wanted to sleep in on this Saturday morning, but decided the best time to catch some of these guys might be today.

Katie opened the door and stepped into the dive where the same greasy aroma of burgers and fries and identical worn chair pads and ceiling tiles greeted her.

Sure enough, Luke was right. She spotted seven older men, all in their late seventies and eighties, sitting around two rectangular tables pushed together. Each man had a cup of steaming coffee sitting on the table. Katie waited for a brief lull in their conversation before interjecting.

"Good morning, guys! How are all you fellows today?" Katie awkwardly burst out.

The men slowly turned their heads to acknowledge her. "Good," gruffly bellowed out one man as he lifted his furry eyebrows along with his cup of coffee. "And how are you doing, young lady?"

"I'm good as well. I just have a favor to ask you gentlemen. I am a teacher at the high school, and we are planning a party. I… I…wanted to see if you guys could dir…dir…direct me to some of the people we…we are wanting to invite." She wanted to slap her forehead. That didn't come out as eloquently as hoped.

"Shouldn't you already know your guest list when planning a party?" asked one of the older men seated at the end of the table.

"Great question!" Katie let out a short laugh. "Usually yes, but in this situation, we are looking for people and trying to get the word out. In a few months, we are going to hold a 75th homecoming for those who had to move off the property currently occupied by Fort Hood."

The men looked dumbfounded. "A 75th anniversary gathering?" the first man questioned again.

"Yes, sir. My grandma is Grace Kathleen Johnson and she has been telling me a lot about what it was like for her family to move during World War II. A few weeks ago, I had her come speak to my 9th grade students at the high school. They came up with the idea of having a 75th reunion for all the people who were affected." Katie gained momentum now that she had their complete attention. "My friend, Luke, mentioned this might be a good place to start to find people who might know my grandma or people who might have had to move as well."

"You shoulda said Grace is your grandma from the very beginning, girl!" A gentleman in his early eighties spoke up. His eyes bright and shining underneath his mostly bald head. "Grace was my teacher back at Oakmont. She taught me and this old guy, David Springer." The older man pointed to a man with a thick head of gray hair sitting across from him. "I think David and I met you one time when you came in here with Luke."

"Oh, that's right. I am sorry I didn't recognize you. Remind me of your name." She stuck out her hand to older man.

"My name is Billy Roberts, ma'am. Nice to see you again," the older gentleman said as he gripped Katie's hand and shook it.

His name sounds so familiar. Where had she heard the name Billy Roberts?

"I think my grandma has mentioned your name before," Katie said, trying to recall at what point in the story her grandma talked about him.

"I guess I was one of her best students, then." Billy winked at her. "Your grandma sure is one of the nicest individuals out there. I will always know her as my teacher, but later as a friend. I eventually worked in the school system alongside her. I retired as the junior high principal," Billy said.

"How old were you when my grandma taught you when the Army moved in?" She sat down at the last available seat left at the long table.

"Oh, I was a first grader, I guess, when my daddy was told he had to move off his land. He was a young guy full of hope and dreams for his property. I remember the day he found out. He came and got me out of school, and I could see the desperation and heartache in his eyes. Every dream he had for his new property was dashed. We traveled around from relative to relative for at least six months waiting to receive the money for his land. He didn't get hardly anything for it." Billy paused as he took a sip out of his coffee.

"And he didn't have enough money to pay court fees to fight and increase the price. He was never the same man again after the day he lost his farm. He eventually was able to buy five acres of land and a small house on the far edge of town. He worked construction and then later worked at a seed supply store until he passed away at the age of sixty. Man, those days were sure rough in the beginning. Glad I don't remember too much of it." Billy put down his cup of coffee and folded his hands over his chest.

"Seems like my grandma was telling me the same thing as what you just mentioned." Katie said unsure what else to say.

Billy took a deep sniff clearing his nose and then his throat. "Well, your grandma knows David and his wife Rebecca pretty good too." He patted the man next to him on the back. "David, what grade were you and Rebecca in when we had to move from Oakmont?"

"Wait, just curious, is Rebecca's maiden name Smith? I remember my grandma talking about Smith's General Store and a young girl named Rebecca."

Billy and David both gave each other a knowing smile. "Yep, my Rebecca used to be a Smith," David said. "We were in sixth grade with Grace's brother, J.J. I used to walk with him to school every day. My parents were able to find a small place just north of Gatesville. My dad continued to farm. I attended Gatesville schools with J.J., Rebecca and one or two others. Most of our classmates were not so fortunate to stay in the area since the price of land was so high and cattle went for so little. I hadn't thought about it being seventy-five years ago. Seems like it was just yesterday."

"Well, Katie, what can we do for you? Is there some way we can help?" Billy questioned.

Another man at the other end of the table with rimless glasses and a short-sleeve plaid button-down shirt spoke before Katie replied.

"Now, Katie are you wanting just Oakmont folk or everyone who had to move? My mama and I lived with my grandparents and great-grandparents out near the Cow House Creek, which was south of Oakmont. I was only four years old when we moved, but my great-grandparents lived on their property for over sixty years. My great-grandpa died of a heart attack when we found out about the move. My grandpa quit farming forever and my mother went to work at Fort Hood leaving me to be raised by my grandparents. There were so many small communities affected in the area. Hundreds of families had to move, but thousands of people."

Wow. Katie was amazed. *Seems like everyone around here was affected. Thousands of people uprooted. Their lives changed, which in turn changed their children's—and their children's children's—future.*

"We want everyone who was affected to come, and we would love for the generations after to join too. I never lived in Gatesville, but I grew up going to the cemetery on Memorial Day weekend with my grandma. I love learning about her past and celebrating all she has survived."

"Great," the man said as he gave a big nod. "I can spread the word at my church, and my son-in-law works at the newspaper. I'm sure he would love to write an article about this."

"Yes, the newspaper would be amazing."

"My granddaughter works at the news station in Waco. I bet she would cover a story for us as well," Billy added in.

"You guys are wonderful! I will continue working with the

high school students and finalizing the date, time, place, and of course the decorations and food."

"Yes, food would be perfect. I think we all would enjoy having some good food and some great company as well. Heck, I'll even bring my smoker and throw on a couple of briskets," Billy said.

"This already sounds like a fantastic party to me!" David said with the others adding in some hearty *Amens* around the table as well.

A smile spread across her face. This was working out better than she imagined. Now, maybe she could get Luke to help her out as well. It was his suggestion to reach out to these guys. At that moment a new idea started forming in her head. Yes, maybe Luke could help her after all.

CHAPTER 38

MARCH 2017

*T*he months passed quickly as Katie and her team of students planned and prepared for the 75th anniversary and reunion at the Gatesville High School gymnasium. On the Friday before the big day, Katie escorted each class period to the gym and allowed them to take part in setting up chairs, airing up and placing gold and silver balloons around the doorways, and creating large banners welcoming guests.

Several restaurants in Gatesville, as well as a few individuals, donated brisket, potato salad, beans, rolls, and homemade desserts. She stared around the gym. To see how the entire community desired to support and love those who had given so much for the sake of security and wellbeing of their country - it was quite overwhelming.

The next morning, Katie woke up and tossed back her covers as her heart fluttered with excitement and anticipation of the day ahead. At 11:00 am, the party would begin. There would be a live fiddle player playing songs while families gathered to feast on the hearty Texan food in the cafeteria. Those families, including children, grandchildren, and great-grandchildren, were invited to bring photos to share with others. Tables and chairs were set up in the gym so they could fellowship with one another about the good times gone past. Reporters from two local news stations, the Gatesville paper, and the Waco paper would all be on-site as well to capture this special occasion.

She threw on her favorite black capri pants and a hot pink sleeveless top. Despite it being spring, the weather anchor the night before had given a forecast of bright and sunny with a high of 85. She straightened her hair and then made loose ringlets with her curling iron hoping the humidity would not flatten all her locks.

As she headed through the house, she wondered if Grandma would be prepared to go. Hopefully she remembered today was her big day. Thankfully, Katie found her dressed and ready in a light blue pant suit and a button-down floral blouse. Her silvery white hair was neatly hair-sprayed in place. A pearl necklace surrounded her neckline and her sparkling diamond wedding ring stood out on her leathery tan hands. Her familiar cane rested on her favorite wingback chair.

She knew Grandma had been anticipating this day of reflecting, reuniting, and remembering for several months. Grandma appeared composed, but Katie could sense her excitement the moment she walked in. Grandma inched forward in her chair and released a wide grin.

"There's bacon and cereal on the counter if you are hungry." She motioned toward the kitchen.

"Thanks, Grandma. I think I will grab a piece of bacon to hold me over," She headed toward the kitchen as the doorbell rang.

"Someone is already here?" Grandma leaned forward attempting to catch a glimpse out the front window.

"It's part of your surprise later today." Katie grinned not giving away any hints to the older woman.

"Well, who is it?" Grandma's head bobbed up and down trying to see out the window across the room.

Katie didn't say a word and went to the entryway opening the front door for their guest. "You're welcome to come in. I'm going to grab a piece of bacon in the kitchen. I'm starving. I haven't had any food yet this morning. Do you want any?"

"No, thanks. It sounds good, but I ate a large breakfast and I want be ready for all that good food at lunch." His husky voice made her heart beat a little faster.

"Okay. Give me a second." Katie dashed off toward the kitchen past her grandma letting their guest enter the living room alone.

"Luke! Are you a part of the surprise?" Grandma said the moment she saw the handsome young man. He wore pressed jeans as well as a pressed dark blue button-down shirt and brown boots. "You look very nice today."

"Thank you, ma'am, but I must say, you're beautiful! Are you ready for your special day?" Luke asked as he assisted the elderly woman to her feet with her cane in her hand.

"Why, thank you. And yes, I am more than ready. I just wish Katie would tell me about this surprise. My stomach is all in knots." She touched her waist with her free hand.

"Oh, it is nothing to be nervous about, Grandma." Katie said as she walked back in the room.

"No ma'am. Don't be nervous," Luke added still not giving any hints. "How about I help you to my mom's SUV that I am borrowing today so we can get going."

Grandma agreed as she shifted her feet toward the door. Her walking had rapidly decreased over the past few months, but she still managed to get around slowly. Luke helped Grace into the front passenger seat.

"Okay, Grandma are you ready?"

"More than ready. Let's go." She helped her close the vehicle door.

Luke drove the two women a few miles down the familiar road; however, instead of going straight past the main entrance of Fort Hood he made a left turn and headed toward the gate. This just might be the best surprise pulled off for Grandma. As the vehicle approached the post, a soldier standing guard waved him on and opened the gate for him.

"Well, that was easy," Grandma said looking back toward the entrance.

"They are expecting us today." Luke pointed toward an old Army truck parked in front of them. "And there is our guide." Luke got in line behind their escort vehicle.

"Grandma," Katie gently tapped her from the back seat. "This is part of your surprise. We wanted you to be able to see the place where you grew up before we headed into Gatesville today. Luke asked around and was able to get it set up for us to come out here. I know you are only able to come on Memorial Day weekend; however, all firing on the range will be stopped for the next hour to allow a special visit for a very special person." She reached forward and held the older woman's shoulder. She wanted her grandma to have the very best. Hopefully, she would find today a very meaningful day.

Grandma didn't say anything. She'd probably known enough to suspect today would be an emotional day, but she seemed overcome with emotion to know her granddaughter had gone through such lengths to make today happen.

"Grandma, we hope this doesn't upset you. We thought you might enjoy a visit here." *Maybe this is too hard for her. She's not saying anything.*

Grandma cleared her throat. "This is a pleasant surprise." She lifted her hand and squeezed Katie's. "Thank you both for going through all the trouble to make this happen." Tears began streaming down the older woman's face. Her eyes got a faraway look, as if as her mind was drifting back in time.

Luke and Katie sat in uninterrupted silence while they gave Grandma time to relive her past.

The light beige single cab Army truck led them down a paved road for about a mile before the driver turned right onto a dirt road. Wildflowers of all various shades and sizes lined the road. As Katie and Luke peered out their windows, they saw empty fields with flowers, large oak trees, and shrubby mesquite and cedar trees.

But Grace's eyes came alive. "Look at the bluebonnets and Indian paintbrushes!" she exclaimed softly. "It's just like I'm walking to school."

Grace seemed to be seeing more out her window than they were.

"There, I can see it, Mr. Lloyd's house. That old dog run is something else. And look! Do you two see Oakmont in the distance?" A smile lit up her face.

"I see the blacksmith shop, the cotton gin, and look there is the good ole Smith's General Store with the gas pump in front."

Luke glanced back at Katie. He seemed unsure of what to say. She crinkled her nose and shrugged her shoulders. The two continued to stay quiet as an intricate description of the town unfolded before them.

"The children are playing in the streets. J.J., Rebecca, David, Billy, and many others. Look the schoolhouse. Oh, the schoolhouse. It's never looked so wonderful," her voice barely audible now. Wet tears clung to Grandma's chin as they rolled down her cheeks.

"Drive me a little further, Edward. I want to see the church building. There it is. Beautiful and white with the steeple straight on top." She pointed to a large oak tree as her mind took her back in time.

Luke continued to drive Grandma along the road as the Army vehicle in front made another turn toward the cemetery.

"Edward, do you see the cemetery? It was just past there where those bushes are down the hill where you proposed to me." She pressed her finger on the glass. "Do you remember getting down on one knee? The children were in the bushes squealing and laughing with delight. I'm so glad you wanted me for your wife, Edward." She released a deep sigh and rested back in her seat.

The Army truck parked on the side of the road just before arriving at the cemetery allowing Luke to pass him so they could have privacy.

The interior of the SUV remained quiet with only the sounds of steady even breathing.

"Grandma, we are here at the cemetery. Would you like to get out now?" Katie asked. Today's event might have been too much for her aging grandma.

"We are at the cemetery?" She looked confused. Her forehead crinkled and her eyes darted back and forth.

"Yes, Grandma. Luke and I, Katie—your granddaughter—brought you to Fort Hood today. Would you like to go place flowers on your grandparents' graves?"

"You thought to bring flowers. My child, you thought of everything today, didn't you?"

Luke flashed a grin back at Katie seeming to understand Grandma was back in present day with them.

"Stay there and I will help you out." Luke jumped out of the SUV and opened the door for Grace, helping her down the step.

Katie walked to the back and grabbed several batches of silk bluebonnets and Indian paintbrushes. Her grandma's favorite as well as her great-grandma's favorite.

The three headed toward the chain link fence of Oakmont cemetery and spent the next twenty minutes remembering those who settled the land long before Fort Hood existed. Grandma repeated stories about her grandparents to the younger two as they listened and placed flowers on the graves.

Before they left for Gatesville, Katie paused. She tried to wrap her mind around the former communities that once surrounded this area. Many were created over a century and a half earlier, but now the only remnants remaining of those bustling farming towns were a few cemeteries.

The hundreds of thousands of Fort Hood soldiers who had passed through here since its opening in 1942 provided comfort and security for millions of Americans over the years. As Katie eyed the area around her, she was thankful for her grandparents, great-grandparents and all they gave as well as all the many people serving in the armed forces. Their histories unknown by many were forever intertwined.

A farming community could be erased off the map forever, but the determination and perseverance of the farmers and their families would never be destroyed.

She looked over her shoulder one last time and then hopped into the SUV ready to attend the long-awaited reunion.

KATIE GLANCED at the dash clock. It blinked 10:58 am. They were just in time. Cars and news anchors lined the entire high school parking lot nearing it to capacity.

Luke snagged an open spot near the front of the school. He assisted Grandma out of the SUV and the three of them walked side-by-side toward the building. What a day. There might not be any more room for emotion in Grandma. Hopefully she could handle it. Once inside the lights were turned on, but there was no sound coming from the gym.

"It sure is quiet, Katie," Grace stated as the three continued walking down the school hallway toward the gym entrance.

"I'm sure there are people around here somewhere." Katie stole a peek at Luke. He gave her a quick wink.

As they neared the entrance, balloons arched across the doorway, but the doors remained closed.

"Here let me get this door for you two." Luke skirted in front of the two of them and popped open the door.

Grandma stopped moving. She appeared stunned at the gym's entrance. The silence disappeared as the gym erupted in cheers and applause. Grandma gripped Katie's hand as her feet slowly began to move. The large crowd parted down the middle as the bystanders whistled and clapped for Grace. The ninety-six-year-old woman gazed around and saw familiar faces surrounding her. Billy Roberts, David and Rebecca Springer, descendants of the Miller and Carter families, Reverend Paul and his family, and many more. Even Grandma's younger brother, J.J. and sister, Ruth, and their families managed to make the trip back to Gatesville for this special occasion. One by one she greeted them and smiled as tears of joy raced down her wrinkled face.

"Thank you, Katie. This has made my tired and worn heart happy." Grandma reached to embrace her granddaughter.

"No, thank you, Grandma. You and the others gave so much. This is the least I could do. I hope you enjoy this 75th anniversary and know just how special you are to all of us."

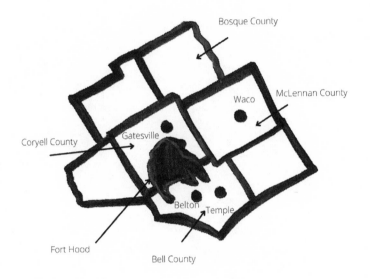

ACKNOWLEDGMENTS

Little did I know, my parents taking me to the Ewing Reunion in Gatesville, Texas, on 4th of July in the 1980s and 1990s as a young child would eventually turn into a subject for a novel I would one day write. It took years for me to fully grasp the importance of this event where both family members and friends faithfully met year after year. As a child, I didn't understand the true sacrifices those from Ewing (and other surrounding communities) made to help our country continue to fight the War.

Though this novel and its characters were formed from my imagination, the people who used to live on this land were real. This book is for all the families who lived on the land that is now known as Fort Hood, Texas. May their stories of sacrifice and struggles here on the homeland during World War II not go unnoticed and not be forgotten. This includes my great-grandparents, Y.W. and Georgia Alabama Williams.

Some of the scenes in the book are based on what really did happened including Grace's home being cut in two and then moved across fields to its new location (Y.W. and Georgia Alabama did this to their home). For those of you who live in

Gatesville, they moved their home to FM 107. The house never did completely recover from the move and someone else bought the land and removed the home years later. I did plenty of online research as well as went to the Texas Historical collection, but stories like the house being cut in two came from my Uncle Kermit, who was there as a young child when the house was being moved. He shared stories and pictures with me about my great-grandparents and life in Ewing and a few of them you will find embedded in the novel. A special thank you to Kermit for always being ready to talk to me about *the move*.

I would like to give my family a huge thank you. For six years, I dreamed, talked, researched, wrote, and then dreamed some more about the publication of this book. Thank you to my siblings (and their spouses and kids) including nieces and nephews who joined me on research excursions for this book. To Jeremy - for answering all my tech questions. To Josh - for always being positive about the book and researching family history. To Larissa - for reading, re-reading, and reading again this book. You were my biggest cheerleader and motivator on finishing this book. Without your continual support, I'm not sure I would have finished. My parents have been also some of my biggest supporters as they listened to me talk for years about the book I was writing and constantly provided encouragement. And thanks, Dad, for reading the book and helping with the final edits.

Special thanks as well to my husband's family who believed in me and provided encouragement to me along the way. Also a special thank you to my Christian writers workshop friends who encouraged me on this journey especially my indie publishing author friend, Mary H., who answered my many questions about publishing. I am also grateful for my writing and author friends, Amy B. and Lindsay H., who provided encouragement through the past few years.

I would like to share a very special thank you to Brandon, my husband, and our daughters, Katelyn and Sophia. My daughters have gone on trip after trip to research this novel and have listened to me talk about the book for the majority of their lives. I am thankful for them caring about the book and even offering insight on ways to make the book better. Brandon has also been a trooper. He never complained when I asked him to take care of the girls so I could have a long night or weekend away to work on it. Even when money was super tight, he encouraged me to keep moving forward until the book was finished. Words can't express how truly thankful I am to have a wonderful best friend, partner, and husband.

And finally and most importantly, thank you to God for giving me this dream six years ago and for walking with me every step of the way. God is faithful - all the time.

ABOUT THE AUTHOR

Carrie Burrows is a fifth generation born and raised Texan and loves researching family and Texas history. Her favorite time of the year is spring when she gets to see all the bluebonnets and other wildflowers covering the fields.

When not writing, her favorite thing to do is to be with her family - her husband, Brandon, and two daughters, and to go on road trips with them. Almost every year for her birthday she will pick to either visit a Texas museum, park, or historical site.